Too Late to Paint the Roses

Too Late to Paint the Roses

Jeanne Whitmee

ROBERT HALE · LONDON

© Jeanne Whitmee 2011
First published in Great Britain 2011

ISBN 978-0-7090-9365-7

Robert Hale Limited
Clerkenwell House
Clerkenwell Green
London EC1R 0HT

www.halebooks.com

The right of Jeanne Whitmee to be identified as
author of this work has been asserted by her
in accordance with the Copyright, Designs
and Patents Act 1988

2 4 6 8 10 9 7 5 3 1

Typeset in 10.25/13.5 pt Palatino
Printed in Great Britain by the MPG Books Group,
Bodmin and King's Lynn

For Matthew, Ellie, Jamie and Rick

Prologue

Manoeuvring his baby grand piano out of the tiny cottage where it had lived for most of its life and into a removal van was something Ian had been dreading. Now he watched apprehensively as the two burly men huffed and puffed, heaving and groaning until at last the body of his precious instrument was safely stowed inside the van. I touched his arm.

'Don't worry. They assured me they'd shifted pianos before.'

Ian sighed and ran a hand through his already tousled hair. 'I hope you're right. The first thing I'll have to do is get it tuned. God only knows how much damage all that shaking up is doing. Perhaps we should have got that specialist firm in after all.'

'I did get a quote,' I reminded him. 'Have you forgotten how much they were asking? And that was just for removing the piano.'

'I know, I know.' Ian sighed. 'We'll just have to hope for the best I suppose.'

Having safely stowed the piano's body into the van, the men were walking back to the cottage, shiny red faces beaming good-naturedly. 'Okay, guv'ner,' the one called Shane said. 'Just gotta get the legs in now and we're all done and dusted – ready for the off.'

Ian watched apprehensively as the piano's bulbous legs, lovingly wrapped in felt and bubble wrap, were wedged into a corner. 'You're sure nothing will fall on it? The piano, I mean,' he said.

The men exchanged an indulgent glance. 'Don't you worry about a thing, mate,' the tallest one said. 'We done this a hundred times or more and never had no casualties yet.'

'There's always a first time,' Ian muttered under his breath as he turned away.

Shane was closing the van doors and securing them. 'Right,' he called out as he climbed into the driving seat. 'Beaumont House, 16 Wellington Avenue – right?'

'Right,' I called. 'We'll see you there.' I slipped a hand through Ian's arm and squeezed it as the van moved off. 'Do cheer up, darling. Everything's going to be fine. Just think of all that lovely space we're going to have. Come on, get in the car. I've packed some sandwiches and a flask.' I put Jamie's violin in its case on the back seat of the car next to Ian's and fastened the seat belt round it but as I joined Ian in the car I caught sight of the troubled look on his face and reached across to kiss him. 'Don't look like that. It's all going to be fine. This is the first day of the rest of our lives, remember, so let's enjoy it.'

The moment I'd seen Beaumont House I'd fallen in love with it. A five minute walk from the seafront, it had been built at the turn of the twentieth century as a large family home, but later used as a guest house. On the ground floor there were three reception rooms, a large kitchen and six bedrooms on the two floors above. Ian had immediately declared it too large.

'It's far too large. We'd rattle around in it. There are only three of us, remember,' he'd pointed out. 'We don't really need all those rooms.'

But a month later our situation had changed dramatically. Unforeseen circumstances made what had seemed like a pipe dream possible. Our casual efforts to upsize suddenly became necessity and Beaumont House fitted the bill perfectly.

When we drew up outside our new house the removal van was already there.

'Hi there!' I called to the removal men. 'Sorry for the delay. We had to pick up the key from the estate agent's.'

Shane jumped down from the driving seat, brushing crumbs from his chin and T-shirt. 'S'all right, missis, we took advantage of the delay to eat our sarnies.' He looked at Ian. 'I 'spect you like us to unload the Joanna first, eh, guv'?'

Ian grinned in spite of himself. 'That would be great,' he said. 'Just let me unlock the door and I'll show you where it has to go.'

He had chosen the smallest of the three ground floor rooms, the one nearest to the front door, as his studio. It would be the most convenient room in which to teach his pupils. He watched anxiously as Shane and his mate carried the piano in, reattached the legs and set it up near the window where he wanted it. Shane wiped his forehead and looked at Ian. 'Right. Gonna give us a tinkle then?' he asked with a cheeky grin. 'Just to make sure we ain't broke nuthin'?'

'I'm sure everything's fine but I think we'll give her time to settle down first,' Ian told him.

'*She*! Blimey! You'd think it was a bird,' Shane said with a grin. 'I've seen blokes treat their wives worse!'

The piano was quickly joined by Ian's desk, his CD player and recording equipment and the cabinets in which he kept his music.

Once the removal men had gone we sat on upturned boxes and ate the lunch I'd packed. Seeing that he was itching to unpack his collection of music and CDs and rearrange everything I left him to it, closing the door of the new studio and standing in the hall to breathe in the atmosphere of our new home.

The hall was what had first attracted me to the house. It was wide and spacious with an elegant staircase leading up to the first landing. At the top of the stairs was a large window with lozenge shaped panes of pink and green stained glass. When the sun reached that side of the house in the afternoon it lit up the window, bathing the whole of the hall and landing in soft pastel colour. That was how we had first seen it and although Ian had laughed at me, I had the warm feeling that the house was welcoming us. In spite of the promised changes to our family situation we were going to be happy here. I just knew it.

I worked hard all afternoon, unpacking enough to make us comfortable for our first night. I loved the big kitchen with its Aga standing in a tiled recess and the built-in dresser. By four o'clock I had washed and put away all our crockery and as I put the last of the saucepans into a cupboard a sudden ring at the front door bell made me look at my watch.

'That must be Jamie,' I told myself hurrying through the hall to let my son in. Jamie was standing in the porch when I opened the door. I laughed, taking in his uncertain expression as he stood in the doorway.

'You don't have to ring the bell, you live here!'

He grinned shamefacedly. 'I s'pose I'll get used to it eventually,' he said. 'It's a lot nearer school – I won't have to get up so early in the mornings. I nearly got on the bus to go to Mableton Park.'

'Well, thank goodness you didn't!'

'The piano survived the journey then?' he observed, his head on one side as he heard Ian running his hands experimentally over the keys. 'Is my violin still in one piece?'

'Of course it is,' I laughed. 'Everything's in one piece. Pop in and see the new studio if you like. Tea will be ready in about ten minutes. Only makeshift I'm afraid.

He looked at me. 'I suppose we couldn't have a takeaway, could we – pizza?'

'Okay, if you like.'

His face lit up as he shouldered off his satchel and dropped it on the floor. 'Wow, wicked! I'm so hungry I could eat an elephant. School dinner was rubbish as usual.'

I went back into the kitchen, telephoned for the pizza and began to lay the table, pausing to look out of the window, my attention suddenly caught by the climbing rose on the front porch. In a few months' time it would be a mass of tumbling blooms. I was reminded, suddenly, of other roses, tumbling over a Cornish wall, one summer all those years ago. I'd been so young and carefree then, happily unaware of the difficult decisions and the heartache that was to come. I paused, praying silently that this new home would bring us good luck and happiness.

One

1997

By the time I left school I was well used to being a disappointment so when I announced that I wanted to make catering my career my mother's displeasure came as no surprise.

From the day I started school it had been made clear to me that she expected no less than that I should be studious and academic, eventually go to university and follow her into the teaching profession. I had let her down at every turn. And she never let me forget it.

Her disappointment in me wasn't only in my failure to live up to her expectations. I had committed the sin of being born a girl and not the son she had wanted so badly. Added to that, my birth had been difficult and complicated, leaving her unable to have more children and I had always been made to feel that I was somehow responsible for that too.

No real rapport ever developed between Mother (never Mummy) and me. Year after year, however hard I tried, my school reports met with disapproving frowns. As a mother she was not harsh but there was always a coolness, an impenetrable barrier that had kept me at arms' length. It was as though she could never quite separate her head teacher persona from motherhood.

Dad on the other hand was made of much softer stuff. It had always been Dad who sneaked upstairs to read me a bedtime story or stroked my brow when I wasn't well; Dad who covered up my small misdemeanours and shared my secret dreams.

As the years went by Mother grew even more remote and unbending. She was especially dismissive when I started secondary school and showed an aptitude for domestic science rather than history and English, which had been her own forte. Even taking extra classes in bookkeeping did not impress her, but Dad argued that a child should be allowed to follow what he or she had a talent for and wanted to do. It would be useless trying to push me into a mould I didn't fit. Needless to say, he got the blame when my interest in domestic science persisted.

When I wanted to study it further after A levels rather than try for a university place she was clearly appalled. It was unthinkable that a daughter of hers should perform what she referred to as 'menial tasks' for a living. But eventually she washed her hands of the whole argument and resignedly accepted my decision to study for a career in catering. To her I was a lost cause.

Greencliffe was a seaside resort on the south coast. The town's only college ran courses in various types of catering and hotel management. I opted for a catering diploma. I had the right qualifications from school and it sounded interesting. Without actually going abroad it could hardly have been further from home and I secretly welcomed the distance it would put between Mother and me. I also looked forward to shaking off the constraints and inhibitions she imposed and enjoying the independence I would have away from the stuffy atmosphere of home.

As there were no halls of residence at Greencliffe College of Further Education I applied for a bedsit I saw advertised in the college newsletter. It was in the house of a mature student, about to join the same catering course as me. I wrote to the address given, enclosing references from my headmistress and the kindly local GP, and to my delight I received a letter by return to say that the room was mine. I was on my way!

But when I actually arrived I found Greencliffe very different from the windswept Yorkshire village where I'd grown up. This seaside town on the fringe of the New Forest had a totally different feel to it. The people were different too. I found to my dismay that I missed Dad and home much more than I'd expected to.

Feeling very much the new girl, I felt out of my depth and desperately lonely in those first weeks. I found an evening job in a hotel bar but the other members of staff seemed aloof and unfriendly and looked askance at me when they heard my northern accent, often perversely pretending not to understand what I said. I vowed to rid myself of it as soon as possible but the more I tried the worse it seemed to get. Halfway through that first term I was so miserable and disillusioned that I was on the point of giving up and going home, and if it hadn't been for my landlady my whole future might have turned out to be very different.

Mary Sullivan was a lively young widow of thirty-five. Her bright green eyes and unruly red hair endeared her to me from the start. She was warm and friendly and almost at once I felt I had known her all my life. Her husband had been tragically killed in a car accident, leaving her with a three bedroom semi on which there was still a mortgage. She confided in me that she was hoping to get a diploma in catering so that she could start her own business.

'Sure, it's a long way off though,' she sighed. 'Looking at things realistically I'll have to get a job in a hotel and work at paying off the mortgage for a few years before I can set up on my own.' She smiled her enthusiastic smile. 'Still, what would life be without a dream, eh? We all need something to work towards.'

When she knocked on my door one evening and found me in tears she reacted with her natural warmth.

'Ah, what's wrong, love?' She came into the room and sat beside me on the bed, slipping a motherly arm around my shoulders. Her kindness was all that was needed to unleash a fresh torrent of tears as I poured out my loneliness and disillusionment.

'There now, don't I know just how you feel,' she said in her soft Irish accent. 'When I first came over here from Ireland I was just sixteen and I felt I might just as well have dropped in from another planet. I had no friends and I felt like a freak. But I'll tell you one thing, darlin'. I never even tried to lose my accent, no matter how much they laughed at it. I've never been ashamed of it and neither should you. Isn't it who we are, after all? People who can't see beyond a way of speaking are too shallow to bother with. You're a lovely girl, so just be yourself. Hold your chin up and smile. They'll soon see you for the lovely person you are.'

After that day Mary took me firmly under her wing. 'Sure, there's only the two of us,' she said. 'So where's the sense in you sitting up there in your room alone? If you like we can take it in turns to cook, and eat together.' Her smile vanished. 'Ah, but maybe that's not to your liking. Maybe you like being on your own.'

'Oh, no! It sounds lovely,' I assured her.

'And as we're taking the same course you might as well drive in to college with me in my old rattletrap of a car? Seems silly you catching the bus when I have to go anyway.'

'Only if you let me share the petrol costs,' I offered.

She laughed. 'Done!' She raised her hand to give me a 'high five'. 'But if you ever want to change the arrangement just you let me know,' she went on, suddenly serious. 'You might not think it right at this minute but a pretty girl like you will soon have a busy social life and I'll not be the one to stand in your way.'

Silently I told myself that there was little hope of that. Mary was good for my flagging confidence. She made me feel worthwhile; a feeling that had been missing from life so far. It was a luxury I wasn't about to throw away.

Things got better after that. My confidence improved with the knowledge that at least there was one person on my side; a kindred spirit who understood how I felt. Mary had suffered the devastating tragedy of losing her husband, the love of her life, in a horrifying accident. She had never had the children she longed for, yet she had the courage and fortitude to start again and make a new life. If Mary could do it, I told myself, then so could I.

I first met Chris towards the end of the first year. I'd noticed him before, of course, lots of times; admiring his cool, clean good looks and tall, athletic build. On this occasion he was queuing in the canteen for lunch and I watched him covertly from my table in the corner, thinking, not for the first time, that he had the brightest blue eyes I'd ever seen. My glances in his direction did not escape the sharp eyes of Cheryl, a girl on my course who joined me at the table. She gave me a knowing grin.

'His name's Chris Harding. Dishy, yeah?'

I blushed. 'Is he? I haven't noticed.'

'Like hell you haven't!'

'He looks arty. Is he an art student?'

Cheryl laughed. '*Art*? God, no! He's doing accountancy.' She grinned. 'A deadbeat number cruncher.'

'Why do you call him that?'

'They're all the same.' Cheryl shrugged. 'You don't get much more boring than accountancy, do you? Everyone says it's for guys with no imagination. That's why so few girls want to do it.' She looked across at him. 'You wouldn't think it to look at him but he's almost as shy as you are. He's been here ages and so far he hasn't dated anyone.'

'He doesn't look shy,' I observed. 'He doesn't look boring either.'

Cheryl laughed. 'No accounting for some people's taste.' She giggled. 'Get the pun? Shall I call him over for you?'

'*No!*'

But before I could stop her Cheryl was beckoning him over. 'Hi, Chris! Come and join us. There's a spare place at our table and I know someone who's dying to meet you.'

'Cheryl! *Don't.*' I blushed ever redder.

Chris hesitated then walked across. 'Thanks,' he said as he sat down and put his tray on the table. 'It's really crowded in here today, isn't it?'

'Don't you want to know who wants to meet you?'

He smiled. 'All right – go on.'

'*She* does.' Cheryl jerked a thumb in my direction. 'This is Elaine Law. She's on the same course as me.' She looked at her watch. 'Gotta go now guys. See ya.' And she stood up, grinning pointedly at me. 'Good luck, kid.'

I stared into my half finished bowl of soup, my appetite suddenly gone. If only I could control my despicable habit of blushing.

'You don't want to take any notice of her.' I looked up to see Chris smiling at me. 'She seems to take great delight in embarrassing people. Soon as she knows you're a bit shy she's onto you. This isn't the first time she's done this to me.'

'That's all right.' Scarlet-faced, I put down my spoon and began to gather up my belongings. 'I have to go now anyway.'

To my surprise he reached out a hand to stop me. 'Don't go yet,' he said quietly. 'I've seen you around and to be honest I've been trying to get up the courage to speak to you anyway.'

Flattered, blushing more than ever and totally tongue-tied, I sat down again. He went on, 'I'm Chris Harding. But you already know that. I'm studying to be an accountant – and hating every minute.'

I looked at him sympathetically. 'Really? Why are you doing it then?'

He shrugged. 'Because my father was an accountant.'

'He pressed you to follow in his footsteps?'

'No. Both my parents died when I was a kid. My gran brought me up. She's been wonderful. I'm doing it to please her really.'

'My mother was a teacher,' I told him. 'She would have liked me to be one too, but I'm not the academic type. My talents are more on the practical side. I thought I might have to do "business studies" but luckily my dad talked her into letting me do the catering course here.'

'Lucky you!' He smiled at her. 'Elaine, isn't it?'

'Yes.' I looked at my watch and saw to my regret that I was already late for a lecture. 'Look, I'm sorry but I really will have to go now. We've got a health and safety lecture at two.' I stood up. 'It's been nice talking to you, Chris,' I said shyly.

As I prepared to leave he said suddenly, 'Come for a drink – or a coffee?'

I paused, my heart racing. 'Oh – er – okay, when?'

'Saturday – tomorrow? Maybe you'd like to see a film or – or something.'

I smiled, feeling my heart lift. 'That would be nice – thanks.' I began to walk away then stopped. 'Oh! Where…?'

He was laughing. 'Outside college. Around seven. Okay?'

I nodded. 'Okay.'

That was the beginning. On the first date we went to a film and then to a café afterwards where we talked non-stop until closing time. At first it seemed that we had a lot in common. We were both only children and had grown up learning to amuse ourselves and finding it difficult to mix and fit in. But as we saw more of each other it became clear that where my shyness hid a longing to be popular and part of a large circle of friends, Chris was quite happy with his own company. He wasn't shy so much as introverted and contented to be so. Although his fellow students liked him he preferred to be alone, me being the only exception. Something that made me feel special. We each drew the other out and often sat up late, talking about our hopes for the future.

'What will you do when you're qualified?' I asked him one evening as we sat in the pub. He pulled a face.

'Get a job with a firm, I suppose. Then it'll be more exams if I want to go all the way with it.' He looked up at me, suddenly serious. 'What I really want, Elaine, is to be a writer,' he said. 'I don't tell

16

many people that. It's what I've always wanted and I'll do it one day, I'm determined.'

I stared at him. 'A writer – a journalist, you mean – on a newspaper?'

'No, a novelist. I want to write thrillers – mysteries. You know, like Colin Dexter or Ian Rankin. I know I can do it. All I need is for someone – just one person to believe in me – give me a chance.'

I frowned, not fully understanding his ambition. The authors' names that he mentioned were like film stars' names to me, remote and obscure. People you actually *knew* didn't write books. 'You'd like to do it as a hobby, you mean?'

'No!' He shook his head. 'As a career.'

I'd never seen him so passionate about anything. There was a new light in his eyes when he talked about it; a vital determination that showed me a different side to the young man I thought I knew. For the first time this was an aspiration I couldn't fully comprehend and it made me feel slightly left out.

Chris explained to me that he had been born and had grown up in Greencliffe with his grandmother who ran a newsagent's shop but when she retired she'd decided to sell the business and return to her Cornish roots. When Chris went off to university she had moved to St Ives where she had bought a cottage.

'I don't see her nearly as much as I used to,' Chris said. 'I miss her, of course, but I go and stay with her in the holidays. It's lovely down there. You'd love it.' He smiled at her. 'Hey, I know – why don't you come with me next time?'

My heart lifted. I was flattered that he wanted me to meet his grandmother, clearly the most important person in his life so far. I'd been dreading the thought of going home for the whole of the long summer break, of the thinly veiled disparaging remarks from Mother and the long silent mealtimes I'd suffered during the short Easter break. 'Oh, I'd love that,' I said. 'But are you sure? Shouldn't you ask your grandmother first?'

He laughed. 'She'll be over the moon. She's been on at me for ages to find myself a nice girlfriend and I think you'll go down a storm with her.'

*

Chris's grandmother, Cecily Harding lived in what had once been a fisherman's cottage perched high above the sea in St Ives. She stood waiting for us at her gate as we climbed the narrow, winding alley to her cottage. She was tall and blue-eyed like her grandson, her white hair stylishly cut to curl gently round her face, nut brown from the sea air. I liked her on sight. She welcomed us in, chattering non-stop as she showed us round her beloved garden and the quaint fisherman's cottage she was so proud of. From my bedroom window there was a breathtaking view of the sea that lay below the tumbling mass of cottages that climbed in zigzag lanes above the harbour. Roses and honeysuckle clambered over sun-baked walls concealing little gardens full of scent and colour. To me it was like something out of a picture book.

Over the meal she had prepared, Cecily, as she insisted I call her, told how she had been born in St Ives and always promised herself she would one day return.

'I had to wait until I'd seen this young man through school,' she said with a fond smile in Chris's direction.

Later, as Chris and I walked along the beach he told me that she had always wanted to be an artist.

'She's really good too,' he went on. 'Watercolour is her speciality, but she never had much time for it when she had the shop. If you want to get into her good books ask her to show you her work. I think she sells some of her pictures to the visitors down here.'

I got the chance to ask Cecily about her painting sooner than I'd expected. The following morning I woke at dawn and couldn't get back to sleep so I got up intending to go for a walk. To my surprise I found Cecily already up and filling the kettle in the kitchen. She smiled when she turned and saw me standing uncertainly in the doorway.

'Have trouble sleeping too, did you, dear?' she asked, getting another cup and saucer down from the dresser.

'I thought I might go for a walk,' I said.

'So did I.' She looked at me, her head on one side. 'Want to be alone or could you do with some company?' The kettle on the Aga began to boil and I stepped forward.

'I'd love some company.' I reached out towards the spluttering kettle. 'Shall I mash?' I blushed. 'Sorry, that's a northern expression. I lapse back into it sometimes.'

She laughed. 'I'm quite familiar with northerners,' she said. 'When we had the shop in Greencliffe we used to get a lot of holidaymakers from up north.' She smiled her warm smile at me and took the milk jug out of the fridge. 'Salt of the earth, I always thought.'

I made the tea and we sat down opposite each other companionably at the round kitchen table. Cecily poured two cups of tea and added the creamy Cornish milk. 'We'll have this first to fortify ourselves, eh?'

'I took a sip of my tea, watching her over the rim of the cup. 'Chris tells me you like to paint,' I ventured. 'I'd love to see some of your work.'

As he had predicted she looked pleased. 'Most of the pictures that you see around the cottage are mine,' she said, 'including the one on your bedroom wall.'

I gasped. 'Really?'

Over the chest of drawers in my bedroom was a painting of St Ives harbour in the very early morning. I'd been impressed by the way the artist had caught the pearly light perfectly and the slight haze over the water; the deep shadows under the harbour wall and the dappled light on the wet sand. There was a wealth of detail in the painting: seabirds clustered round the lobster pots, a fisherman in the distance unloading his early catch. 'But that's a brilliant picture,' I said.

She laughed. 'Don't sound so surprised!'

'Oh no!' I blushed and stammered, 'I wasn't. It's just—'

'It's yours if you'd like it,' she said as she rose to put the used cups in the sink.

'Oh no, really, I couldn't.'

'Yes you could.' She laughed. 'I can easily do another. I've got so many I can't count them, sheer self indulgence. I've waited so long to come down here and paint and now I can't get enough of it.' She pulled a wry face. 'To the detriment of the housework, I'm afraid.'

She locked the door and we negotiated the steep steps and winding lanes, emerging at sea level as the tide was coming in, lapping the ridged sand with gentle wavelets. The sun was already warm and it promised to be a hot day. I looked at Cecily as I took a deep breath of the fresh salty air.

'I can see why you love it so much here.'

She nodded. 'I miss Chris, of course, but then he'd be making his own life now anyway. You have to let go sometime.'

I looked at her. 'You brought him up?'

She nodded. 'From the age of three.'

'What happened?' I asked. 'Chris has never said.'

'I don't suppose he remembers much of it.' She sighed and shook her head. 'George, my husband, had been poorly and needed a break. We couldn't both leave the shop so Paul and Helen, my son and daughter-in-law, suggested that he went with them on a caravan holiday along with little Christopher.' She smiled 'George doted on his little grandson.' She paused and I saw the pain in her eyes. I put my hand on her arm.

'Please – if it's too painful to talk about....'

'It's all a long time ago.' She took a breath and went on, 'They were on their way when they collided head on with a coach that had burst a tyre. All three killed instantly. By some miracle Chris survived with barely a scratch.' She shook her head. 'Seems he was asleep. The ambulance man said it looked as though George had shielded him with his own body.' She shook her head. 'That little boy saved my sanity. I don't know what I would have done if it hadn't been for him. We needed each other and I needed to keep the shop on to feed and clothe us both or I might have gone under.'

'It must have been so awful for you – hard too.'

'It would have been but for my boy. He's been more like a son than a grandson.' She sighed. 'But there – I've done the best I can for him and now it's up to him.'

I wondered silently if she knew about his ambition to be a novelist and, as though she read my thoughts she said, 'Ever since he was quite small he's had this bee in his bonnet about writing. I know the feeling because I used to feel the same about my art but I've told him – there's plenty of time for dreams.' She smiled fondly. 'When you're young you want everything now. Every year as summers came and went and I watched the flowers bloom and fade I'd tell myself that I'd lost my chance to be an artist. It was too late for me to paint the roses and the sea and all the other beautiful things I longed to paint. But Chris was worth the sacrifice and everything comes to he who waits.' She smiled. 'And I've proved it, haven't I? When I could see how keen he was on making a career of the writing though, I did make one condition. Chris's father was an accountant so what could be more suitable than that Chris should study accountancy too? You can't live on dreams, I told him. Train for a good profession that will stand you in good stead; plenty of time for dreams later.' She took my hand and squeezed it. 'I'm glad he's found you, dear. You're a sensible girl and I know you'll keep his feet on the ground and persuade him to stick to his studies.' She stopped on the quayside and took a deep breath, looking out to sea. 'Anyway, as I always say, you have to live life before you can start to write about it. Don't you agree?'

I did agree but I knew all too well that Chris didn't see it that way. Cecily was right, he wanted everything now. I felt the weight of responsibility. Cecily had faith in me; a faith I wasn't sure I could live up to. Back at college I knew he was writing short stories when he should have been studying and that most of the time his mind was elsewhere during tutorials.

'Accountancy is so mundane,' he told me exasperatedly. 'So lacking in inspiration and imagination. Three years at uni' studying maths was bad enough and I only just scraped through with a 2.2. Now there's this.' He ran a hand through his hair. 'I just don't know how to stick it, Elaine.'

'But it's not for much longer, is it?' I insisted. 'Once you've done this course you'll be able to earn good money, then you'll be able to relax and write as much as you want.'

'No, I won't. It takes ages to get fully qualified. I'll still be studying for exams even after I've started working. Years of studying stuff I loath. I just don't know that I can face it.'

Inevitably our relationship developed to a deeper level. Chris said he loved me and there was no question that I loved and trusted him. When he was unhappy he often begged me to stay the night with him in his tiny bedsit.

'It's only you that makes life worthwhile here,' he'd say with that hint of desperation in his voice. 'I honestly don't know what I'd do without you, Elaine.' So I'd stay and we'd make love. It seemed to calm him and make him happy.

But although I fell more and more in love with him I sensed that I was only a diversion. There was always the feeling that he kept something of himself back and I suspected that I would always come a poor second to his burning ambition to be a writer.

I talked to Mary about it, knowing that girls like Cheryl at college would laugh at me, thinking I was taking it all too seriously.

Mary was hesitant. 'I know you, darlin',' she said. 'You're not like some of the girls I know, lookin' on sex as a bit of mindless fun. I know that to you it means more. Are you sure he's as committed as you are? If you are and you really love each other, okay. The only advice I can give you is, be careful. I don't want to see you hurt and there's many a heart broken and, yes, life wrecked too, by giving in to what turns out to be just a physical urge. You'll be qualifying next year. You have to think of your own future.'

We were about three weeks into the new term when I arrived at college one Monday morning to find Chris absent. No one seemed to know where he was. We hadn't seen each other over the weekend as he had promised me he'd get down to some serious revision for a coming exam. Slightly concerned I went round to his room at lunchtime. I knocked on the door twice to no reply but I could hear movement from inside the room. Finally I called out, 'Chris! It's me, Elaine. I know you're in there. Open the door.'

When he opened the door I could see at once that something was seriously wrong. His eyes were red-rimmed and he looked shaky. My heart gave a lurch.

'What's wrong? Chris – talk to me.' As he turned I followed him into the room and put my hand on his arm. 'Please – what's happened?'

When he spoke his voice was so quiet I could barely hear him. 'It's Gran,' he said. 'She's – she's dead.'

I thought I must have misheard him. Not Cecily, so vibrant and enthusiastic, so full of life. He couldn't mean her. I stared at him. 'Cecily? She – she can't be.'

He sat down abruptly on the bed. 'Apparently she wanted to paint that wall with the roses tumbling over it before the summer was over. She tripped going down the steps and fell – broke her hip. That was a couple of days ago and they were going to operate yesterday. I was packing to go down there, then this morning they rang from the hospital to say she'd died suddenly in the night.' He spread his hands helplessly. 'A heart attack, they said; delayed shock.'

'Oh, my God, Chris. I'm so sorry. Why didn't you ring me?'

He shook his head. 'I don't know. I never got round to it, I suppose.'

His face crumpled and I put my arms round him. '*Chris*! Oh, Chris, you didn't have to bear this on your own. I'm here for you. You know that.' A thought occurred to me. 'Are you going down to Cornwall? Would you like me to come with you?'

He looked at me. 'Would you? Would you really do that for me?'

'Of course I will.'

He shook his head. 'There's nothing we can do.'

'You're her only relative. There'll be a lot to do, Chris.' I remembered when my own grandparents had died and how much there'd been for Dad to do at the time. 'You need someone. Let me help.' I looked round the room at the clothes strewn around and the half filled suitcase. 'Let me help you pack a few things then I'll go home and throw some things into a case. We'll go this afternoon.'

I borrowed the fare from Mary and we caught the afternoon train. It was all very sad. The funeral was a quiet affair and afterwards a few of Cecily's friends joined us for a bite to eat and a cup of tea at the cottage. Next day Chris spent the morning with Cecily's solicitor. When he returned he was quiet. I asked him if he would like me to stay and help him clear the cottage but he refused.

'You should get back to Greencliffe,' he said. 'Bad enough one of us missing college but no need for you to stay on too, after all she was nothing to you, was she?'

His words stung a little. True I had only spent a few days in Cecily's company but even in that short time I had become fond of her. But Chris insisted that he could manage alone so I caught the train the following morning, leaving him to the bleak task of disposing of Cecily's belongings.

When a week went by and he hadn't returned or been in touch I rang.

'Chris, it's me, Elaine. Are you all right?'

'I'm fine.' He sounded odd.

'You haven't been in touch and I wondered – when are you coming back?' When he didn't reply I went on, 'You could put the cottage in the hands of an estate agent. You don't have to stay on and—'

'*I'm not coming back.*'

His words stopped me in mid sentence. 'Sorry – you're not...?'

'Coming back,' he repeated. 'I've let the college know.'

'But – why? You've only got another few months to go on your course. You don't want to have to start again.'

'Gran left everything to me; the cottage and all her savings. With what she got for the business it amounted to quite a bit, enough to keep me going for a couple of years at least until I establish myself.'

Establish himself! I felt as thought all the breath had been knocked out of me. 'But – what about your accountancy?'

'You know how I feel about that, Elaine.'

'But it was what *she* wanted, Chris. You'll be letting her down.'

'She'd understand. She had a dream too but for her it was too late. I feel this is like fate. It's an opportunity I can't pass up. If I did I'd regret it for the rest of my life.'

'And if you don't succeed in a couple of years – what then?' I swallowed hard, my heart thumping dully in my chest as I thought about the faith Cecily had had in me. What could I say to make him see sense?

'If I take this opportunity to concentrate on it, I believe I will succeed. And if the worst comes to the worst I'll still have the cottage to sell.'

I was stunned as the reality of the situation became clear and I could see everything slipping away from me. 'I see. So you're saying that it's over between us then?'

He paused. 'You could always join me here – if you want to.'

'You could sound more enthusiastic.'

'I still love you and want to be with you, Elaine,' he said warmly. 'That hasn't changed. But I can't have any encumbrances at the moment.'

'I understand that.'

'I don't feel it's fair to ask you to give up your course. Even if you joined me down here after you'd qualified there'd be no work for you and anyway I'd—'

'Be busy,' I finished for him. 'Too busy to bother with a silly girl hanging around.'

'It's not like that, Elaine, you know it's not. There's nothing I'd like more than to have you with me.'

'As what?' I asked. 'A housekeeper?'

'You have no idea how inspired I am down here,' he went on excitedly, oblivious to the irony of my remark. 'I'm getting up at the crack of dawn and writing like crazy. It's pouring out of me. I *know* this is the right decision.'

'And that's all you need; you don't need anything else?'

He paused. 'I still want you, Elaine.'

Want, not *need*! Suddenly I was angry; angry and frustrated with him. Who had ever heard of Chris Harding? How would he ever get anyone to take him seriously? I'd read some of his stories and I hadn't been that impressed. And what would he do once the money ran out?

'You knew you were going to do this when you sent me back, didn't you?' I accused.

'I knew it was a possibility,' he hedged. 'I needed time alone to think it through.'

'Okay, Chris, have it your way,' I snapped. 'You stay down there alone and scribble away to your heart's content. You throw away your future and everything your grandmother worked so hard for. You go ahead and let everyone down and good luck to you!'

'I'm sorry you feel like that, Elaine,' he said, calmly. 'But I did mean what I said. If you want to be with me you have to take me as I am.'

I slammed the receiver down without saying goodbye then I ran up to my room and threw myself down on the bed in a torrent of tears. How could he be so *selfish*? How could he say he loved me when all he really wanted was to write? If I did go down to Cornwall and join him it would just be to cook his meals and wash his clothes. Why should I give up my future for that, especially when his head was full of silly rubbish – dreams that would never come true?

But as the days went by and my resentment cooled I missed him terribly. It was unbearably painful, like a red hot poker burning a hole in my heart. Maybe life in St Ives wouldn't be so bad, I told myself. I could get a job in one of the little cafés in the town and earn some money to keep myself. Chris clearly wasn't ready for marriage but that wouldn't matter. I'd take what time and attention he could spare me. Perhaps he needed to get the idea of writing out of his system and grow up. When he did I'd be there for him. I rang him again.

'Hello – Chris Harding.' He sounded slightly impatient at being disturbed.

'Chris, it's me. Look, I've thought about it and if you want me, I'll come.'

'*No!*' His abruptness shook me. 'I've thought too, Elaine. It wouldn't be right to ask you to give up your future, especially as you don't share my faith that I can make it as a writer.'

'I do, Chris.' I sounded unconvincing even to myself.

'No, you don't. Even if you did it wouldn't be right to ask you to sacrifice your future. You love what you're doing too. It wouldn't be fair.'

'But if I'm willing to do it – for you.'

'Right now it might seem like a good idea. You miss me and I miss you,' he said. 'But better if we make this goodbye – at least for a while. Maybe I'll get in touch again when things start happening for me. Maybe by then….'

Fury rose in my throat almost choking me. '*Goodbye, Chris!*' I slammed down the receiver. Was he really so arrogant that he thought I'd waste my youth waiting for his impossible dreams to come true?

I confided in Mary. She didn't say much but I knew that as the weeks went by she worried about me. My mood alternated between anger and self-pity. I couldn't eat and I wasn't sleeping very well. Even I could see the dark rings under my eyes and my dull, limp hair. I lost weight and to make matters worse I went down with some kind of tummy bug that wouldn't clear up.

One morning as I staggered out of the bathroom I found her waiting by the door with something in her hand. She pushed it towards me.

'Indulge me,' she said. 'Just put both our minds at rest, will you darlin'?'

It was a pregnancy testing kit. I stared at it, then at her, and shook my head. 'I can't be!'

'Well I only hope you're right, sweetheart, but just let's make sure, shall we?'

I took the box from her and read the instructions. Later I stared at the tell-tale blue line in stunned disbelief as Mary and I sat opposite each other at the breakfast table.

'What do you want to do?' she asked. 'Will you go to him now? Will you ring and tell him?'

My first instinct had been to do just that but when I thought about it I knew I couldn't. He would see it as a trap. He might even think I'd done it on purpose. If I was the cause of his dreams being dashed he would never forgive me. For the rest of our lives he would resent me – and the unwanted child. I knew only too well what it was to be unwanted and resented. I'd suffered from that all of my life and I didn't want to go down that road again.

'No,' I told her emphatically. 'I shan't be telling Chris.'

'He does have a right to know,' she reminded me.

'Believe me, Mary, it's the last thing he'd want to hear.' I didn't need to say more, she knew about Chris's single mindedness when it came to living his dream and she clearly understood my reasons. She considered for a moment, her eyes on my face.

'Would your mum and dad be supportive?'

I shook my head in horror, trying to imagine the scenario: Dad's disappointment in the way I'd let him down; Mother's disgust and secret triumph. Tears ran down my cheeks. There was no choice. Going home was out of the question.

Mary reached out a hand to me. As always she was non-judgmental and coolly practical. 'In that case you have to think seriously about your options, pet,' she said. 'You don't have to go through with it, you know. It's very early days. No one need ever know.'

I swallowed hard at the lump in my throat. '*I'd* know,' I said. 'For the rest of my life I'd know. I couldn't live with that, Mary.'

She sighed and raised an eyebrow. 'So…?'

I shook my head. 'Maybe adoption.' I looked at her. 'I realize I can't stay here, Mary. You've been so good to me. I feel I'm letting you and everyone else down. And as for college—'

She held up her hand. 'Woah! Slow down! Let's not get ahead of ourselves. Now,' she counted on her fingers, 'the baby will be born next spring, right?' I lifted my shoulders. I hadn't even thought about dates yet. She went on, 'You can carry on till Christmas – the end of this term at least. After that we can see how things are going and think again.'

I looked up at her. '*We* can – you mean…?'

'Yes, of course "we".' She looked surprised. 'Because you're staying here with me. There's no two ways about it. Did you really think I'd chuck you out at a time like this?'

Two

Somehow I got through most of that term without anyone guessing I was pregnant but when it began to be obvious tongues began to wag. Most people knew that Chris and I had been an item and guessed that he was the father. It wasn't an easy time.

'Is that why he scarpered, the bastard?' Cheryl asked with characteristic bluntness.

I told her he knew nothing about it and I wanted it kept that way but she clearly didn't believe me.

My morning sickness gradually wore off and I began to feel better, though I tired easily and I found some of the coursework exacting. Mary looked after me like a mother. She made sure I ate properly and went for regular antenatal check-ups. The doctor pronounced me fit and well, the pregnancy progressing normally. Then we broke up for Christmas and I had to write to Mother and Dad and break the news that I wouldn't be going home.

By return I had a brusque letter from Mother, saying that going home was the least courtesy I could pay them after not going home in the summer. She reminded me that she and Dad were still supplementing me financially and that it was the least I owed them. I wrote back saying that I hadn't been well and that as the Christmas holiday was short it wasn't really worth making the long journey up to Yorkshire.

It was two days before Christmas Eve and I was alone in the house as Mary had gone to do some Christmas shopping. I was making a cup of tea when there was a ring on the front door bell. I went through the hall to answer it and my heart lurched when I opened the door to find my father standing on the doorstep.

'*Dad*!'

The smile froze on his face as he took in my newly rounded figure. For a moment we just stood there, the two of us, staring at each other. I was the first to recover.

'Come in, Dad. It's cold and you've come all this way. I was just making tea and—' As I closed the door he grasped my arm and turned me round to face him.

'My God, Elaine, why didn't you tell us?'

Tears pricked the corners of my eyes. 'I'm so sorry, Dad. Surely you realize why.'

'Who is the father?'

'He's – out of the picture. He doesn't even know.'

We sat over the pot of tea at the kitchen table and I told him the whole story.

'I did love him, Dad – very much. I still do. If I hadn't I would never have....'

'I know, love.' He squeezed my hand. 'I know, and I still think he should shoulder his responsibility.'

'No, Dad. It was a mistake. It would just make matters worse. It's better this way.'

He sighed. 'So what are you going to do?'

'Try to finish my course and get my diploma before the birth and then have the baby adopted,' I told him. 'They've been very good at the college. They're going to let me study at home for the last few weeks – just go in for the exam. Luckily it's in April.'

'When's the child due?'

I bit my lip. 'April the 10th.'

He winced. 'That's driving it close.'

'I know, but most first babies are late, so they say. I'm keeping my fingers crossed.' Suddenly I couldn't believe I was talking to my father like this. He was taking it all so well. 'With a bit of luck I'll be able to come home for Easter. It's late next year.' I looked at him. 'Mother need never know about it. I think you'll agree that would be best.'

Suddenly he stood up and came round the table to pull me to my feet. His arms around me, he hugged me close and I felt his tears wet against my cheek.

'You're talking about my grandchild,' he said huskily. 'The one I'm never going to be allowed to see.'

It was the first time I'd thought about the baby I was carrying as a real live entity and it brought me up sharply. I wiped his tears away with my thumbs. 'Dad, I can't keep the baby. You know what Mother is like. She's never had much time for me anyhow and she'd never forgive me for shaming her – letting her down. I'd never be able to come home again. And if I'm not there she'll make life hell for you. You were the one who stood up for me. When I've got my diploma I'll be able to get a good job down here and I'll pay back every penny you've spent on me. You have to agree that it's best Mother never knows.'

'She *has* to know,' he said firmly. 'It's time she faced up to life in the twenty-first century. I don't like the way things are nowadays any more than she does, but you are our daughter.' He shook his head at me. 'I can't believe you've been through all this alone and felt you couldn't come to your own family.'

'I haven't been alone, Dad,' I told him. 'I've got the most marvellous landlady and friend. She'll be home soon. You must meet her. And I'm sure she'll insist that you spend the night here. You can't make the journey back to Yorkshire tonight.'

Mary was surprised to find Dad sitting in her kitchen when she came home, but as always she rose to the occasion and treated him like an old friend. They seemed to take to one another on sight. She insisted that he stayed the night and made up the bed in the tiny third bedroom for him.

After I'd gone to bed the two of them sat up talking till late. Lying in bed I could hear the buzz of their conversation in the sitting room below my room. It continued until I fell asleep. I had no idea what they discussed but Dad seemed happier in the morning. I took an hour off and went to the station to see him off. Before he boarded the train he hugged me.

'Mary'll take care of you,' he said. 'You're so lucky to have found her. She's a real gem. Take her advice, love. It'll be sound common sense.'

I looked at him. 'You won't really tell Mother, will you?'

'I've told you, love; she has to know.' He sounded adamant. Looking at my troubled expression he added, 'Just you let me worry about her.' He grinned wryly. 'I might be tougher than you realize.' He kissed my forehead. 'Take good care of yourself and keep in touch. Goodbye, and have a happy Christmas.'

Crossing to the station exit I stopped halfway across the bridge to watch the train pull out. With tears in my eyes I watched until it disappeared into the distance, my heart heavy. This wasn't how I meant things to be at all.

Christmas came and went. I had a letter from Mother. She wrote that my news had come as a shock but no real surprise to her. She'd always known that I was weak-willed and irresponsible, but she wished me no ill will. She made it clear that I would not be welcome at home until after my 'condition had been restored to normal' and suggested that I might write and let them know when that day came.

It was no less than I had expected.

The new term began and the exam date was set for 8 April. By the time January was halfway through I found standing behind the bar all evening too tiring and Mary persuaded me to give in my notice even though I desperately needed the money. I worked hard at home from the beginning of March and with Mary's help and encouragement I was confident that I had a fair chance of getting my diploma.

On the morning of the 8th I awoke at 5.30 with a dull pain low in my back. I said nothing to Mary at breakfast, telling myself it was just exam nerves and trying to ignore it. We travelled in to college together in the car.

The first contraction came as I turned over my paper half an hour later. All morning as I worked on the written paper I was aware of the pains growing relentlessly stronger but I carried on. During the lunch break I tried not to let Mary see when the pain came but there was no fooling her. She kept asking me if I was all right. I insisted that I was.

The afternoon was taken up with the practical exam, hygienic food preparation, care of equipment and kitchen management. Somehow I got through it but when at last I eased myself with relief into the passenger seat of Mary's car she looked at my ashen face with concern.

'You're not all right, are you?'

I winced as another pain seized me in its grip. 'N-not really, no.'

'It's the baby – yes?'

'I think so.'

'So do I.'

I looked at her apologetically. 'I'm sorry, Mary.'

She frowned. 'For God's sake, what have you got to be sorry about? Have you been in pain all day?' I nodded. She switched on the ignition and let in the clutch determinedly. 'Right, we'll drop in at home for your case and then it's straight to the hospital with you, my girl!'

My baby son was born six hours later. He weighed seven pounds four ounces and had my dark hair. The midwife assured me that although his eyes were blue they would no doubt turn to brown like mine in a few weeks' time. It was irrelevant to me. Soon he would belong to someone else. I turned my head away, terrified of seeing Chris's blue eyes looking up at me.

Mary had stayed with me throughout the labour and delivery. The nursing staff took her for my mother and neither of us bothered to correct them. Later as she beamed proudly into the cot at the tiny sleeping face she might as well have been my mother anyway.

'Oh, Elaine, he's such a little angel,' she said softly. 'Don't you want to hold him?'

My arms and my heart ached to hold him but I refused to look at him. 'He's not going to be mine,' I said. 'I had a normal delivery so they'll let me come home tomorrow. I don't want to get to know him only to have to say goodbye.'

When she looked at me the expression on her face said it all. 'If you could just imagine what I'd have given to have had one like this,' she said softly.

'*Don't!*' I said angrily, swallowing the lump in my throat. 'Where is all that common sense now, Mary? You *know* I can't bring him up on my own without a father. What kind of life could I offer him? You've seen the single mothers from the council flats near the college, out with their children, down at heel, exhausted and irritable with the kids; struggling to manage on state benefits. I don't want that. Not for me – or for him.'

She said no more, just tenderly stroked the baby's cheek with one finger, hugged me and went home. But later that night after the lights were out and the tiny scrap in the cot at the end of my bed wailed unceasingly, tiny fists waving, his little face red with exertion, I was at the end of my tether. I'd rung the bell several times but no nurse appeared.

At last the woman in the bed opposite sat up and hissed across at me, 'Oh, for Christ's sake, girl, give him a cuddle or a feed or some-thing. Shut him up and let's all get some sleep!'

Reluctantly, I slid out of bed and scooped up the furious, wriggling bundle. To my surprise he stopped crying at once, fixing me with his wide blue, unfocused eyes. I took him into bed with me and felt strangely moved when he nuzzled his face against my neck. A nurse appeared at the end of the bed.

'Give him the breast,' she suggested. 'There won't be much yet but it'll comfort him.'

'But I'm having him adopted,' I whispered.

'I know, but you're still his mummy tonight,' she said.

Her words were like a knife slicing through my heart and combined with the sweet scent of the tiny baby and the feel of his little face against my skin, burrowing so determinedly made some-thing deep inside me give way like a dam bursting. My tears welled up and once they began to flow they wouldn't stop. The nurse stepped forward.

'Give him to me. I'll take him to the nursery.'

I held him fast. 'No! Leave him,' I said, clutching him closer. 'He's *mine*.'

Mary knew of course that I'd never be able to let him go.

The following evening after she'd driven me and the baby home and I'd put James Edward, as I'd decided to call him, to bed upstairs in his makeshift cot in my room the enormity of what I was taking on suddenly hit me.

'Oh, God, what have I done, Mary?' I asked, looking at her despairingly. 'How on earth am I going to manage? All I hope is that I get my diploma. I'm going to have to find a job and a good nursery for James as soon as I can.'

'I was going to talk to you about that,' Mary said. 'As long as I get mine too I'm going to set up in that little catering business I told you about, so how would you feel about becoming my business partner?'

'*Me*?' I thought I must be dreaming. 'You're asking me?'

She laughed. 'Who else? We get along, don't we? There'll always be a home for you both here with me too. If you want it, that is.'

'Of course I want it.' I stared at her in surprise. 'I can't believe my luck. But the catering business, Mary…?'

'As I've told you before, it's something I've always wanted to do; one of the reasons for taking the course.'

'Well, I know that, of course, but setting up is bound to cost a bomb. Are you sure you can do it, Mary?'

'I've looked into it and made notes on all we'll need to do. I'll need to register the business, have the premises inspected by the local environmental health service. Then there's all the equipment to buy and—'

'You're avoiding my question,' I put in. 'How will you finance it – a bank loan? Will they give you one? Don't you think you should make sure you can afford it before you offer me this partnership?'

She paused. 'Okay – there's something you'll have to know. Your dad is lending us the money to get started.'

'*Dad* is?' I stared at her. 'You discussed this with Dad?' A suspicion entered my mind. 'Did the loan depend on my keeping his grandson?'

Mary looked shocked. '*No*, absolutely not! We got along very well, your dad and I and we both agreed on that particular issue. The decision was to be yours alone. No one had the right to influence you on it. We talked about a lot of things that night and when I mentioned the little business I'd always dreamed of starting he offered the loan right away.'

'Conditional on you asking *me* to be your partner?'

Mary shook her head. 'Elaine – you know how much I think of you – or you should by now. This isn't something I could do alone and there's no one I'd rather work with than you.' She laid a hand on my arm. 'You surely believe that, darlin'?'

I nodded, my throat too tight for words. Mary went on, 'The money will be paid back with interest. I insisted that it was all arranged properly through a solicitor, but I'm not saying that you keeping baby James won't be a huge bonus for your dad. It's my bet that he'll be coming to see his new grandson very soon.'

She was right. Dad came and stayed for the weekend a month later when James was christened. He apologized for Mother's absence but he told me that he was sure that she was secretly pleased to know she had a grandson. I wasn't altogether convinced – about that or about the message he said she had sent to say that I could take James home for a visit whenever I was ready.

'She hasn't been too well,' he confided. 'Angina, the doctor says. Not life threatening but she has to take it easy.'

Privately I wondered if she blamed me for that as well.

Dad was besotted with James. He couldn't get enough of him and he was pleased and flattered that I had chosen his own name, Edward, for a second name.

Sitting round the table together in the evening, Mary outlined the business plan she had drawn up. Dad's loan would be used to have the kitchen re-vamped; to buy a large fridge, a freezer and two new ovens; a refrigerated van and all the cutlery, glass and crockery we would need.

'We'll need a computer too,' she said, looking at me. 'You're the one who's good at that so how about enrolling for some evening classes so that you can learn how to build us a website?' I agreed and she began to count off the tasks ahead on her fingers. 'Right, then there'll be advertising. We'll start with the Yellow Pages and the local papers and when we get off the ground we might splash out on an ad in one of the upmarket county magazines.'

I laughed. 'You've thought it all through, haven't you?'

'If a thing's worth doing, it's worth doing properly,' she said, 'I've been thinking and planning it for years. I just never thought it would happen this soon.' She smiled. 'It's funny how things work out, isn't it? If it hadn't been for you my dream might have come to nothing. Now I've got the cash to get started and a ready made, qualified partner.' She smiled. 'I've also got a surrogate daughter and grandson, because that's how I think of the pair of you now.' She smiled across at Dad. 'Not to mention a fairy godfather.'

It was the day before Dad's visit was over that the postman brought our exam results. Mary opened hers at once and found to her relief that she had passed. I hardly dared open mine, remembering the trauma and pain of the day I'd sat the exam. Surely under the circumstances I must have failed. Eventually Mary grew tired of seeing me sitting there, chewing my lip, the unopened envelope in my hand. Reaching across the table she snatched it from me and tore it open. Before she pulled out the slip inside she looked at me.

'I want you to know one thing,' she said. 'This is only a formality. It's immaterial to me whether you've passed or not.' I said nothing, just held my breath as she pulled out the slip then beamed up at me. 'Passed – and with credit!' she said. 'Congratulations – *partner*!'

There were hugs all round and Dad produced a bottle of champagne because he said that as far as he was concerned it was a foregone conclusion anyway.

In the early days there wasn't a lot I could do. James took up so much of my time, both by day and night. Mary helped as much as she could but most of her time was taken up with organizing the new business. She set about employing a builder she knew to refurbish the kitchen. She managed to buy all the cutlery, glass and crockery we'd need, plus a large commercial freezer at the auction sale of a hotel that was closing down. The refrigerated van was purchased second hand from a local butcher. The rest we bought new. Dad's loan more than covered everything and the money that was left was put in the bank for anything we might have overlooked. During the early days when baby James took up so much of my time and energy I made sure that the house was cleaned and the meals cooked daily, leaving Mary free for the important task of preparing to set up the business.

One evening as we were finishing our meal Mary mentioned getting some stationery printed. I looked up at her and asked, 'What are we going to call our new venture?'

She looked taken aback. 'Would you believe it – I haven't even thought about a name.'

'We'll have to think of one soon,' I told her. 'Can't have stationery printed until we have. And it has to be something catchy – memorable.'

We tossed possible ideas back and forth, some of them so ridiculous that we were in fits of laughter. Suddenly I thought of the perfect solution.

'Why not call it *Mary-Mary*?'

She thought for a moment. 'But I wanted something that would include us both.'

'Mary is my second name,' I told her. 'So it does!'

We set about designing a leaflet, wondering how ambitious to be. Mary decided to advertise catering for parties and corporate events such as board meetings and business breakfasts.

'Corporate dos won't involve large numbers of people,' she said. 'And it looks good on the leaflet.'

She worked tirelessly, canvassing, doing market research, ferreting out the best suppliers and sitting for hours with pencil and paper costing out menus and working out what was profitable and what was not. Leaflets were sent out to businesses in the town and throughout those long summer evenings we walked the streets dropping off leaflets, James dozing contentedly in his buggy.

Between us we divided up the responsibilities. Books would need to be kept and records of food safety kept up to date. We decided that as I'd done a bookkeeping course I would take care of the clerical side of the business. The tiny breakfast room off the kitchen was designated as an office and the computer was duly set up there along with the new business telephone line.

Mary babysat James while I began web-building computer classes in the evenings and gradually began to build our *Mary-Mary* website. The business was registered with the local environmental health service, the premises visited by an inspector and passed. We were 'ready to roll', as she put it.

A week later the telephone rang and our first assignment was booked. We were in business.

By the time James's first birthday came round we were in profit; just as well as the *Mary-Mary* account was already overdrawn at the bank. By the time he was two we had begun to build a regular client list. I'd found a reliable young mother a few doors away who agreed to take James for me when Mary and I were out working. At the end of that year we decided that we could safely afford to draw a proper salary each and enjoy some of the benefits of our hard work.

James grew from a chubby baby into a bright-eyed, inquisitive toddler. He was a happy child. At three he started nursery, leaving me more time for the daily cooking and baking sessions Mary and I needed for the constant restocking of the freezer. He was bright and intelligent, constantly asking questions and interested in everything and it was around his fourth birthday that he discovered the piano.

Mary's house was a spacious semi built at the turn of the century. The large ground floor room at the front was rarely used except for

Christmas and special occasions. It contained a three-piece suite, the china cabinet full of nick-knacks that Mary had inherited from her mother-in-law and the upright piano that had belonged to Derek, Mary's late husband. Finding the door ajar one afternoon James wandered in and climbed up onto the piano stool. Cautiously lifting the lid he began to try out the keys. Mary heard him from the kitchen and laughed.

'Would you just listen to that,' she said. 'You know, I'd swear that kiddie has a real feel for music.'

James could do no wrong in Mary's eyes. She was in danger of spoiling him as I was always telling her. 'He knows he's not allowed in the front room, Mary,' I said. 'He should get a scolding.'

Mary looked at me in horror. 'Poor lamb! Don't you dare scold him for a little thing like that. I'll go and get him. A biscuit and a drink of juice should tempt him away.'

But she was wrong. Once James had discovered the piano and the sounds it could make there was no tempting him from it at any price. He wanted to play all the time. Mary, who had a rudimentary knowledge of the piano, taught him how to play a few simple tunes with one finger and his joy in the instrument knew no bounds. At five and a half he learned from school that as well as people who taught sums, reading and writing there were others who could teach you how to read music and play the piano properly – *With both hands, Mummy*! After that momentous discovery he constantly pestered me to find him one of these magical beings.

When the inquiry came to cater for the Langley wedding Mary and I were excited. The bride, Jessica Langley was the elder daughter of one of the town's leading solicitors. Tom Langley was a well respected town councillor, heavily tipped to be the next mayor. Mary and I were invited along to meet the bride and her mother at the family home. We went armed with our choice of menus and the folder of photographs we'd accumulated, taken on various successful occasions. We'd catered for weddings before but not one on this scale and as we got out of the car in the wide, tree-lined avenue my stomach churned with apprehension. But Mary seemed unfazed by the affluent house and its setting. Looking up at the large mock-Tudor house she winked at me.

'If we get this job and make a success of it we'll be well on the way to the big time, darlin',' she whispered.

The wedding reception was to be held in the Langleys' large garden in a massive marquee. We learned that a florist had been engaged and a small group of musicians would be playing for the reception and again later for the evening dance.

Jessica and her mother seemed happy with the choice of menus we suggested, both for the wedding breakfast and the buffet for the evening dance and we left triumphantly with a firm booking and a cheque for the deposit. As we drove home Mary could hardly contain her excitement.

'Flowers!' she said. 'One day we'll provide flowers as well. That's the way to go. We'll have our own team of waiters and waitresses *and* a selection of marquees to offer for hire.' She looked thoughtful. 'By the way, remind me to have a word with the photographer and whoever is in charge of this band they're engaging. It might be a good idea to get a little circle of useful contacts together – you know, recommend one another.' She grinned at me. 'Can't do any harm, can it?'

I laughed. 'You don't let the grass grow under your feet, do you, Mary?'

She raised her eyebrows at me. 'Who wants grass when you can have deep pile carpet? There's no stopping us now, girl!'

The wedding went off without a hitch. We'd hired six waiters to help us serve the three course meal, two barmen and two waitresses to help with the evening buffet, plus a couple of washers-up to deal with the dirty dishes. Luckily there was a large dishwasher in the Langleys' kitchen, which helped. During the interval between the wedding breakfast and the evening dance, during which most of the guests went home to change, our team set about rearranging the marquee whilst I drove home to collect the boxes of buffet food. I was having a cup of tea and a five minute break in the kitchen later when Mary came through with a young man in tow. He was tall with dark hair which he wore unfashionably long. He looked elegant in his dinner jacket but I thought he was a little too thin, as though he didn't always remember to eat. But he had warm brown eyes and a wide, sensitive mouth, both of which completely transformed his face when he smiled.

Mary looked slightly hectic, her cheeks pink and her red hair tousled. She had a habit of running her fingers through it when she was working, which did nothing for her coiffeur.

'Oh, there you are, Elaine,' she said, though she knew perfectly well where I was. 'This is Ian Morton. Ian, this is my business partner, Elaine Law.'

I stood up and we shook hands solemnly. I had no idea why I was being introduced to this man. I'd been too busy all day to notice him along with the other musicians playing the piano on the dais at the end of the marquee until Mary rather impatiently pointed this out.

'It's his band that was playing,' she said frowning at my puzzled expression.

'Not exactly mine,' Ian put in. 'I'm a freelance musician. I get a few of my friends together for occasions such as this. This afternoon it was light classics – mainly strings; this evening we'll be joined by a sax and a double bass for the dancing.'

'Not your band?' Mary looked a bit nonplussed. 'But you'd have no objection to us recommending you?'

He smiled. 'Absolutely not, Mrs Sullivan. And if the delicious plate of food I enjoyed after we'd finished playing is anything to go by I'll certainly recommend you.' He paused and looked slightly apologetically at me. 'Not that I meet that many people who are looking for caterers.'

Mary looked disappointed. 'Oh – well, if you'll excuse me I'd better go and make sure the waitresses know what they're doing this evening.'

When she'd gone I glanced at Ian who was looking uncomfortable and slightly bewildered. 'Would you like a cup of tea?' I offered. He accepted eagerly and seemed to relax.

'Thanks, I'd love one.' He sat down at the table.

'Don't take too much notice of Mary,' I told him. 'She's very ambitious for our business and wants to make as many contacts as she can.'

'She seems nice,' he said sipping his tea.

'She is,' I told him. 'She's one of the best.' I looked at him. 'We were very busy during the reception, of course, but from what I heard your – band…?' I looked at him hesitantly.

'Quintet,' he supplied.

'Your quintet was very good. You're a freelance musician, I think you said.'

He nodded. 'I used to play with the Greencliffe Symphony Orchestra; in the first violin section, but I've always been more interested in teaching really.'

'You're not with the orchestra now then?'

'No. I decided to take the plunge and give in my notice. I've got quite a lot of pupils and I augment my income by doing this kind of thing.'

'I see. That was a brave decision.'

'Not really,' he said. 'I have no commitments you see, no wife or family, just a little cottage out in the sticks.' He smiled. 'Teaching is what I like to do.'

I caught my breath as an idea occurred to me. 'How old are your pupils?'

He shrugged. 'All ages. Why do you ask?'

'I have a small son. He's desperately keen to learn to play the piano.'

'How old is he?'

'Five and a half.' I waited for him to laugh away the idea but he didn't.

'The perfect age to begin,' he said. 'No inhibitions, no problems with self confidence.'

I took my courage in both hands. 'Would you come to the house and meet him?' I asked. 'See if you think he's ready to start – if he has any – any aptitude?'

'Of course I will.'

When I told Jamie that a music teacher was coming to see him he was over the moon.

'How soon will I be able to play? When is he coming?'

I laughed. 'He's only coming to meet you to start with,' I explained. 'We'll have to see how you get along and what he thinks. He might think you should wait a little while.'

His face crumpled. 'But I don't *want* to wait!'

'Well, just let's see what he says, shall we?'

Ian joined us for tea the following Sunday afternoon. He'd suggested we make it all as informal as possible so we sat in the small living room where we spent most of our free time. Jamie stared up at Ian as though he was some kind of god, solemnly shaking the hand he offered and once tea was over Ian took both of Jamie's hands in his, examining them, both palms and backs, and taking special note of the fingers.

'So you'd like to learn to play the piano, Jamie?'

Jamie nodded. 'I can play already,' he said proudly. 'A little bit.'

'Can you really? I'd like to hear that.'

Jamie took his hand, pulling him in the direction of the front room. 'Come on. I'll show you.'

In Mary's front room Jamie sat on the piano stool, his little legs dangling, too short to reach the pedals. He ran through his repertoire of one-fingered tunes and looked up into Ian's face, eager for his approval.

'That's very good.'

Jamie beamed with delight. 'It'd be better with two hands though, wouldn't it?'

'It certainly would. Would you like to learn to play with all of your fingers and both hands, Jamie?'

'Oh, yes *please*!'

'And read music just like you read a story book?'

'Ooh, can I? How long will it take?'

'Quite a long time,' Ian warned. 'And you'd need to practice very hard – every day.'

'I already do,' Jamie assured him.

Ian smiled at me. 'Well, I don't think there's any more to be said, do you? Now, if you'd like me to come here to the house I suggest you get the piano tuned,' he said.

Mary, who had been hovering in the doorway, stepped forward. 'I'll see to that,' she said.

Ian reached into an inside pocket and took a card from his wallet, passing it to her. 'I can recommend this chap. He's very good, and quite reasonable.'

Mary took the card and held out her hand to Jamie. 'You come with me, young man, and let Mummy make all the arrangements for you.'

When Jamie had trotted off with Mary Ian smiled at me. 'He's clearly very keen,' he said. 'And he has very good hands, long fingers and strong wrists for his age.'

'He's been playing the piano in his own way for ages,' I told him. 'He loves it more than any of his favourite toys. It's all he wants to do when he gets home from school.'

We discussed fees and then Ian said,'I should warn you they do often reach an age when they lose interest,' he said. 'Even the very keen ones. Lessons suddenly become boring and practising is a time-wasting chore, especially when they discover things like football and later …' he grinned, 'girls.'

'I know, but somehow I can't see that happening with Jamie.'

'Well, forewarned is forearmed. All we can do for now is to give him what he wants, which is to learn.'

'And you're happy to take him on?'

He nodded. 'More than happy. Kids that keen are a delight to teach. Shall we say Monday afternoons – after school, about 4.30? Give him time to eat.'

I laughed. 'If I know Jamie he'll be far too excited to eat.' I held out my hand. 'Thank you so much, Mr Morton.'

He frowned. 'Ian, please.'

Three

Jamie loved his music lessons. He could hardly wait for Monday afternoons to come round and getting him to practice was never a problem. He progressed quickly and by the time he'd been taking lessons with Ian for a year he'd already passed his grade one exam.

Life was busy and eventful. *Mary-Mary* went from strength to strength. Mary achieved her ambition of creating a syndicate of tradespeople and we all met for informal meetings once a month to plan future strategies. The meetings usually took place at Mary's house because it was more convenient and as well as useful work contacts our new colleagues soon became a circle of friends. Collectively we now had in our circle a florist, a photographer, a young man who had recently put all his redundancy money into a marquee hire business, a taxi firm that specialized in wedding cars and last but not least, Ian and his freelance musician friends.

We had all been working together for about eighteen months when Brian Maxey, the photographer, came up with the suggestion that we combine to form one firm. The suggestion certainly gave us food for thought and we all decided to go away and think about the idea.

At first Mary was doubtful. '*Mary-Mary* is our baby,' she said. 'We created it, you and I. I don't want to see it swallowed up.'

'I don't see why we should be swallowed up,' I pointed out. 'Brian's plan would surely only apply to weddings. We'd still be free to work independently on other kinds of function.'

She brightened up. 'I suppose that's right. And the same principal would apply to the others as well. We could form a separate company; one in which we'd all participate. We could even call it something different.'

After Jamie's lesson the following Monday afternoon I put the idea to Ian.

'I like it,' he said. 'Not that it'll make any difference to me, of course. I'd only ever play at weddings and anyway, most people nowadays prefer a disco for the evening do.' He glanced at me. 'Which brings me to what I've been meaning to ask you.'

I looked at him. 'Yes?'

'A friend of mine is getting engaged and he and his fiancée are having a small party to celebrate. It's on Friday evening. If you're not working I wondered if you'd like to come with me.'

I was slightly taken aback. Ian had been part of our every day lives for over a year now and he'd never asked me out before. He looked at me, clearly troubled by my hesitation.

'Just say no if you'd rather not,' he said quickly. 'It was only an idea.'

'I'd love to go with you, Ian,' I told him.

'You *would*?' The look on his face made me laugh.

'Of course I would. Thank you for asking me. Luckily we don't have anything booked for Friday evening.'

He beamed. 'Great! It's Harry Spencer, you might remember him. You've met him once or twice. He and I used to play in the orchestra together. I'll pick you up about eight o'clock then, if that's all right.'

When I told Mary she pulled a face. 'Well, not before time. I thought he'd never ask you. To tell you the truth I'd begun to wonder if he might be gay,' she said.

I was shocked. '*Mary!* Didn't it ever occur to you that he might not find me attractive?'

Her eyebrows shot up. 'All I can say is that if he didn't find *you* attractive he had to be gay!'

'Not all men are keen to rush into dating a single mother with a growing son,' I said.

Mary snorted. 'Ian is devoted to Jamie, you know that.'

'As a music pupil, yes.'

When I came downstairs on Friday evening, dressed for the party, Jamie, now a precocious 7-year-old, whistled.

'Wow, Mum, you look really cool.'

'Thank you.'

'Are you and Ian going out together now then?'

'Of course not. It's just a party.'

He looked disappointed. A ring at the doorbell sent him scurrying towards the front door. 'Oh! That'll be him. I'll get it.'

'Don't you dare say anything to Ian about it,' I called after him. To my relief he didn't.

It was a warm evening and as we drove to Harry's house Ian put me in the picture.

'Harry is first clarinet in the Greencliffe Symphony Orchestra,' he told me. 'He's been married before but his wife left him a couple of years ago – ran off with an old flame who turned up out of the blue. They live in Australia now. I thought Harry would never get over it at the time but now he's met Celia and they seem to be made for each other.'

'It's nice to hear of a happy ending,' I remarked. 'Marriage nowadays seems a dicey business.'

'Yes.' He glanced at me. 'I've often wondered – you and – Jamie's father….'

'We were never married,' I finished for him. 'In fact he doesn't even know Jamie exists.'

Ian looked shocked. 'You never told him?'

'He was fiercely ambitious,' I explained. 'We were at college together. He was studying accountancy but longed to be a writer. His grandmother died suddenly and left him all she had including a cottage down in Cornwall. He decided to gamble everything on trying for a writing career. He opted out of college and made it clear that he needed to do it alone – with "no encumbrances" as he put it. I only discovered that Jamie was on the way after we'd parted. I knew it would mean the end of all his dreams, so I decided not to tell him.'

He frowned. 'Don't you think you should have at least given him the choice?'

'What choice?' I asked. 'He was risking all he had on making a success as a writer. Babies take a lot of money and a lot of time and attention.' I looked at him. 'It would have ruined everything for him. I just couldn't do it to him, Ian.'

'It was a big sacrifice on your part.'

'Not really. As I saw it our relationship would have been doomed from the start. He'd have ended up resenting me – possibly Jamie too.'

He was silent for a moment. 'You must have loved him very much,' he said at last.

I shrugged. 'I thought I did. I know now though that it was just a girlish infatuation. I've never regretted having Jamie though.'

'It couldn't have been easy.'

'It wasn't, but it could have been a lot harder. I owe everything to Mary, and to my father for lending us the cash to start *Mary-Mary*.' He was silent and after a moment I looked at him. 'You still disapprove?'

He shook his head. 'Not at all. I only wish my own mother could have been as unselfish as you.'

I would have liked to ask him more but we had arrived at Harry's house so the conversation came to an end.

I enjoyed the party very much, realizing suddenly that it was years since I'd had any kind of social life. Harry's fiancée, Celia, was an attractive girl of about my own age. She was very interested in the catering business and asked me if she could get in touch about her own wedding to Harry, which was planned for later in the year.

Once everyone had arrived Celia produced an appetizing buffet supper. Many of Harry's musician friends were there and it didn't take long for them to begin 'jamming'. Ian was on the piano, while Harry got out his clarinet and two other guests who had brought their own instruments joined in. They played everything from pop tunes to snatches of opera and classics and the evening ended with everyone joining in, some more tunefully than others. As the evening wore on everyone became quite high spirited and I realized that for the first time in years I was actually having fun.

Later, as we drove home I asked Ian if he missed his friends and being in the orchestra.

'No,' he said firmly. 'I love what I do now. And I still keep in touch with the friends I made while I was there.'

I glanced at him thoughtfully, wondering whether I should ask what was on my mind. 'Ian – you mentioned your mother earlier. You said you wished she'd been less selfish.'

He sighed. 'And more of a mother. In fact she never was a mother to me. I was brought up by her sister, my Aunt Janet.'

'Why was that?'

'As far as she was concerned I was a horrible mistake,' he said unable to hide the hint of bitterness in his voice. 'My mother was an actress. She was very ambitious, determined to make the big time. Having me was a disaster. I never even knew my father. Amanda decided to keep his identity to herself, which was why I spoke as I did earlier about Jamie's father. I'm sorry about that.'

'Don't be.'

'It's true though,' he went on. 'I got in the way of her career and she would be the first to admit it. But she was lucky. Her sister, Janet had always wanted children and was unable to have any. As it happened, Amanda – my mother – only had to take a few months off, hand the unwanted bundle over to her sister and carry on working. Problem solved.'

'Your aunt and uncle adopted you?'

He shook his head. 'It was what Aunt Janet wanted, naturally, but Amanda held out. She wanted the best of both worlds.'

'Oh, Ian, I'm so sorry.'

He shook his head. 'Oh, no. I still think of Aunt Janet and Uncle George as my parents. No kid could have had better. They gave me a wonderful childhood.'

'And your mother?'

'Oh, she'd appear from time to time, in between jobs, descending like some exotic perfumed angel with gifts and kisses, only to disappear just as fast the moment the phone rang with a better offer. It was very confusing for a small child. It would have been less disrupting if she'd kept away.'

I made no comment. It was obvious that Ian still resented his mother and her abandonment and I suffered a sudden pang, thinking of Jamie.

'Is she still…?'

'Oh, very much so; living on her state pension in a smart apartment building and still waiting for the phone to ring. She never made the big time but she still gets the occasional bit part on TV.'

'She never married?'

'Good heavens, no! Husbands were no more on the agenda than children, not that there weren't plenty of lovers.'

'But you and she still keep in touch?'

'Oh yes, a couple of years ago when she decided to retire and live in Greencliffe it suddenly suited her to acknowledge that she had a son.' He gave a cynical little laugh. 'She only gets in contact when she wants something, though.'

'And your aunt and uncle?'

'Uncle George died a couple of years ago but Aunt Janet's still fine, bless her.' He looked at me. 'What about your parents. You mentioned your father.'

I nodded. 'Dad's great. I only wish I could see more of him but Yorkshire is so far away and life is so busy here with *Mary-Mary*. Dad can't get down to visit us very often. My mother's health isn't good and he doesn't like to leave her.'

'You're obviously close to him. What about your mother...?'

I sighed. 'Mother is something else. I've never really hit it off with her. She always wanted a son and I've always been a disappointment to her – never managed to do anything right.'

'So ... when you had Jamie...?'

'It was no more than she expected of me,' I told him. 'She wasn't interested in the circumstances. I've only been home twice since Jamie was born; both on flying visits.'

'Did Jamie melt her heart?'

I shook my head. 'The first time he was quite a small baby. I think she found him noisy and disruptive. The second time was after he'd begun to show an interest in music and she found that slightly more agreeable. She felt he'd inherited it from her.'

'She was musical?'

I smiled. 'I remember her knocking out the odd tune on the piano. I'd hardly call it musical.' Eager to change the subject I asked, 'Tell me more about your aunt.'

'She's great. She *is* musical, in fact she was the one who got me started. She used to be a professional singer. I'll take you and Jamie to meet her one of these days.' He bit his lip. 'God! What am I saying? As if you'd want to be involved with my life.'

I touched his arm. 'Ian – don't say that.'

By now we were almost home and he pulled the car over and stopped, turning to look at me. 'Elaine – do you have any idea how much you and Jamie have come to mean to me over these last couple of years?'

Lost for words I reached up to touch his cheek and suddenly he pulled me into his arms and his lips were on mine. When we drew apart we were both a little breathless. He laughed shakily. 'I've wanted to do that for ages.'

'Me too,' I whispered.

'Really?' He looked at me incredulously. 'I've always seen myself as a bit of a loner.'

'Why?'

He shook his head. 'I've never thought of myself as the kind of guy a girl would fancy – especially a girl like you.'

'What's so special about a girl like me?'

He sighed. 'Well, for starters, I can't see any reason why you'd be interested in me. I'm not good looking, I've got no head for material things and I'm never going to make a million. All I've ever really wanted from life is my music – at least till now.' He looked at me. 'You deserve the best, Elaine; designer clothes, exotic holidays, diamonds and—' I put my finger against his lips.

'No! You've got me all wrong,' I told him. 'I've got an interesting life – a partnership with my best friend in a flourishing business and a wonderful young son.'

'And that's enough for you? You life is complete?' His eyes searched mine.

'I used to think so. Now I'm not so sure.'

'So – what's missing?'

'Well, someone special to share my life with; someone who'd laugh away all my secret fears; who'd be on my side even when I was wrong.'

'Someone to love you, in other words?'

I nodded. 'That would be the icing on the cake.'

'Consider your cake well and truly iced.' He pulled me close. 'I love you, Elaine. I'd like to be with you more. Maybe if we both thought really carefully we could think of a way.'

It was a week before Jamie's eighth birthday when he came home from school one day with the question I'd been dreading.

'Why haven't I got a dad?'

Mary and I exchanged glances over his head as we sat at the tea table. I took a deep breath. 'Lots of children don't have a dad in their lives,' I told him.

'A lot do, though.' He spread Marmite on his bread thoughtfully.

'Even when he doesn't live at their house they still see him. Daniel's dad has a flat near the park and he goes to stay there sometimes at the weekend.' He looked up at me with his wide blue eyes. 'I've never even *seen* my dad.'

I swallowed hard. 'No.'

'Why, Mum? Where is he? Is he dead?'

'No.'

Mary and I had discussed this question many times, knowing that it was only a matter of time before it came up. We'd agreed that when Jamie did ask he should be told the truth, but I'd hoped that he would be old enough to understand before the situation arose. Was seven old enough? I smiled at him.

'Finish your tea. We'll talk about it later,' I told him.

When he was in bed I tucked him in and sat on the edge. He looked at me expectantly with the expression I knew so well. There was no way he was going to be fobbed off with some half-truth. No one ever got away with trying to pull the wool over Jamie's eyes.

'Mum, I know that everyone has to have a mum and a dad,' he said. 'So I know I have to have one somewhere.'

'Of course you do.'

'So where is he? And why doesn't he come and see me?'

'Jamie – it's hard to explain but sometimes babies come when they're not supposed to.'

He frowned. 'Wasn't I supposed to be born then?'

'You were – a surprise,' I told him. 'A lovely surprise for me, but....'

'Not lovely for my dad?'

'Your dad had something he wanted very badly to do. Having a wife and baby would have meant he wouldn't be able to do it.'

'So he didn't want me?'

I shook my head. This was even harder than I'd foreseen. 'The truth is, Jamie, your dad doesn't know about you. He has never known. It was my decision. I knew that having a family would stop him from doing what he wanted, so I chose not to tell him about you.'

He was quiet, so quiet that I began to worry. Then he looked up at me. 'Where is he?'

'He lives a long way away from here.'

'So can we go and find him?'

'I don't think so. He might have moved by now – gone abroad, anywhere. Maybe by now he's even got a wife and children.'

'You could try and find him and tell him about me.'

'Not really. It's too late. It was all a long time ago.'

He frowned. 'So isn't he *ever* going to know about me?'

'Probably not. It's for the best.' I took his hand. 'We have each other, Jamie, you and me, and we have Auntie Mary and a nice home to live in. You have your music and your friends at school. It's enough, isn't it?'

He considered for a moment. 'I s'pose so,' he said at last.

'You are happy as we are, aren't you?'

'Y-yes.' He looked up suddenly. 'Mum, does a dad always have to be the man who – you know – *borned* you?'

I hid a smile. 'Not always. Some children get adopted and some have a stepfather.'

'What's that?'

'That's a man who marries someone's mother and takes the father's place.'

'Oh!' His face brightened. 'Ian could be my stepfather then, couldn't he?'

The question took my breath away. 'Ian? Oh, I don't know about that.'

He sat up in bed, his face eager. 'But you like him, don't you, Mum? And he likes you. I can tell he does. Can he, Mum – *can* he – *please*?'

I pushed him gently back against the pillows. 'That kind of thing is for grown-ups, Jamie.'

'Shall I ask him?'

'*No!* It's something that takes a lot of thinking about; a very big, important step.'

'But it might happen – yes?'

I looked into the big blue hopeful eyes and felt my heart wrench. Bending forward to kiss him I said, 'We'll have to wait very patiently and see. And, Jamie…?'

'Yes?'

'Promise me that you'll say nothing about this talk we've had to Ian.'

'Couldn't I just…?'

'Not a word. Promise me.'

He sighed. 'Okay, I promise. But I do think grown-ups are funny. If you want something why can't you just ask?'

I bent forward to tuck him in. 'Because it isn't always the best way to go about things,' I told him.

Downstairs Mary was waiting to hear how the conversation went. I told her about Jamie's wish and she laughed.

'Out of the mouths of babes,' she quoted. 'Though I have to confess it's no more than I've been thinking for some time.' She looked at me. 'What's your view on the subject?'

I shrugged. 'Somehow I don't think Ian is the marrying kind, though I wouldn't be surprised if he asked us to move in with him.'

'Move in!' Mary bridled. 'What a cheek! If he does I hope you tell him where to go,' she said. 'I know things are different now to when I was your age, but I still think there's nothing like having a ring on your finger and a respectable marriage certificate.'

'It's just a piece of paper and a chunk of metal.'

'No. It's a commitment.'

'I know.' I didn't want to point out that Ian hadn't asked me to marry him, or that if he had I'd have said yes right away. Instead I said, 'I've got used to being single. It doesn't bother me whether we get married or not.'

Mary narrowed her eyes at me. 'Are you saying he's already asked you to live with him?'

'No, but it's a sort of unspoken possibility between us.'

'And what about that child?' Mary asked. 'Don't you think he deserves better than a hole-in-the-corner arrangement like that?'

I sighed, suddenly tired. Hearing that Ian had never known his father and the conversation I'd had with Jamie had made me examine my decision not to tell Chris he was to become a father. It had seemed right at the time but now I wasn't so sure. Was it really right to deprive a child of his father? Was it moral to keep from a man the knowledge that he had a son? The thought suddenly weighed heavily on my conscience. 'It wouldn't be hole-in-the-corner,' I snapped. Mary raised an eyebrow at me and I added wearily, 'Anyway it's all hypothetical so why are we arguing about it?'

*

Ian and I had to snatch time together when neither of us was working. Sometimes we'd take Jamie out together on a Sunday afternoon but any time we spent alone together was mostly at the beginning of the week. Gradually it became a habit for Ian to eat with the three of us after Jamie's music lesson on Monday afternoons then snatch a couple of hours together after Jamie was in bed. The following Monday he told us over tea that he had arranged to visit his Aunt Janet the following Sunday.

'I'd love you and Jamie to come too,' he said. 'And Mary too if you'd like to.' He looked at her across the table but she shook her head.

'No thank you, Ian. You three go. Now that I'm getting to be an old lady I like my Sunday afternoon snooze.'

Although she laughed as she said it I knew that the real reason for turning down Ian's invitation was that she thought he was merely being polite in including her.

'That's a shame. I'm sure you and Janet would have a lot in common,' he said. But Mary was already clearing the table.

'I'm sure we would. Some other time maybe.' She smiled. 'Off you go, you two and enjoy yourselves,' she said. 'Jamie and I will watch *Coronation Street* and then I'll chase him off to bed.'

We drove out to a favourite pub for a quiet drink. Ian was thoughtful and when I asked him if he had something on his mind he answered with a wry smile.

'Only what's been on my mind for some time,' he said.

'Which is…?'

'Which is how I'd like to spend more time with you, and wondering how you'd react if I asked you to move in with me.' He looked at me. 'There, I've said it.'

I laughed. 'So you have!'

He ran a hand through his hair. 'It's just that we only seem to see each other once a week.' He shook his head. 'It's funny, I used to be so content with my own company. Now I miss you all the time.' He frowned at me. 'Do you realize, woman, that you're ruining my concentration?'

'Really? We certainly can't have that, can we?'

'Are you laughing at me, you cruel woman?'

'No.' I covered his hand with mine and squeezed it. 'I'm very flattered.'

'So – is that a yes – about moving in, I mean?'

'I'd love to, Ian, but I have Jamie to think about.'

'Well of course I meant him too. That goes without saying.'

'Then there's Mary. She's got rather old fashioned views about such things.'

'It's your life, though.'

'I know, but she's been a big part of it for a long time. I owe her so much.'

In the car he pulled me close. 'I love you, Elaine,' he whispered. 'I want to be with you – all the time, not just now and then.'

'Me too,' I told him. 'And nothing would please me more than to come and live with you in your cottage. It's just that I have two other people to consider.'

'Would you like me to speak to them?'

I thought of the conversation I'd had with Jamie and his longing for a father-figure. Fearful of what he might say if Ian broached the subject I shook my head.

'No, let me do it. It would be better coming from me.'

'I'm sure Jamie would enjoy doing his practice on my baby grand piano and there's a nice little bedroom at the back of the house. I could do it up – make it nice for him. It's full of my junk at the moment but—'

'I'm sure he'd love it,' I interrupted. 'Just be patient and leave it with me.'

I spoke to Mary first. She wasn't surprised but she was still slightly disapproving.

'I'm not being a prude,' she assured me. 'I just don't want to see you get hurt. There's Jamie to think of, too. He adores Ian. If it were all to fall through….'

'I'll have to make sure he knows it might not be permanent then, won't I?'

Mary tutted exasperatedly. 'If you believe it might only be temporary why are you doing it?' she demanded. 'And what do you think it will do to Jamie if it doesn't work out?'

'Who can be sure of *anything* nowadays, Mary?' I said impatiently. 'Even marriages aren't for ever nowadays.'

'Oh, I don't know!' She threw up her hands. 'It's a funny old world. That's all I can say.' She reached out a hand to me. 'But you know there's always a home for you here if things don't work out.' She shook her head. 'I'm being an old fuddy-duddy, aren't I? And I suppose I have to admit that I'm dreading the thought of losing the pair of you.'

I put my arms around her. 'You're not going to lose us, Mary,' I told her. 'You and I will still be working together every day and as far as Jamie is concerned you're the only real grandmother he's ever had.'

'Well he certainly feels like a grandson to me,' she said. 'By the way, what about this Aunt Janet person?'

I laughed. 'I've yet to meet her so I don't know, but you needn't feel she's going to usurp your position in any way.'

'Well, she'd better not,' Mary said. 'That's all I can say!'

Janet Morton still lived in the house where Ian had grown up. Inglewood was a lovely unspoilt village six miles out of Greencliffe and as we drove there the following Sunday afternoon Ian told Jamie about some of the mischief he and his schoolmates used to get up to.

'I was in the church choir,' he said. 'And we used to have some super outings to the seaside. Once I tried to climb up the cliff, halfway up I got stuck, too scared to go up or down and the vicar had to climb up and rescue me. I don't know which of us was the most scared.'

Jamie laughed delightedly. 'Did you get into trouble?'

'You bet! I went home in disgrace and was sent to bed without any supper, though Aunt Janet did sneak me up a sandwich later.'

'What else did you do?' Jamie wanted to know.

Warming to the subject Ian opened his mouth. 'Well, there was one time when—' I stopped him.

'I don't think we need to hear any more of your juvenile exploits at the moment,' I said with a frown. 'I don't want Jamie getting ideas.'

'Oh Mum!' Jamie piped up from the back seat. 'You are a spoil-sport.'

'Well, we're here now,' Ian said, turning the car in through open double gates. He turned to Jamie with a sly wink. 'We'll resume our conversation some other time, eh?'

The house was a late Georgian villa, built of warm red brick with a blue slate roof and latticed windows. The garden was pretty with flowering shrubs and a spreading cedar tree in the centre of the lawn. From one of the lower branches hung a home-made swing. Jamie's eyes widened.

'Wow, a swing! Can I have a go?'

'You must come in and say how do you do first,' I reminded him. 'And ask permission.'

Janet Morton stood at the open door to meet us, smiling a welcome. She was tall and slender with twinkling blue eyes. Her grey hair was caught back into a chignon and she wore a tweed skirt and pale blue sweater.

'Come in, all of you. The kettle's on.' She held out her hand to me. 'You must be Elaine. It's so nice to meet you at last and be able to put a face to the name.' She looked past me at Jamie. 'And this is Jamie, of course. Hello, Jamie. I hope you like iced buns.'

He nodded shyly. 'Yes, thank you – er ...' he glanced at me. 'Can I have a go on the swing?'

Janet laughed. 'Of course you may.' At that moment a small wire-haired terrier shot past her, a ball in his mouth, which he dropped at Jamie's feet. Janet laughed. 'Oh, here's Brownie come to play with you. He's brought his ball for you to throw.'

As Jamie ran off with the dog Janet ushered us into the house. The hallway was dim and cool, the stone-flagged floor scattered with rugs. A door to the right led into a spacious, comfortably furnished living room. It had a low ceiling and French windows which led out into the garden and in one corner stood a piano, the lid open and music on the stand as though someone had recently been playing it. Tea was laid out on a trolley; three kinds of cake and a selection of sandwiches, plus the iced buns Janet had mentioned to Jamie.

'I know what small boys like,' she said as she saw me looking at them. 'I should. I've had plenty of practice.' Looking out into the garden where Jamie was playing with the dog she said, 'He's a lovely looking boy. You must be very proud of him.'

I smiled. 'I am.'

'He's a very promising music student,' Ian put in.

We talked. Janet was interested in the catering business and wanted to hear the story of how Mary and I had started.

'I think you're so brave, starting a business on your own,' she said.

She looked out of the window to where Jamie was swinging perilously high.

'Oh dear. Ian, I think you should go out and make sure that the child is safe,' she said. 'He's going awfully high and I'd hate anything to happen to him.' When Ian had left the room she looked at me. 'I hope you don't think me an old fusspot.'

'Not at all. I always feel I'm in danger of being over protective,' I said. 'I suppose most single mothers are the same.'

She refilled my teacup thoughtfully. 'Ian is very fond of the boy,' she said glancing up at me.

'I know.' I took the cup from her. 'And it's mutual. Jamie couldn't have a better music teacher. He adores Ian.'

'I shouldn't ask – but are you and he…?'

'Yes,' I told her. It was a tricky moment. 'I don't know whether he's mentioned it to you but he's asked us to move into the cottage with him.' I held my breath, wondering whether she would share Mary's views. To my relief she smiled and nodded.

'Well, yes. I confess that he has hinted that he hoped it would happen and I'm so pleased for you both, my dear. Ian has spent far too much time on his own since he decided to leave the orchestra. I know he keeps in touch with his musician friends but he really needs someone who understands and cares for him.' She shook her head. 'Do I sound like an interfering old busybody?'

'Not at all.'

'It's just that I don't think he….'

'Eats enough?' I suggested. She laughed.

'Exactly! He forgets to get his hair cut too, and he's always forgetting things like dental appointments and paying bills.'

'Well, I think I can promise that he won't in future.'

'I'm so glad he's found you,' Janet said. 'I hope you don't mind but he's told me what happened between you and Jamie's father. It was a very brave decision you made.'

'It didn't feel brave at the time,' I told her. 'I felt I had no choice. But I was lucky. I had a good friend who helped me.'

'And now you've got Ian.'

'I have and I'm very lucky. I love him very much, Mrs Morton.'

'Janet, please. Aunt Janet if you prefer. He loves you very much too, my dear. You can be sure of that.'

'Ian told me you used to be a singer. That must be where he gets his musical talent from.'

She smiled. 'There was always music in the house when he was little and Ian has loved the piano ever since he was big enough to reach the keys,' she said. 'I gave him his very first lessons but when I could see he had real talent I found him a proper teacher.'

'He was lucky to have you and his uncle.' I glanced at her. 'He told me about his mother.'

'Amanda? Ah, yes.' Janet sighed. 'But then who are we to judge? None of us can help who we are, and Ian has always been the son George and I would never have had if Amanda hadn't been the way she was.'

I looked at the photograph on the mantelpiece. It showed a younger Janet and Ian at about six; with them, his arms around them both, was George Morton, tall and dark-haired with laughing brown eyes.

'Is that your husband?' I asked, nodding towards the photograph. Janet nodded.

'He adored Ian. They were inseparable.'

Ian came back in with Jamie, the little dog at his heels and Janet chased them off to the kitchen with orders to wash their hands while she made a fresh pot of tea.

Jamie tried each of the sandwiches in turn and did justice to the iced buns while Brownie, the dog, sat beside him, watching every mouthful with appealing brown eyes. I wondered if Janet noticed the titbits that Jamie occasionally posted into his open jaws.

'You must be quite a connoisseur of sandwiches and cake,' she said, 'with Mummy and your auntie running a catering business. I bet you get to scrape the bowl all the time.'

'Oh, they don't let me do that,' Jamie proclaimed airily. 'I'm not even allowed in the kitchen when they're cooking.'

Janet looked at me inquiringly.

'Health and safety,' I explained. 'The rules are very strict, although Jamie doesn't starve, I can assure you.'

She laughed. 'I can see that.'

When tea was cleared away Janet looked at Ian. 'I've got something for Jamie,' she said. 'It was yours and I'm sure you'll want him to have it.' She went out of the room and the three of us looked at each other, Jamie fidgeting on his chair with excitement.

'What is it?' he whispered to Ian, but Ian shook his head.

'Your guess is as good as mine,' he said.

Janet came back into the room with a leather case under her arm. She opened it and took out a junior-size violin and bow which she handed to Jamie.

'You'll have to get Ian to teach you to play it,' she said. 'It's been languishing in the cupboard ever since he grew out of it and it's high time someone played it again.'

Jamie's face was a picture of delight as he fingered the instrument. He looked at Janet. 'Is it really for me?'

She laughed. 'Yes, if you want it.'

He nodded eagerly. 'Thank you.' He looked at Ian. 'Will you teach me to play it?'

Ian laughed. 'I can see I'm going to have my work cut out. It's a good job you're coming to live with me.'

Jamie looked at me, his eyes wide with delight. 'Are we? Wow! That'll be really cool!'

He fell asleep on the back seat of the car on the way home, the violin case cradled in his arms like the precious possession it was. Later as I tucked him up in bed he opened his eyes and smiled at me.

'Are we really going to live with Ian?' he asked.

I nodded.

'And will he really teach me to play the violin? I didn't dream it – it did all really happen, didn't it, Mum?'

I laughed. 'Yes, it did.'

'And is the violin really mine – for keeps?'

'Yes, it is,' I said gently removing it from under the duvet. 'Now go to sleep.'

Downstairs I kissed Ian. 'Thank you for today, darling – and for everything. Jamie is over the moon.'

'No, thank you. When will you move in? I've got rid of all the junk in the spare room and I thought maybe next weekend I'd paint it.'

'I'll come and help. The sooner we get it done, the sooner we can move in.'

He hugged me close. 'I can't wait.'

Four

We painted Jamie's room a bright sunshine yellow. It was at the back of the cottage and overlooked the garden, which, Ian admitted, was an overgrown disgrace. I made him promise that we'd get to work on it as soon as we settled in. Jamie passed his grade three piano exam and Ian began to give him violin lessons which he took to as eagerly as he had the piano.

Virginia Cottage was not 'in the sticks' as Ian had described it, but in a pleasant suburb of Greencliffe, about five miles out of town. It was an end of terrace Victorian two up, two down house which had been updated by a previous owner. It was clear from the beginning that Jamie and I were going to feel quite cramped, especially after being used to Mary's spacious semi.

Downstairs, the two rooms had been knocked into one and a kitchen built on at the back. A lot of space was taken up by Ian's baby grand piano, which Jamie adored on sight. The kitchen was big enough to use as a dining room so it was clear from the start that I would be spending much of my spare time there. Upstairs the tiny third bedroom had been converted into a bathroom. The house fitted the three of us like a tight shoe. Ian promised that we would look for a larger house as soon as we had saved enough money.

On the weekend before we moved, Dad came down from Yorkshire to meet Ian. To my relief they seemed to take to each other on sight. I begged Dad to stay longer but he shook his head.

'I'd love to but I can't leave your mother for too long,' he said. 'She's not at all well and she seems to need me more and more these days.'

I was quite shocked. In all her life Mother had been completely independent. She was what people call a 'private person'. In other words she preferred to shut everyone else out and favoured her own company. As far as I could see she'd never been much of a companion to Dad and it didn't seem fair that she was making demands on him now. But perhaps this was how he liked things; maybe it was what he had always wanted, a wife who needed him.

'How bad is she, Dad?' I asked him.

'Well, as you know it's her heart,' he told me. 'And it's not going to get any better. She's all right as long as she takes things very easily. No excitement or extra exertion.' He grinned good-naturedly. 'I do most of the cooking nowadays. I'm getting to be an elderly Jamie Oliver. We have a cleaning lady once a week and in between I run around with the Hoover. We manage just fine.'

I squeezed his hand. 'I wish there was more I could do, Dad. I'd bring Ian up for a visit but I know she'd disapprove of us living together and I've no wish to upset her.'

He shook his head. 'It's your life, love. As long as you and young Jamie are happy that's all I want for you both. I'm afraid your mum will never change.' He patted my shoulder. 'And for what it's worth, I think you've got one of the best in Ian. He's a grand lad.'

On the morning we moved out, Mary was quite tearful. She stood on the front step as we packed the car, clutching a handkerchief and when I went to kiss her goodbye she clung to me, choking back a sob.

'Oh dear, I promised myself I wouldn't do this,' she said crossly, dabbing at her eyes.

I hugged her. 'Mary! I'm not off to Siberia. I'll see you tomorrow,' I said. 'I'll be here bright and early every day, reporting for work just as usual.'

She nodded, swallowing hard. 'I know, but it won't be the same. I've got so used to having the two of you around the house and I'm going to miss you like crazy.'

'Go on,' I chided. 'I bet you're secretly sick of the sight of us and longing for some peace and quiet.'

She shook her head. 'You want to bet?'

Jamie loved his new room. He'd brought all his favourite posters, books and toys and in no time he'd made the room his own. Downstairs I looked round the kitchen. Ian was very fastidious and everywhere was spotlessly clean, but as I told him, the place could do with a lick of paint and some new curtains. He laughed.

'In other words, the woman's touch!'

I frowned at him. 'Don't you dare suggest anything so sexist!

A month later both kitchen and living room had been decorated and I'd made new curtains for both rooms. My portable TV was installed in the kitchen and we moved the sofa in there, buying a new one for the living room. Virginia Cottage began to feel like home.

Our individual routines worked well. In the daytime while I worked with Mary and Jamie was at school, Ian taught his pupils at the cottage or drove out to teach them at their homes. If one of Ian's gigs coincided with a *Mary-Mary* event Jamie would stay the night with his friend, Daniel, whose mother Cathy had become a good friend.

After a few weeks of struggling with unreliable public transport I bought myself a little second-hand car so that I was able to drop Jamie off at school before going on to Mary's. In our spare time at weekends Ian and I cleared the garden and planted bulbs ready for the spring.

With the arrival of winter the question of Christmas arose. After some discussion we decided to spend it at Mary's, which was what she had suggested. She extended the invitation to Ian's Aunt Janet, who happily accepted. I asked Ian about his mother but he shook his head.

'Amanda and Janet together in the same house for more than half an hour is a recipe for disaster,' he said.

'But they're sisters,' I argued.

'Exactly!' He laughed. 'As far as I can see that only makes matters worse. Anyway, Amanda never seems short of invitations. I vote we just don't mention it.'

Ian had been putting off a visit to his mother ever since Jamie and I moved in. I'd always known they didn't enjoy the closest of relationships so I didn't press it, telling myself he would suggest introducing me to his mother when he was good and ready.

Jamie came home from school, excited at the prospect of auditioning for the school orchestra and when he was accepted two days later I don't know who was the more delighted – him or Ian. Life was good and I fell more and more in love with Ian as the weeks went by. He was loving and considerate, easy-going and wonderful with Jamie, who adored him. We were a family.

We were having supper one evening at the beginning of December when Ian suddenly looked up and said, 'I had a letter from Amanda this morning.'

I looked up. 'Your mother? Is that unusual?'

'It tends only to happen when she wants something,' he said dryly. 'And this is no exception.'

'Oh, what does she want?'

'Oh, she's very subtle.' He took the letter from an inside pocket and passed it to me across the table. 'You have to read between the lines.'

I unfolded the single sheet of notepaper and read with interest.

My dear Ian,

I am rather surprised that you have not had the courtesy to introduce me to your partner yet. I wonder what the reason for this can be. Surely you are not ashamed to be living with an unmarried mother and her child in this day and age! As you know, I am very broad-minded on the subject. I would love to meet her and, as you know, I am always here – mostly alone at the flat. I don't get many visitors so it would be a treat to have a visit from you.

I shall be spending this Christmas alone, alas. It is very sad to be old and unwanted as you will surely discover one of these days. But there – I know you are busy with your own life and who could blame you if you forget sometimes that you have a mother.

Hoping that you might find a few minutes to spare for me one of these days, I remain, your affectionate mother, Amanda.

P.S. I am always out at my bridge club on Wednesdays and Fridays.

'To be fair, I suppose we should have gone to see her before now,' I said, folding the letter and handing it back.

Ian pulled a face. 'If I were you I'd reserve judgement on that.'

We decided to go and visit Amanda the following Sunday after-noon. Ian suggested that, on this first occasion, it would be better if it were just the two of us so it was arranged that Jamie would stay with Daniel for the afternoon.

Amanda's flat was on the fourth floor of Ocean Heights, the private block of flats on the cliffs overlooking the sea. We took the lift up to the fourth floor and as I glanced at Ian I noticed to my surprise that he was nervous. I reached for his hand.

'Don't worry.'

He shook his head. 'The trouble with Amanda is that she always has an agenda. You never know what she's going to come out with. She seems to think she has the right to be "open and honest" as she puts it, whether she offends people or not.'

I gave his hand a squeeze. 'I don't take offence easily. What can she say anyway?'

'Mmm,' He pulled a wry face. 'You'd be surprised.'

She opened the door to our ring immediately, almost as though she'd been waiting behind it. Unlike her sister, Janet, she was tiny and doll-like and had obviously been very pretty in her youth. But unlike Janet she was clearly refusing to accept the advancing years gracefully. She wore a long black velvet skirt and a glamorous white blouse with a profusion of lace ruffles at the neck. Her blonde hair was swept up in a girlish explosion of curls with tendrils escaping over her forehead and neck. But her efforts to retain her youthful looks only enhanced her age and although she was only two years older than Janet I would have guessed that the age difference was greater.

The china blue eyes were openly appraising, sweeping me up and down as Ian introduced us. She offered a small white hand, heavy with rings.

'How nice to meet you,' she said, touching my hand briefly with her scarlet fingertips. 'Though not before time, I must say. Still, better late than never – even if I did have to write to you, Ian.' She gave him a withering look then led the way on four-inch heels into the living room, which was furnished with a pink velvet-covered chaise longue and two rather uncomfortable looking chairs. One wall was entirely covered with signed photographs.

'All my showbusiness friends,' she explained with an airy wave of her hand. 'Do feel free to look at them. I'm sure you'll find many famous names that you'll recognize among them.'

A coffee table was laid for tea with delicate eggshell china and embroidered napkins but no actual food.

'I'll go and bring in the tea,' Amanda said. 'Make yourselves at home.'

When she'd gone Ian let out his breath. 'Phew! I told you she was heavy going.'

'Shhh, she'll hear you,' I told him. 'She's fine.'

'She's in her best leading lady mode,' he warned. 'So don't say I didn't warn you.'

Amanda returned with a plate of minute sandwiches and a chocolate Swiss roll. 'I hope you like fish paste,' she said. 'I'm afraid I'm not a domestic goddess like my sister. I have to rely on the supermarket, but do help yourselves.' She looked at me. 'Where is your child? A boy, isn't it? Nothing *wrong* with him, is there?'

Her tone indicated that we might be hiding the fact that he had two heads and Ian answered for me. 'There's nothing at all wrong with Jamie. He's a very promising pupil of mine.'

'I see.' Amanda poured extremely weak tea from a silver teapot. 'And is that how you two met?'

'Not exactly,' I told her. 'Ian and his quintet were playing at a wedding where my friend and I were doing the catering.'

'Oh.' She looked up at me. 'So – you're a waitress?'

I refused to look at Ian. 'No,' I said calmly. 'My friend and I run a catering business. It's called *Mary-Mary*.'

She raised a delicately plucked eyebrow. 'Really, how quaint.' She passed me a cup half full of pallid liquid. 'So you're really a glorified cook?'

'We do prepare most of the food ourselves,' I conceded.

She passed me the plate of fish paste sandwiches. 'Of course, I know nothing about such things,' she said airily. 'I spent most of my life on tour and living in hotels where things like that were done for me.' She gave a tinkling little laugh. 'I can't boil the proverbial egg, darling. Nowadays I exist on microwave meals and takeaways. Unless, Henry, my gentleman friend takes me out to dinner, of course, which fortunately he does several times a week.' She looked pointedly at Ian. 'Which brings me to the question of Christmas. What are your plans, Ian?'

'We're invited to spend it with a friend of Elaine's,' he put in.

'You're going out?' She looked quickly at me. 'I would have thought you'd have liked your child to have Christmas in his own home,' she said.

'Oh, he will have,' I told her. 'Mary is my business partner. Until we moved in with Ian, Jamie and I lived with her. It'll be like going home for him.'

'I see. Well, as I haven't met this – er – Jamie yet, how about asking your friend if she can squeeze one more in for Christmas?'

Realizing that I'd walked right into it I hardly dared glance at Ian.

'It's not for us to invite extra guests,' he put in quickly. 'We couldn't impose.'

Amanda's eyes were steely as she pressed another fish paste sandwich on him.

'Well you won't know if it's an imposition until you *ask*, will you, darling? I don't really think it's your decision.' She took up a pearl handled cake knife and began to attack the Swiss roll. 'You know, darling, you really must try to lose the habit of speaking up for your girlfriends. I'm sure that's why they all leave you in the end. You can be very domineering.'

Ian flushed. 'No I'm not.'

'Yes, you are.' She looked at me. 'They never stay with him for long, you know dear.' Her eyes shot back to Ian. 'What about that lovely girl you were seeing last year – what was her name? She tipped her head sideways like a predatory bird listening for a worm. 'Petronella?'

'Patricia,' Ian mumbled, his cheeks still red.

'Oh yes.' She glanced at me. 'Now she *was* a pretty girl; footloose and fancy free too. Quite a catch I would have thought. What on earth did you do to put her off, Ian?'

He swallowed hard, hanging on valiantly to his patience. 'It wasn't last year. It was two years ago. It wasn't serious anyway. It was just a couple of dates.'

'Mmm …' Amanda shrugged. 'You can make as many excuses as you like but I wouldn't mind betting that she got tired of you bossing her about.' She smiled at me. 'Just you stand up for yourself, dear,' she advised. 'Men! They'll walk all over you if you let them.' She nibbled delicately at her cake. 'Now – what were we saying? Ah yes, Christmas. I wouldn't need putting up. I don't mind if it's only for the day. You can come and pick me up, Ian, and run me home later in the evening.'

'You're not planning to spend Christmas with Henry then?' Ian ventured.

Amanda shot him a venomous look. 'Clearly not! I'd have thought that much was obvious.'

'Ian's Aunt Janet will be joining us,' I said.

'*Janet!*' Amanda glared at Ian. 'You've asked *her!*'

'We're returning her hospitality,' I said quickly, trying to pour oil on troubled waters. 'She invited us to her house and prepared a wonderful spread—' I stopped short, biting my tongue as I realized that I was making matters even worse.

'Oh, I'm *sure* she did!' Amanda said sharply. 'Always one to get in first with the grovelling.' She dabbed at the corners of her mouth then threw down her napkin. 'Well now you can return *my* hospitality too, can't you?' She glared at me. 'That's if you consider my meagre spread good enough to call hospitality!'

'Of course,' I said, stumbling over my words. 'Ian and I have had a lovely tea. Anyway, we came to see *you*, didn't we, Ian?'

She stood up, making it abundantly clear that the visit was at an end. 'Well now you have!' She began to walk towards the door. 'So if you'll excuse me I'm feeling rather tired. It's been nice meeting you, *Alice*; quite an – er *entertainment*. I only hope you last longer than Ian's last paramour.'

Ian didn't speak at all as we travelled down in the lift. It wasn't until we were in the car that he gave vent to his anger.

'Now perhaps you can see why I put off taking you to meet her,' he said running a hand through his hair. '*Alice*! She really is impossible!' He looked at me. 'I'm so sorry darling.'

'It was me who put my foot in it. There's no need to apologize.'

'There is! I've let you and Mary in for putting up with her on Christmas Day, not to mention Janet. How I'm going to break the news to her I don't know.'

'No, really, it was my fault. Anyway, it's only for one day. Surely they can get along for a few hours.'

'I wouldn't bet on it. I don't know how I'm going to face Janet.' He let out his frustration with an exasperated growl. 'Urhh! Calling you a glorified cook!'

'There's nothing wrong with being a cook.'

'And all that about her being undomesticated and living in hotels,' he went on. 'Her theatrical career amounted to no more than playing second leads in weekly rep in godforsaken holes at the back of beyond and as for hotels! Grubby back street digs was all she was used to.'

'What about all those photographs of her showbusiness friends?'

'She's never even *met* half of them. It's all a front. She's been boasting about her career in the theatre for so long I swear she half believes it herself.'

'I think that's quite sad.'

He looked at me. '*Sad* – Amanda? Never!'

We were still sitting in the car park and I looked up at the apartment block. 'She must have had some quite well paid jobs during her stage career to be able to afford a flat like that for her retirement,' I said.

'She doesn't pay for it,' Ian said. 'You heard her talk about Henry, her "gentleman friend" as she calls him. He pays the rent, presumably in return for her company at those cosy dinners she mentioned. The mind boggles at what else.'

'I see. She's not tempted to marry him then?'

'Marriage has never been on Amanda's agenda.'

'But I would have thought that at her age she'd be thinking about security.'

'She probably thinks *I'm* her security,' Ian said bitterly. 'Not that I owe her anything. She only acknowledges our relationship when it suits her.'

I slipped my hand through his arm. 'Don't let her get to you, darling.' Suddenly I asked mischievously, 'By the way, why have you never mentioned the glamorous Petronella?'

Ian sighed. 'Trust her to bring that up. It was ages ago – water under the bridge, and her name was *Patricia,* as she knows quite well. She was a girl I dated a few times, nothing serious.'

'Serious enough to take her to meet your mother,' I teased.

'Amanda is only my mother through some ghastly biological error,' he said through gritted teeth. 'That title belongs to Janet and always will. And I never took Pat to meet her. We ran into her once in the street, that was all,' he said. 'Even now I cringe with embarrassment every time I remember it!' He looked at me. 'I'd have told you about Pat if it had been any big deal. You do believe that. Don't you?'

'Of course I do.' I reached up to kiss him. 'I'm only teasing. Of course you had relationships before we met just as I did. Haven't I got Jamie to prove it? All that matters is that we have each other now.'

He pulled me close. 'You're right. Nothing can touch us, can it?'

We sat for a moment, his arm warm around me and my head on his shoulder.

'We don't spend nearly enough time together,' he said suddenly. 'We should try to get away for a few days – just the two of us.'

I knew what he meant. In all the time we had known one another we'd hardly spent any time alone. I knew he loved Jamie almost as much as I did but getting away together would be nice even if it were only for a long weekend.

'It's not the best time of year,' I said.

He looked down at me. 'How about after Christmas? Maybe we could have a few days in the Cotswolds or somewhere.'

'That sounds wonderful,' I told him. 'Maybe we could do it after the New Year bookings have quietened down.'

'Do you think Mary would have Jamie?'

'I'm sure she'd jump at the chance.'

He hugged me close. 'It'll be something to look forward to,' he said. 'Something to get us through the Christmas Day fiasco.'

I laughed. 'Don't meet trouble halfway!'

He switched on the ignition and started the car. 'Believe me, where Amanda's concerned trouble rushes to meet you like a hungry lion!'

Mary took the news that we were to have an extra guest for Christmas Day in her stride. She and I were going to do the cooking and we were used to catering for large numbers. Six was a mere nothing. Janet, on the other hand, was a different matter. We went to see her the weekend after our visit to Amanda and Ian broke the news that she was to have the company of her sister on Christmas Day. As he had expected, her face fell.

'Oh, Ian.'

'I know, he said quickly. 'But you know what she's like. She wouldn't take no for an answer.'

Janet sighed. 'Oh well, I suppose I'll just have to try and make the best of it.' She looked at me. 'You must think I'm awful, but Amanda really isn't the easiest person to get along with even though she's my sister.'

'I gathered that. But you've done so much for her. When she had Ian for instance; what would she have done without you?'

'She would have had him adopted,' Janet said.

'She wouldn't have gone through with it once she'd seen him,' I told her. 'I know I couldn't when Jamie was born.'

'Amanda would,' Janet said. 'Back then she wouldn't allow anything to get in the way of her stage career.'

I was about to ask about Ian's father – whether Amanda had ever given him any say in what happened to his son, then I remembered how I had kept Chris in the dark. It may have been for different reasons but it came down to the same thing in the end. Was I no better than Amanda? I shuddered at the thought.

Mary had made the house look wonderful for Christmas. All the downstairs rooms were decorated with evergreens and a big Christmas tree stood in the hall decked with red and gold; tiny pin-point lights twinkling among the branches.

Ian, Jamie and I were to stay with her over the holiday in our old rooms. When Mary had first invited Janet she had declined, saying that she would need to be at home because of Brownie.

'Bring him too,' Mary had suggested. 'I know Jamie would love to have him. He's never stopped talking about your dog ever since the day he came to have tea with you.'

The three of us arrived on Christmas Eve and it was well after ten before we managed to persuaded Jamie to go to bed.

'Are you going to hang your stocking up?' I asked as I tucked him in. He gave me a pitying look.

'Mum! I'm nearly nine. I don't do that kind of stuff any more.'

'I see. Does that mean you don't want any presents?'

He grinned. 'I never said that.'

'Thought not.' I ruffled his hair. 'Okay, where shall I ask Santa to put them then.'

'Oh, *Mum*!'

'What?'

'There isn't any Santa. Everybody knows that.'

I feigned shocked surprise. 'There *isn't*? Oh dear, it looks like Christmas won't be happening this year then, doesn't it?'

'Well....' He sat up in bed and looked at me thoughtfully. 'I suppose I could be wrong.'

'You think so?'

'Daniel still believes in him.'

'Then I suggest you do too,' I said. 'Just for one more year. Better to be on the safe side than to wake up to no presents, eh?'

'But you buy them – don't you?'

'Whatever gave you that idea?'

'D'you think I'll get a bike?'

I pushed him back against the pillows and tucked him in again. 'I think you should go to sleep then it'll soon be morning and you'll find out,' I laughed, kissing his forehead. 'Night night.'

''Night, Mum.'

As I switched the light out I wondered how much longer Jamie and I would keep up this yearly pretence. He was growing up so fast that I was no longer aware of who was humouring whom. Would Ian and I have a child of our own? I wondered. Only time would tell.

Ian went to fetch his Aunt Janet first on Christmas morning. Jamie begged to go too so that he could sit in the back of the car with Brownie on the way back. We'd decided to wait until after lunch to open our presents, although Jamie had already had his bike and ridden it round the garden a few times with Ian holding onto the back of the saddle.

Mary and Janet hit it off on sight. I'd always known they were on the same wavelength. And Brownie won Mary's heart right away with his cute ways and melting brown eyes. Jamie had bought him a new bowl and he was soon tucking into biscuits out of it in a corner of the kitchen.

Mary suggested that Janet sit by the living room fire with a magazine while she and I got to work preparing the vegetables. Predictably, she wouldn't hear of it.

'Oh, can't I help?' she asked. 'Sitting around reading magazines really isn't my thing. Besides, I'd rather have your company.'

So when the time came for him to go and collect his mother, Ian left the three of us in the kitchen happily preparing the Christmas dinner.

'I was going to ask Jamie to come with me,' he said ruefully, looking out of the window to where Jamie was throwing a ball for Brownie in the garden. 'But it seems he's otherwise engaged.'

When he'd gone Janet looked at Mary. 'Have you met Amanda yet?' Mary shook her head. 'Well all I can say is that I hope she's on her best behaviour,' she warned. 'She's got a vicious tongue. My advice is to try and ignore her little barbed remarks.'

Mary laughed. 'It's Christmas,' she said. 'She's sure to be in a good mood. Besides, once we've all got a few drinks down us I'm sure we'll all be the greatest of pals.'

Janet shot me a rueful look. 'Mmm, well I hope you're right.'

By the time Ian arrived with Amanda preparations for the meal were well under way; the turkey sending out a mouth-watering aroma and the pudding bubbling away happily whilst piles of vegetables stood ready in bowls waiting to be cooked.

Under her fur coat Amanda was dressed in a floating pale blue creation, her hair swept up in gloriously contrived disarray. She kissed the air an inch away from Janet's cheek and was royally gracious as Ian introduced her to Mary.

'How do you do. I've heard so much about you and your lovely sandwich business,' she said, extending the scarlet fingertips.

Mary took the barb on the chin whilst Janet turned away to hide a smile. Just at that moment Jamie opened the back door, letting in an exuberant Brownie who rushed straight at Amanda and jumped up at her in a doggy welcome. She let out a piercing shriek.

'Oh, my *God*! Get the wretched creature off me.' She glared at Janet, brushing frantically at Brownie's paw marks. 'Why on earth did you have to bring your filthy animal with you?' she complained. 'Not everyone wants to live in a zoo!'

Janet grabbed a roll of paper towels and gave it to Jamie. 'Take Brownie outside and wipe his paws for me, will you, Jamie?' she said quietly. She turned to Amanda. 'Just leave the marks alone, Amanda. They'll brush off easily when they're dry.'

But Amanda continued to fuss with her dress. 'It's all right for you,' she said glaring at her sister. 'Not all of us go around wearing baggy casuals all the time. Some of us prefer to dress for the occasion.'

Mary stepped forward. 'There now, I'm sure there's no real harm done. Suppose we all go into the living room and have a sherry?' she said. She looked at Ian. 'Will you do the honours?'

I hung back, opening the back door and looking for Jamie who was standing under the window clutching Brownie in his arms.

'Is that lady still cross?' he asked. 'I didn't do it on purpose.'

'No, it wasn't your fault,' I said. 'Come in, you'll catch cold standing out here.'

As I closed the door behind him he looked up at me indignantly. 'Brownie isn't a filthy animal, is he, Mum?'

'No, of course he isn't but it might be as well to leave him in the kitchen just for the time being.'

Mary had pulled out all the stops to make Christmas dinner a success, laying the table in the dining room with a pristine white cloth and scarlet napkins. In the centre she'd created a festive centre-piece with holly and tall red candles. All the food was cooked to perfection and everyone enjoyed it apart from Amanda. To begin with she refused the prawn cocktail starter because she claimed she was allergic to shellfish. Mary apologized for not having checked and conjured up some home-made soup. When it came to the main course Amanda declined the turkey because she said she had once eaten undercooked turkey and suffered horrendous food poisoning. She took one sip of her wine and wrinkled her nose, pointedly pushing her glass away. When it came to the pudding she announced that she could not tolerate dried fruit. Mary, who had been up and down from the table all through the meal, jumped up once again and returned from the kitchen with a platter of cheese and biscuits. I could see both Ian and Janet quietly fuming.

After the meal I offered to make coffee and escaped gratefully to the kitchen whilst the others repaired to the living room. After a moment Jamie appeared and tugged at my sleeve.

'Mum, can I stay out here in the kitchen with Brownie?' he begged. 'He'll be lonely all by himself.'

Reluctantly I agreed. I had hoped we would all spend the after-noon together but it was the lesser of two evils. The atmosphere between Ian, his aunt and his mother was beginning to sizzle. It was clearly not going to be much fun for a child.

In the kitchen I made Brownie his own version of a Christmas dinner and Jamie settled down to watch him enjoy it while I returned to the living room with the tray of coffee.

I poured and handed round the coffee and we all sipped in silence for a few minutes. I could see by Janet's face that she could hardly contain her anger and after a few tense moments she turned to her sister.

'How is Henry Ingram these days?'

Amanda stiffened. 'Why do you ask?'

Janet shrugged. 'Why not? He's your friend, isn't he?'

'He's perfectly fine,' Amanda said, hiding her flushed face in her coffee cup.

'I happened to run into him a couple of weeks ago,' Janet went on. 'I was out to dinner with some friends and Henry was at the same restaurant.' She drained her coffee cup and looked across at Amanda. 'He was with a woman.'

Amanda glared at her. 'You were probably mistaken.'

Janet smiled. 'He was extremely attentive. The chef brought in this beautiful cake and all of us were sent a little piece to celebrate *Mrs Ingram's* birthday. They looked the perfect couple.'

'It's a common enough name.' Amanda snapped. 'As I said – you must have been mistaken.'

'There was no mistake. I went and had a word with him when his wife had gone to powder her nose, actually. I was surprised to hear that he and you had been finished for months,' Janet said. 'He begged me not to say anything to his wife as she had found out about his little … *indiscretion* and he was trying his hardest to make it up to her.'

'That's rubbish. I don't believe you!' Amanda slammed her cup and saucer down. 'You're making it all up!' Amanda had turned from pink to puce.

'Shall we drop the subject now?' Ian put in.

But Janet was well into her stride. 'It explains the sudden resurgence of interest in your family. So what about your flat, Amanda? Who's paying your rent now?'

Again Ian attempted to intervene, 'Aunt Janet, don't you think…?'

Amanda rounded on him. 'Shut up, Ian!' She turned back to Janet. '*I'm* paying it of course!'

'*You?*' Janet laughed. 'With what, may I ask?'

'I'm not exactly a pauper you know. My television appearances pay very well.'

'Your *television appearances!*' Janet scoffed. 'Blink and you'll miss them! A couple of walk-ons twice a year can hardly be called *appearances!*'

'Amanda! Janet! *Please* – that's enough. Remember where you are!' Ian looked upset and I reached for his hand.

Janet turned to him. 'I'm sorry, Ian, but your mother has behaved abominably today. She's exceeded even *her* standards of nastiness. She was downright insulting over the meal. I think Mary and Elaine deserve an apology.'

Amanda's face darkened. 'Can I help it if I have a delicate stomach? The truth is, Janet, you hoped to have centre stage today and you're jealous because Ian chose to invite me too. The truth is, you've always been jealous of me. I've always had everything you wanted – looks, talent, men, and you can't stand it, can you, even now?'

The colour left Janet's face. 'I suggest you leave it right there, Amanda,' she said quietly, 'before you say something you'll regret.'

'Why stop now, Janet?' Amanda said, half rising from her chair. 'After all, you started it.' Her eyes were glinting and she was visibly shaking. 'And of course in the end you had every reason to be jealous too, didn't you?' she said triumphantly.

The colour left Janet's face. 'That's enough.'

'Well, I don't think it is! Why did I refuse to tell anyone who Ian's father was?' She stepped forward to deliver her fatal blow. 'Because it was George – yes, *your husband*, Janet. That was something to be jealous about, wasn't it?'

Deeply humiliated, Janet shrank back in her chair, her eyes filling with tears. A white-faced Ian sprang to his feet. 'Get your coat, Amanda. You're going home.'

She got up and began to fumble in her handbag. 'Yes, I'm only too glad to – and don't worry, you can relax. I'll ring for a taxi.'

'You bet you will!' He bundled her out into the hall and Mary and I looked fearfully at Janet. Mary went to her and took her hand.

'My dear, I'm so sorry. Can I get you anything – a brandy?'

Janet shook her head. 'I asked for it, didn't I? I must apologize to you both. I shouldn't have goaded her. She always brings out the worst in me. But she was so rude to you – after your kind hospitality too. It was unforgivable and I'm so ashamed.'

'But what she said to you.' I moved to sit by her side. 'What a terrible thing to say.'

Dry-eyed, Janet looked at me. 'It's true,' she said. 'I always knew right from the start. George confessed everything to me at the time and begged for my forgiveness. Amanda knows that and she always has. It was what she couldn't handle. She thought George would leave me, you see. In retaliation she refused to enter his name on Ian's birth certificate and held out against our legal adoption of him. She told us that if we ever told Ian that George was his father she'd claim him back and have him adopted.' She squeezed my hand. 'All that she said just now was purely for your benefit. She hasn't hurt me. That pain healed years ago. Today it's Ian she's hurt – *again.*'

That night after we were in bed I encouraged Ian to talk, which he did, well into the small hours.

'I can't bear the thought that George was really my father and I never knew,' he said again and again. 'We were always so close and now I know why – now that he's gone and it's too late to tell him how proud I am to have been his son, and how much he meant to me.'

I held him close. 'But you had him all those years when you were growing up,' I told him. 'He knew you were his son and he had the privilege of bringing you up. You might have been adopted by strangers and never known who your real parents were.'

'I'll never forgive Amanda for what she did to us all,' he said passionately. 'How could she be so cruel – not only to me but to the very people who supported her?'

There was nothing I could say so I just held him close. 'Just let's be grateful that we have each other,' I said. 'You must try to put it behind you or it will spoil our future together.'

He looked at me. 'You're right. From now on there's only the future.'

Long after he fell asleep I lay awake, thinking about Amanda's behaviour today and her shocking revelation. It was such a complex situation. Janet forgave her husband for cheating on her with her sister but even taking into account Amanda's imposed condition they could never have revealed to Ian that George was his father without giving away his betrayal. It would have soured their relationship and ruined any chance of happiness for them as a family. Why had Amanda allowed it to happen, I wondered? Could she really have hated her sister that much or did she have some other deeply buried motive? Maybe one day I would find out.

Five

After Christmas and throughout the New Year period *Mary-Mary* was booked solid. Every weekend was packed with functions of one sort or another and Mary and I were rushed off our feet. The business was really doing well so when Janet tentatively asked if we needed any help Mary jumped at her offer. It turned out that when she gave up her singing she took up cake making as a hobby. She turned out to be extremely skilled. The specimen cake she made for us impressed and surprised us. The icing was spectacular; easily as good if not better than the local confectioner we normally commissioned to make our wedding cakes and we decided to ask Janet to join us. She turned out to be a quick and eager learner and it was invaluable to have her help.

Ian and I finally managed to book a weekend away at the beginning of March. We booked into a hotel in the delightful little village of Bourton-on-the-Water in the Cotswolds and spent four days just relaxing and enjoying being together. Since Christmas we hadn't seen or heard from Amanda. Ian hadn't even mentioned her and when I confided in Mary that I had thought of paying her a visit on my own she advised against it.

'Let sleeping dogs lie, darlin',' she said. 'Family loyalty is complicated. If you take my advice you'll stay well out of it, and when all's said and done, it's really nothing to do with you.'

'But Ian is,' I said warmly. 'He was devastated by what she said at Christmas. There has to be more to it. I might be able to make him understand better if I talked to her and heard the other side of the story.'

But Mary was still dead against the idea. 'It's all in the past. If her attitude at Christmas was anything to go by she'd only send you off with a flea in your ear! If you want to make Ian happy concentrate on the future,' she said.

I decided that she was probably right and put the idea on a back burner.

At Easter Jamie was playing with the school orchestra at a concert. As well as playing in the second violin section he was to play a solo piano piece. It would be the first time he had ever played in public and he was very excited about it. I telephoned Dad to ask him if he could come but he said he couldn't leave Mother, especially at Easter.

Ian and I went along with Janet and Mary. We had seats in the front row and Ian and I held hands nervously as the time came for Jamie's solo. He walked onto the platform and took a bow just as Ian had taught him, then he took his place at the piano with all the confidence of a seasoned performer. He played the piece, a Chopin waltz, to perfection and received loud applause.

Later he confided that he was so nervous that he'd been afraid his fingers were going to fall off but he was elated that it had gone so well. All the parents were invited to stay after the concert to have coffee with the teaching staff so Ian and I attended while Mary and Janet took Jamie home. It was while we were chatting to another pair of proud parents that the headmaster came up and introduced himself.

'Mr and Mrs Law?' He held out his hand. 'Jeremy Kenton, Jamie's headmaster.'

We shook hands. 'I'm Ian Morton, Mrs Law's partner. I'm not Jamie's father,' Ian explained.

The Head nodded. 'I see. I just wanted to have a word with you about Jamie. He did very well this evening. He's extremely talented.'

'Thank you,' I said. 'As a matter of fact most of the credit is due to Ian. He's Jamie's music teacher – has been ever since he was five and a half.'

'Really? Well, I must say you're doing a wonderful job. I don't know whether you're aware of the fact that St Cecilia's School offers a scholarship every year to a talented music student.' He looked at Ian. 'You'll know, obviously, that St Cecilia's is a local private school that specializes in music.'

Ian smiled. 'I certainly do know. It's my old school. I went there until I moved on to the RCM.'

The Head smiled. 'Then you'll know that their academic record is second to none. Specializing in music takes nothing away from their general curriculum.' He looked at me. 'Do you see a professional future for Jamie in music?'

I glanced at Ian. 'He's still very young. What do you think, Ian?'

'We could ask him.'

'Have a think about it,' the Head suggested. 'Talk to Jamie. He's very mature for his age. Let me know what you feel about it. If you like I can put a word in for you, recommend Jamie and let you have the details.'

'Thank you,' I said. 'It's very kind of you to take an interest.'

He nodded. 'I always like to encourage talent.' He was about to turn away, then he paused and looked at Ian. 'Weren't you in the Greencliffe Symphony Orchestra?'

Ian nodded. 'I left because I wanted to teach.'

'Really? Where are you teaching at present?'

'I'm self-employed, teaching privately,' Ian told him. 'I have a full list of pupils. I get the odd engagement to play too, at functions of various kinds.'

'I see.' Mr Kenton looked thoughtful. 'Off the record, John Franklin, our music teacher, is leaving at the end of this school year. Would you be interested in applying for his job?'

Ian looked taken aback. 'Oh – I don't know – perhaps.'

'Well, applications should be in by the end of next month. If you're interested let me know later, when you've decided about Jamie's scholarship.'

We put off speaking to Jamie about Mr Kenton's suggestion for a couple of days. Ian pointed out that we should wait until the euphoria of his first successful public performance had worn off as it might colour his decision. When we did broach the subject to him he flushed with excitement.

'St Cecilia's? *Wow!*' He frowned. 'But doesn't it cost a bomb to go there?'

'That's the whole point of a scholarship,' I told him. 'They give a free place each year to someone they think has talent.'

His eyes widened. 'Have *I* got talent?'

I smiled. 'Well, Ian and I think you have but we would, wouldn't we? After all, I'm your mum and Ian is your teacher. But now Mr Kenton thinks so too, so you must have.'

He was quiet for a moment as he digested this piece of news then he looked up. 'What would I have to do?'

'An audition,' Ian put in. 'Just like the one you did to get into the school orchestra, but as well as that you'd have to sit an entrance exam.'

'What's that?'

'They'd test you on your other school work.'

'What, you mean like maths and English and that?'

'Exactly.'

He looked doubtful. 'Would it be hard?'

Ian grinned. 'I don't think it'd be too hard. But if you want to get that scholarship I suggest you start studying as well as practising.' He raised an eyebrow at Jamie. 'Well, what do you think? Are you up for it?'

Jamie's grin was so wide that his face almost split in half. *'You bet!'*

He raised his hand to Ian's for a high five and we all laughed.

'Right,' I said. 'I take it that's settled then!'

After thinking long and hard Ian decided to apply for the music teacher's post at Jamie's school.

'After all, I've got you and Jamie now, haven't I?' he said. 'And we want to save for that larger house.'

I looked at him. 'Ian, you're a talented musician. If you're really thinking of taking a permanent job why not go back to performing? Have you really given up all idea of making a career of it?'

He shook his head. 'Teaching is a career.'

'I meant as an artist in your own right.'

He smiled. 'Teaching is what gives me the most fulfilment,' he said.

We made an appointment and went along together to see Mr Kenton in his office late one afternoon after school. He was delighted that Ian had decided to apply and gave him the necessary application form. He was also pleased that Jamie was to enter for the St Cecilia's School scholarship. He told us that the entrance examination would be towards the end of the summer term. We filled in the necessary forms there and then and left in high spirits, celebrating with a cream tea at the Copper Kettle on the way home.

It was about a week later that I realized that I might be pregnant. Life had been so busy that I hadn't noticed the weeks slipping by, and when I looked in my diary I was shocked to see that it was two months since my last period. I decided not to say anything to Ian until I'd done a test but the thought of being pregnant revived my desire to go and see Amanda again – to hear her side of the story of Ian's birth. I remembered Mary's remark about Amanda sending me off with 'a flea in my ear', and decided that she was more than probably right. Was I prepared to risk that? I decided that I was.

After thinking about it for a few days I decided to go one afternoon while Jamie was at school and Ian was busy with a pupil. I wouldn't mention it to anyone, just in case Mary was right and it was a mistake.

I found the apartment block again quite easily, took the lift up to the fourth floor and rang the bell, my heart beating a rapid tattoo in my chest as I waited for the door to open.

She was longer answering my ring this time and I thought briefly about Janet's remark about Amanda's 'gentleman friend' not paying the rent any more. Could she possibly have moved out without letting Ian know her new address?

I was on the point of turning away when I heard a movement on the other side of the door. When it opened a crack I was shocked. The Amanda who peered at me through the small space was very different from the woman I'd been expecting to see. Her face was devoid of make-up and her hair was drawn back and tied loosely, the parting showing tell-tale grey roots. Although it was the middle of the afternoon she wore a crumpled dressing gown.

'Oh – it's you.' Her eyes widened with surprise and she glanced anxiously over my shoulder, obviously relieved to see that I was alone.

'May I come in?' I asked.

'Why, what do you want?'

'We hadn't heard from you since Christmas and I wondered if you were all right.'

With reluctance she held the door open for me to pass her into the hallway. Closing it behind me, she looked at me. 'Don't I look all right?' She held up her hand. '*No!* Don't answer that. I look like shit and I know it. I'll be frank with you, I object to people who drop in on me without any notice.'

'I'm sorry. I didn't think.'

'Clearly!' She pulled the dressing gown around her and pulled the belt tighter. 'Well, now that you're here I suppose you'd better come through.' She led the way into the living room and I saw that there was a bottle of prescription tablets on the coffee table and a bottle of cough medicine. I looked at her.

'You're not well?'

'Ten out of ten for perception!'

'I'm sorry. Did I get you out of bed?'

'No, I was just getting changed,' she lied.

'Can I do anything for you – make a cup of tea?'

'Oh for God's sake, it's only a dose of flu,' she snapped. 'Nothing terminal! And I'm not senile – or helpless.'

I was getting nowhere but I decided to persevere. 'This is a lovely flat,' I said in an attempt at conversation.

'Look, if you're here to tear me off a strip about ruining your Christmas, for God's sake get it over and done with,' she said suddenly.

'I wasn't—'

'Having someone challenge me about it is better than being ostracized,' she went on. 'If there was an unpleasant scene it wasn't of my making.'

I wondered if this was a grudging attempt at an apology. 'Actually I'm not here for that,' I told her. 'At least, not directly.'

'So what then? Come on, I haven't got all day even if you have. Spit it out and let me get back to b … to getting changed.'

'To be frank, I couldn't understand why you wanted to hurt Ian so badly,' I said. 'What has he ever done to deserve it?'

To her credit she looked ashamed. Her sharp eyes slid away from mine. 'It wasn't my intention to hurt him,' she mumbled. 'It was Janet. Like I said, she started it all. She wound me up. She always does.'

'I think she was angry with you,' I ventured.

'*Huh!* When isn't she angry with me?'

'Have you and she always disliked each other so much?' I asked.

She shot me a hostile look. 'What the hell has it got to do with you?'

'Quite a lot, actually,' I said. 'I happen to love Ian very much and I hate seeing him unhappy. If you really want to hear the truth from my point of view I'll tell you. You invited yourself to Mary Sullivan's house on Christmas Day. Mary is my best friend. She's kind and generous and hospitable and I hated seeing her insulted. And yes, since you mention it, you *did* ruin Christmas – for all of us. And it *was* your fault.'

For a moment I thought she would lash out at me again, but as I watched, her belligerent expression vanished and the corners of her mouth drooped. She bit her lip as she fumbled in her dressing gown pocket for a handkerchief. 'All right, I know,' she muttered. 'It *was* and what's more, I'm ashamed to say that I got a kick out of it – at the time. As soon as I knew Janet was going to be there I made up my mind I was going to show her up. Trouble was everybody else got the fall-out.' She blew her nose noisily and shoved the handkerchief back into her pocket. 'There! I've said it. It was despicable. I'm a bitch and I know it.'

I hid a smile. 'Was that meant to be an apology?'

'It was an admission and that's as far as I'm going!' She straightened her back and stared at me. 'Anyway, I thought you were going to make me a cup of tea.'

I stood up, relieved that at last I seemed to have broken through the barrier, 'Okay,' I said. 'Milk and sugar?'

'Just milk.'

'Right. Biscuits?'

'Cupboard next to the cooker.'

As we sat with our tea I tried again. 'What is it between you two? Has Janet really always been jealous of you?'

She dipped her biscuit into her teacup thoughtfully and took a deep breath. 'You want the truth?'

'Of course.'

She paused. 'This is just between you and me, right?'

'No one else knows I'm here.'

'Good. Let's keep it that way.' She looked at me. 'I like you,' she said. 'You call a spade a spade like I do and I can tell it's no use trying to pull the wool over your eyes.'

The soggy half of the tea-soaked biscuit suddenly fell into her teacup with a plop. '*Shit!*' she said. 'Look at that; the bloody story of my life.'

'I thought you'd had a wonderful life, Amanda,' I said gently.

She sighed. 'Janet was never really jealous of me,' she said. 'It was the other way round. She was the clever one at school, always in favour with our parents. She was the one with the musical flair, playing the piano and singing – showing off all the time, getting all the praise. She had the looks too; classical looks, not Barbie doll pretty like me. I couldn't be bothered to study hard at school – knew I'd never better her in that. I was a complete dud at music so I decided to be a stage and film star. I thought I'd show them all in the end.'

'And you did. Didn't that make you feel you'd evened the score?'

She sighed. 'To tell you the honest truth it never quite worked out. I wasn't the big star I made out to be. Oh, I tried. I slept with all the right people to get the parts I wanted but in the end I never amounted to anything more than a jobbing actress. Number three tours; weekly rep. Meantime, Janet made an effortless success of her singing, damn her! *And* hooked herself a dishy husband into the bargain.'

'I see.' All this was a revelation to me. Amanda looked up at me. 'So what did I do in desperation to get the better of her? I seduced her husband.' She gave a dry little laugh. 'Poor old George. He never stood a chance once I got my hooks into him. But it all went wrong. Did he leave her? Like hell he did! It was only the once and, eaten up with guilt he confessed all to her, the silly sod, and she, like the saint she is, forgave him. As for me – soon afterwards I found out I was up the stick! Talk about hoist with my own petard!'

'You never considered an abortion?'

She shrugged. 'I was in denial, bloody stupid. I kept thinking that if I ignored it, it would go away. By the time I was forced to face up to the truth, it was too late.'

'But at least George and Janet brought up your child,' I said.

She looked at me. 'They took the only thing I ever did that was any good from me, you mean.' She said bleakly. 'Oh yes, I thought it was the perfect answer at the time. They'd take the baby and I could carry on striving for that big break. Then he was born.' She raised her eyes to mine. 'You of all people must know what it's like when you look at that tiny life you've just been through hell to give birth to. I adored him on sight. The thought of giving him away ripped my heart out.'

'Yes, I do know how it feels,' I told her. 'I meant to have Jamie adopted but when it came to it I couldn't have parted with him to save my life.' I looked at her. 'You did though.'

'I compromised,' she said. 'I wouldn't put George's name on the birth certificate. That, believe it or not was for Ian's sake – mine too if I'm truthful. It wasn't a pretty story for a child to grow up with. I compromised – let them change his name to theirs by deed poll on condition that he must never know George was his father. But I wouldn't let them adopt him legally. That way he would still be mine and I'd get to see him when ever I wanted to.'

'Wasn't that selfish?'

'Maybe. But they had the best of the deal. Janet got the child she wanted so badly. George got off the hook and Ian had a good home and loving parents.' She looked up and suddenly I saw past the glittering defiance to the pain behind it. 'How do you think it felt seeing her forming a mother-son bond with my boy? The bond they still have and that he and I will never share. Whatever you might think, I've never stopped loving him, you know.'

'But you had the best of both worlds, didn't you? You had to sacrifice something.' Another thought suddenly occurred to me. 'Did Janet give up her singing career to take Ian?'

'I don't think she was ever that keen – or that good either in my opinion.' She shrugged. 'Anyway, it was her choice.'

'And your choice to withhold the knowledge of who Ian's father was,' I said. 'Until last Christmas Day, when you told him yourself – out of spite.'

She frowned. 'I know, and do you think I haven't agonized over it ever since? she said. 'If I could turn the clock back I would, but it's done now.' She sighed. 'I've been hoping he'd come and see me so that I could explain it all properly.'

'I'm sorry, Amanda but I'm afraid it might be some time before he forgets the shock of hearing it the way he did.'

'Maybe you'll put in a good word for me,' she said. 'Tell your friend, Mary that I'm sorry. And speak to Ian for me. You know what it is to be a mother.'

'I've already told you, no one knows I'm here.'

'But now that I've told you the truth surely you'll be on my side.'

'I'm only on one person's side and that' Ian's,' I told her. I looked at my watch and stood up. 'I'll have to be going. It's time to pick up Jamie from school.' I headed for the door and Amanda stood up.

'You're so lucky to have him,' she said wistfully. 'Thank you for coming, Elaine. I'm glad we've had this little chat.' She touched my arm as I reached for the door handle. I turned to look at her. She looked small and shrivelled – pathetic, and I felt a tug of pity.

'So am I,' I said. 'And I hope you'll feel better soon.'

Going down in the lift I thought over all she had said. I thanked heaven that I had Jamie and that Ian had had someone like Janet to bring him up. When all was said and done there were two sides to every story. In this one there were no winners.

About a week after I'd been to visit Amanda Ian was invited to go for an interview at Jamie's school. It was to take place one afternoon after school and Jamie and I waited eagerly for his return. He didn't say much when he came home, although he seemed impressed by the school's interest in music.

'Not many primary schools have an orchestra *and* a choir,' he said.

'I didn't know they had a choir,' I said.

'We don't,' Jamie chimed in.

'They're about to start one next year,' Ian told him. 'So whoever gets the job will have to be choir master as well as orchestra conductor.'

Jamie pulled a face. 'I don't fancy being in a choir,' he said.

'Well maybe you won't be asked,' I pointed out. 'Anyway if you get that scholarship to St Cecilia's you won't even be there.'

Two days later Ian received a letter offering him the job. We went out to celebrate with Jamie to the local café with sticky buns and lemonade.

As summer got under way we had the usual rush of weddings to cater for. To our delight we were engaged to cater for the reception at the wedding of the Langleys' younger daughter, Frances. As before the reception was to take place in a marquee in the garden of the bride's home. For the first time we suggested that the wedding cake could be provided by us and showed Frances and her mother photographs of Janet's work. To our delight they accepted and commissioned Janet to make the cake.

Ian was asked to provide the music as before but he turned the offer down. He'd promised to take Jamie to a school cricket match and he didn't want to let him down.

The Saturday of the wedding dawned fine and sunny. When I got up at six to drive over to Mary's there was a fine mist over everything. By seven o'clock it was already warm and by the time we were packed and ready to go the heat had become oppressive. Ever since early that morning I'd had a niggling pain but I'd said nothing. After all it was a big day and I was sure it would wear off as the morning went on.

We picked Janet up and drove to the Langleys where the marquee was already up. The hired furniture was already in place and the florists were busy with their arrangements. Janet and I laid and decorated the tables while Mary unpacked the food and began the preparation in the kitchen. As we worked Janet kept looking at me, eventually she asked if anything was wrong.

'Are you all right, Elaine? You're looking a bit peaky.'

'I'm fine,' I told her. 'I think the heat is getting to me.' I laughed. 'Can't afford to be anything else but fine today, can I?'

She touched my arm. 'My dear – I've been wondering lately – tell me to mind my own business but you're not...?'

'Pregnant?' I finished for her. 'Well, between you and me I think I just might be. But not a word to anyone because I haven't even told Ian yet.'

'Have you done a test – seen a doctor?'

I shook my head. 'I've had other things on my mind, to tell you the truth. We've been so busy. I thought I'd wait until the third month.'

She looked doubtful but she said nothing more.

The wedding was at twelve o'clock. We were serving a three course meal and by 12.30 the starters were already on the tables. The bridal party arrived just before one and our hired waitresses circulated with trays of drinks. All morning the pain had been worsening and by the time all the guests were seated I hardly knew how to bear it. The main course was served and I heaved a sigh of relief. That was the worst over. The desserts were cold and everything was plated up and ready. In the kitchen Mary looked at me.

'Elaine, you're not very well, are you?'

I forced a smile. 'I'm fine.' But even as I said it the pain seized me again and I gasped, doubling up. Mary looked alarmed.

'Darlin' what is it? You look terrible.'

I gritted my teeth. 'I think I might be pregnant, Mary. You don't think I could be losing it, do you?'

'Why on earth didn't you say something before?' She was pulling off her apron. 'Right, that's it,' she said. 'I'm taking you straight to A and E.'

I shook my head. 'We can't leave Janet here on her own.'

Janet, who had been listening, stepped forward. 'Yes you can, we've done most of the work. I can manage the champagne for the toasts with the help of the waitresses. I think we should get an ambulance.'

'We can't have an ambulance turning up here. It will put a damper on the wedding,' I muttered.

'Blow that!' Mary said. 'You're going to the hospital. I'm going to go and find Mrs Langley and explain to her. I know she'll agree with me.'

As it happened it was Mary who drove me to the hospital. 'Where's Ian?' she asked, looking at me anxiously as she drove. 'I rang the house before we left but there was no reply.'

'He's taken Jamie to a cricket match out at Little Basset,' I told her. 'He's got his mobile with him though.'

'Right, we'll just get you to the hospital and then I'll ring him.'

'Not yet,' I begged her. 'Not until we know. It might just be a false alarm.'

In A and E things happened fast. The pain grew so severe that I could hardly bear it and I began to drift in and out of consciousness. I was vaguely aware of being wheeled somewhere to be scanned. Later I learned that it showed that the embryo had been developing inside a fallopian tube which had ruptured causing me to bleed internally. I was rushed up to the theatre, anaesthetized and knew nothing more until I came round in the recovery room where a nurse explained gently that there was no baby and that I'd had what was known as an ectopic pregnancy. Barely able to take it in I drifted off again.

Next time I woke I was in a small side ward hooked up to a transfusion drip. Ian was sitting by the bed, holding my hand and looking anxious. When I opened my eyes he looked relieved.

'Hello, darling – how are you feeling?'

I managed a smile. 'Better for seeing you.'

He leaned across and kissed me. 'You gave us all such a fright,' he said. 'Darling, why didn't you tell me you were pregnant?'

'I wanted to wait until I was sure.' My eyes filled with tears. 'Anyway, I wasn't really, was I – not properly?' I thought of my baby struggling to grow in the wrong place and an overwhelming sadness engulfed me. 'Was it something I did? Was it my fault?' Helpless tears rolled down my cheeks and Ian pulled a tissue from the box on the locker and dabbed them away.

'Shhh. Of course it wasn't your fault. Don't cry.' He kissed me and stroked my hair. 'Nothing you did could have made this happen so stop worrying. I love you, darling. All that really matters to me is that you're all right. I'm going to let you get some rest now before Sister throws me out. She told me five minutes only. But I'll be back again later. Get some sleep now and let the transfusion do its work. I'll see you this evening.'

Mr Frazer, the obstetrician came to see me a couple of hours later. He explained in more detail what had gone wrong and reassured me again that it could not have been avoided.

'When can I go home?' I asked.

'We'll need to keep you another few days,' he told me. 'You've had a very severe haemorrhage and we want to make sure you're completely well.'

'When will I be able to have another baby?' I asked.

He sighed and sat on the edge of the bed. 'Unfortunately I'm afraid you're unlikely to conceive again,' he said gently. 'In most cases only one tube is affected but in your case we found that the other one was damaged too.'

The tears began again and he patted my shoulder. 'I believe you already have a young son.' I nodded. 'Then at least you're lucky enough to have him,' he said.

'My – my partner,' I muttered.

'I've already had a word with him,' he told me. 'He was naturally very worried about you and asked to speak to me this afternoon after we'd operated.'

'I see. So he knows.'

'Yes.'

When he'd gone I lay staring at the wall. Would Ian still want me now that he knew I would never be able to give him a child of his own? It wasn't something we'd discussed although there was a tacit understanding between us that we'd start a family at some point in the future. I dreaded visiting time when he'd come again. I'd know how he felt about it the moment I saw his face.

As it happened I was asleep again when he arrived. I woke to see him sitting at the bedside, a huge bunch of flowers and a box of my favourite chocolates on the table at the end of the bed. He smiled.

'Hi there. You look much better.' He bent to kiss me. 'Jamie wanted to come but I said better wait until you came home. I didn't want him to be scared. Sister said only one visitor for today.'

'Mr Frazer came to see me.' I looked at him. 'He said he'd spoken to you.'

'That's right. It was earlier. I asked to see him.'

'He told you – that I wouldn't be able to....' I couldn't bring myself to frame the actual words but Ian cupped my cheek gently with his hand.

'I know, and you're not to worry about it,' he said quickly. 'You're okay and that's the most important thing. There's something I need to ask you. I know I should probably wait until you're feeling better but I can't.'

'What is it?' I asked fearfully.

'I want us to be married,' Ian said. 'As soon as possible, and – if you're agreeable – I'd like to adopt Jamie legally, as my own son.' He held my hand tightly in both of his and looked into my eyes. 'How do you feel about it?'

I looked at him for a long moment. 'Ian – are you sure you've given this enough thought. I mean, you're not asking because – because you're – because of this?'

'It has nothing to do with what's happened today. It's awful of course but it makes no difference to the way I feel. I've been trying to get up the courage to ask you for ages. I wasn't sure you'd want to make that kind of commitment – make our relationship that perma-nent. And as for Jamie, he's exactly the kind of son I've always dreamed of having one day. He's like me in so many ways he could almost be mine.' He bent and kissed me. 'And he's yours, so that makes him doubly perfect.' When he looked into my eyes I knew there was no doubt that he was sincere. After a moment one eyebrow twitched in the way it always did when he was asking me something important.

'So, what do you think? Could you bear to have me around for the rest of your life? Do you think Jamie would approve of me as a father? When they let you come home shall we ask him?' I continued to stare at him, my mouth and throat too dry to speak. He frowned. '*Elaine*! For God's sake *say* something! How long are you going to keep me in suspense?'

Reaching up I wound my arms around his neck and pulled his head down to mine.

'Is this a yes?' he asked.

'Oh, Ian, of course I'll marry you,' I said, my words muffled against his neck. 'I – I thought you'd never ask!'

Six

The following afternoon I had a visit from Mary. She brought surprising news.

'You'll never guess who rang me yesterday.'

'I'm in no condition for guessing games,' I told her. 'Just tell me.'

'Ian's mother,' she said triumphantly.

My eyes opened wide. 'Amanda?'

'The very same. She rang to apologize for her unacceptable behaviour at Christmas.' Mary sniffed. 'Though I must say it took her long enough to make up her mind to do it.'

'Is she better?' I asked without thinking.

Mary raised an inquiring eyebrow. 'I didn't know she'd been ill.'

I felt my colour rise. 'I meant, was she in a better mood,' I hedged, but it was too late. There was no pulling the wool over Mary's eyes.

'You went to see her, didn't you?' she accused. 'And after all I said.'

'It was when I suspected that I might be pregnant,' I conceded. 'I felt I had to know her side of the story. No one is all bad, Mary.'

She drew in her breath sharply. 'Maybe not, but she has a damn good shot at it, that's all I can say.' When I made no comment her curiosity got the better of her and she said. 'So – what did she say? Nothing that wasn't a pack of over dramatic lies, I'll bet.'

'You might have been surprised,' I told her. 'I caught her off guard. She was suffering from flu or a heavy cold so her defences were down. She was a bit vulnerable.' I shrugged. 'No make-up and a grubby dressing gown. She was resentful at first, but she softened – even said she liked me in the end.'

'Huh!' Mary grunted. 'Very magnanimous of her, I'm sure! What's not to like about you?'

I laughed. 'There are two sides to every story, Mary. She told me hers.'

'And made herself sound hard done-to, I'll bet.'

'No. She was honest. I believe what she told me was the truth.' I explained a little of what Amanda had told me. 'She's no saint, Mary, but she's not a monster either – not deep inside.'

But Mary didn't look convinced. 'She manipulated the situation for all it was worth if you ask me,' she said. 'How could she punish Janet and her husband when all they were doing was trying to help her? And as for keeping the identity of Ian's father from him all those years....'

'I've told you how she explained it to me,' I said. 'You yourself said that families and their loyalties are complicated. None more so than in this case.'

'Well, I'll never be able to trust the woman,' Mary said. 'To me she'll always be a vindictive, embittered bitch.' She looked at me. 'Just watch she doesn't make trouble between you and Ian. She's obviously eaten up with jealousy.'

Eager to change the subject, I reached for her hand. 'Mary – I've got some exciting news. But if I tell you, you have to promise to keep it to yourself, at least for a few days.'

Her eyes lit up. 'Ooh! Go on tell me. I promise I won't say anything.' Her fingers tightened round mine.

'Ian and I are engaged,' I told her. 'We're going to be married. And even more exciting, Ian wants to adopt Jamie legally as his own son.'

She gasped with delight. 'Oh, that is good news,' she said. 'I guessed it would happen soon, though. The two of you are made for each other and Jamie adores him. I know he'll be over the moon to have a daddy at last.'

'You won't say anything to him though, will you?' I begged. 'They're talking of letting me go home tomorrow and we want to sit him down and ask him how he feels about it. It has to come from us first.'

'Of course it does. I won't say a word,' Mary promised. 'But I'd love to be a fly on the wall when you tell him.'

'*Ask*, not tell,' I corrected. 'He's old enough to have a say in the matter. I'm pretty sure he'll be pleased but there's no way we'll impose it on him if he isn't.'

*

The hospital discharged me the following day. Ian came to collect me and as we sat in the car in the hospital car park he took a little box from his pocket and gave it to me.

I looked at him. 'What is it?'

'Open it and see.'

Inside the box was a lovely ring; an oval amethyst in an antique setting. Ian took it from me and slid it onto my third finger. It fitted perfectly. 'There,' he said. 'That seals it. No going back now. You're the future Mrs Morton.'

I kissed him. 'Oh Ian, it's beautiful but it must have cost a fortune. You shouldn't have spent so much money. I don't need a ring.'

'Well I happen to think you do,' he said. 'So that's that.'

On the way home we picked Jamie up from school. He was strange, almost shy when he saw me in the car.

'Hi, Mum. Are you better?' he asked as he climbed into the back seat.

'I'm fine,' I assured him. 'Good as new.'

Ian shot me a look. 'She's not *quite* as good as new,' he corrected. 'We've got to take good care of her for a while.'

'Yeah, I know.' Jamie gave me a little half-smile and rummaged in his satchel to avoid my eyes.

Ian hadn't told him about the baby, considering an ectopic pregnancy too much for him to take in. Instead he'd explained that I'd had an operation and needed time to recuperate. At home he seemed almost afraid to touch me or even come too close and at bedtime when I reached out to hug him he stiffened. I looked at him.

'It's okay,' I assured him. 'I won't break.'

He turned a grave little face up to mine. 'Daniel's gran had an operation,' he said. 'And now she has to be in a wheelchair.'

I laughed. 'Daniel's gran had a hip replacement operation,' I told him. 'Mine was nothing like as serious as that. And she won't be in a wheelchair for long so tell Daniel not to worry either.'

After we had eaten Ian looked inquiringly at me and I nodded. We'd both agreed earlier that we'd speak to Jamie that evening. He was about to disappear upstairs with his homework when Ian said, 'Sit down a minute, Jamie. There's something your mum and I want to talk to you about.'

Jamie hesitated, an apprehensive expression on his face. 'It's not the St Cecilia's exam, is it? They haven't cancelled it?'

'No, nothing like that. Just sit down.'

Jamie dropped his satchel in the doorway and came to sit in the space between us on the settee. 'Don't look like that,' I said. 'You're not in any trouble.'

He looked anxiously up at me. 'You're not really ill or anything, are you, Mum?'

I put my arm round his shoulders. 'No! Just let Ian tell you.'

Ian cleared his throat. 'Jamie, I need your permission to ask your mum to marry me. Would that be all right?'

Affected by Ian's serious expression Jamie looked at me and then back at Ian. 'If that's what Mum wants I s'pose it's okay,' he said.

'And there's something else,' Ian went on. 'When your mum and I are married I would like very much to adopt you. Do you understand what that means?'

Jamie looked at me and I saw the colour rise in his cheeks. 'Does it mean that you'd be my dad?'

'It does – legally,' Ian said. 'Your proper dad with papers to prove it. You'd have my name and everything. It would make us a whole family.'

There was a moment while Jamie took this in then he said, 'So I'd be Jamie Morton instead of Jamie Law?'

'That's right. So how do you feel about it?'

Jamie digested the prospect, looking first at me then at Ian, then suddenly he gave a loud whoop and punched the air. 'Wow! *YES!*' he shouted.

Ian and I laughed. 'So you approve then?' Ian said.

'I think it's really cool!' Jamie said. 'When will it all happen?'

'As soon as we can arrange it all. We can have the wedding fairly soon,' I explained. 'Once you've broken up for the summer holidays. But the adoption thing might take a bit longer.'

'Oh.' Jamie's face dropped a little then he looked at Ian. 'So I can't call you Dad yet then?'

Ian swallowed hard. 'Not legally, but I don't mind what you call me. Once your mum and I are married it'll be a new start for all of us.'

There was so much to do in the weeks that followed. First, and taking priority, was Jamie's entrance exam to St Cecilia's. He had already taken the written exam but he still had to play for the head of the music department, which would be the deciding factor. Ian was coaching him in the pieces he would play both on piano and violin. The two of them were closeted together every evening after Jamie had finished his homework. There was his music theory to study as well and we had decided that our wedding plans must certainly go on hold until after the exam.

'He's going to need a full sized violin soon,' Ian said one evening. 'I'll have to ask around to see what's on offer.'

'How much will that cost?' I asked.

Ian shook his head. 'To get a good worthwhile instrument won't be cheap and Jamie has promise. He deserves the best. But don't worry, I'll be earning a regular salary once I start my teaching job and we can probably pay for it in instalments.'

I looked at him. 'Ian, don't you ever miss the orchestra?'

'Not a bit.'

'But – haven't you ever had a dream?'

He laughed. 'What kind of dream?'

'Well, you're talented, haven't you ever wanted to become a soloist?'

He shook his head. 'I've told you darling. Teaching is what I love; besides I don't think I could handle the competition; all that aggressive rivalry. You say I have talent but so have hundreds of others. It's a jungle out there. No, watching youngsters like Jamie growing up into first class musicians is more than enough reward for me.'

On the day of the exam Jamie was too nervous to eat any breakfast. He sat at the table pale-faced, his untouched boiled egg and soldiers in front of him.

'Try and eat something, darling,' I said. 'You really do need something inside you.'

'I can't swallow, Mum,' he said. 'My mouth has gone all sort of dry.'

I sat down opposite him. 'Listen, Jamie,' I said, taking both his hands. 'There's no need to be scared. Just go in there and do your best. Pretend you're at home, practising with Ian. If you don't get the scholarship it's not going to be the end of the world. No one's going to chop your head off and Ian and I will never stop being proud of you whatever happens.' I glanced up at the clock. 'Better go and wash your hands now. It's time you were leaving.'

He grinned at me and I felt reassured. 'Thanks, Mum. Ian always says, "Blow their socks off", so I'll do that, shall I?'

'That's right, you blow their socks off. I'll be keeping my fingers crossed for you – really tightly – all morning.'

I waved them off from the window. I knew Ian was as nervous as Jamie but he was trying hard not to show it. During the hour that followed I hung around the house, unable to concentrate on anything and when the telephone rang I welcomed the diversion. I recognized her slightly husky 'actressy' voice at once.

'My dear, I had to ring and say how sorry I was to hear about your sad loss,' she said.

I swallowed hard, still finding it hard to hear it put into words. 'Thank you, Amanda. How kind of you to ring.'

'Not at all. It's odd, isn't it, the way nature lets us down sometimes. If there's anything I can do….'

'There's nothing, but thank you anyway.'

'If you want to come and see me again – or perhaps we could meet one day for lunch…?'

'That might be fun. I'll be in touch, Amanda, and thanks again for ringing.'

I replaced the receiver and looked at my watch. At least another hour before I could expect them back. I went into the kitchen and laid the table. I'd planned to get Jamie's favourite, chicken nuggets and chips for lunch, with a chocolate Viennetta to follow. If the news was good it would be a celebration – if not it might help to cheer him up.

At twelve o'clock I heard the car draw up outside and I ran to the front door. Jamie was out of the car almost before it had stopped.

'I passed, Mum!' he yelled. 'I did it. I got in!'

We had our celebration lunch and Jamie had to go to school afterwards, much to his disgust. Ian and I went with him and went to find Mr Kenton, the headmaster, to tell him Jamie's news but he already knew. The headmaster of St Cecilia's had already contacted him.

'He's done remarkably well,' he said as he invited us to take a seat. 'He's getting in a year ahead of the age they usually accept scholarship students. Not that it will make any difference because they take children from year three upwards so you needn't worry that he'll be overstretched. They were very impressed with him.' He smiled. 'And we're looking forward to having you on board next term, Ian.'

Ian smiled. 'I'm looking forward to it too. I've already made lots of plans.'

Mary refused point blank to let me work over the month that followed.

'You've had a bad time,' she said. 'And there's a lot going on in your life, not to mention having Jamie at home for the school holidays. Just concentrate on your wedding plans for now. Janet and I will manage fine.'

It was kind of her but I couldn't help feeling a bit left out and really I'd have liked something to take my mind off the loss of the baby or the fact that Ian and I would never have a family of our own. Although we didn't discuss it, the sadness was never very far from my mind.

We decided on the last weekend before the new term began for our wedding. When I told Mary she frowned.

'That's short notice.'

'We're planning something very quiet,' I told her. 'It won't take much organizing.'

'But what about a honeymoon?'

I laughed. 'We don't need a honeymoon. It's a waste of money.'

She shook a finger at me. 'You may not need a honeymoon but you need a holiday, my girl. You've had an extremely traumatic time.'

'And it doesn't help being reminded of it all the time,' I said, a bit more sharply than I intended. 'Sorry, Mary. I didn't mean to snap. Maybe we'll manage a few days at half term.' I grasped her arm. 'Oh, and by the way, I'm coming back to work next week, even if it's only to share some cooking sessions with you.'

'Oh, all right. You win,' she said. She gave me a brief hug. 'I don't mind admitting that I've missed having you around, but definitely no functions until after the wedding.' She grinned. 'And by the way, your wedding reception is to be my present to you both.' She held up her hand. 'No arguments. You might be planning a quiet wedding but the reception is going to be a wow – so there!'

I went shopping for my wedding outfit by myself, determined not to be influenced by anyone else's taste. It didn't take me long to choose. I found what I wanted almost right away; a plain cream dress with a pretty matching jacket. I found shoes to go with it and to finish the afternoon I treated myself to a visit to the hairdresser and emerged with a new short feathery hairstyle which, the stylist assured me, accentuated my eyes and cheekbones. At home Ian was flatteringly appreciative.

'Wow! You look fantastic. So where's this outfit?'

'You're not seeing that until the day,' I told him. 'And you better get yourself a new suit – and take Jamie with you to get his.'

Jamie looked up from what he was doing with a loud protest. 'Oh no! I won't have to wear a *suit*, will I?'

'You certainly will.'

'What, with a tie and everything? Can't I just wear my jeans?'

'Of course you can't. Tell you what, let Ian help you to choose a nice pair of trousers and a white shirt. You'll need new shoes too. Your old ones are all scuffed.'

He groaned. 'Well at least you're not expecting me to wear a *kilt* like Daniel had to at his sister's wedding. All this fuss just to get married. Why can't you just go and get it done, like having a check-up at the dentist's?'

Ian roared with laughter. 'I notice your son hasn't inherited your romantic streak,' he spluttered.

Mary had arranged the wedding reception at her own home. Our marquee supplier had agreed to install a marquee in her garden and she had contacted some of Ian's friends to supply the music. I was touched when she told me that they had all insisted on giving their services free of charge by way of a wedding present.

When Ian and I sat down to write the invitations the question of what to do about Amanda came up.

'We have to invite her, Ian,' I said. 'She is your mother after all.'

He shook his head. 'After the way she behaved last Christmas?'

I moved round the table to sit next to him. 'Ian, I didn't tell you but I went to see her.'

He looked at me in surprise. 'When? You didn't mention it.'

'It was when I suspected I might be pregnant. It made me wonder how she felt when you were born. I felt I wanted to hear her side of the story.' I took his hand. 'I didn't mean to go behind your back or

Janet's either. I just wanted to know if she was really was hard as she seemed.'

'I see.' His mouth hardened. 'And what did you discover?'

'That she has a vulnerable side,' I told him. 'On the day I went she was ill, suffering from flu. She was annoyed with me for calling unannounced and finding her not at her best, but she came round in the end and we had quite a heart-to-heart.'

He shook his head disbelievingly. 'I'm sorry, Elaine, but you don't know her like I do. She never really stops acting, flu or no flu. Whatever she said would be for your benefit – designed to get your sympathy.'

'I don't think so. I believe she told me the truth. She didn't try to make herself look innocent; quite the reverse.' I outlined what Amanda had told me that afternoon and was rewarded by the stunned expression on his face. 'People are complicated animals, Ian,' I went on. 'None of us are ever quite what we seem on the surface. And, as Mary always says, there are two sides to every story.'

'You can't deny that she's selfish,' Ian put in. 'She tried to get the best of both worlds after I was born. She didn't give a damn how much it hurt Janet that she could never call me her son. Neither did she care that I never knew George was my father.'

'Of course she was very wrong,' I said. 'She must have hurt a lot of people in her time, but it's all in the past now. She's not young any more, Ian. If you'd seen her as I did, feeling ill and alone....'

'It's no more than she deserves.'

'I know. I know.' I leaned forward and kissed him. 'But I'd still like to invite her to our wedding.'

He raised an eyebrow at me. 'Even if she misbehaves again and shows us all up?'

'I don't think that will happen again.'

He sighed. 'All right, if you really want her there.'

I kissed him again. 'Thank you, darling. I'm sure she'll be good. I think she's mellowed.'

He smiled ruefully. 'Well, I wouldn't hold my breath if I were you.'

I bit my lip as something occurred to me. 'You don't think Janet will be annoyed that we've invited her, do you?'

He gave me a long look. 'You've talked me round so I'll leave it to you to talk to Janet. Maybe it'll be a lesson to you that you can't please everyone!'

I decided that if Janet and Amanda were to be reconciled it was up to me so I invited each of them to meet me for lunch, carefully not mentioning it to the other. I knew it could easily blow up in my face but I decided I had to take that risk.

We met at a small restaurant on the seafront. The promenade was always pleasant at the end of the season when most of the visitors had gone home. It was a beautiful sunny morning with the sun turning the sand a rich gold and the sea a deep sparkling blue. I was early, determined to arrive first. As I sat waiting with a glass of wine I couldn't help feeling nervous. Janet was the first to arrive. From the table in the window I caught sight of her walking down the promenade, her upright figure trim in a neat navy blue suit, a bright yellow and white scarf at the neck. She smiled as she came through the door and saw me already waiting.

'Elaine! Good morning, dear. I'm not late, am I?'

'No. I'm early. I wanted to be here first,' I told her. 'I took the liberty of ordering you a dry sherry. Is that all right?'

She smiled. 'Thank you, dear, how delicious.' She sat down opposite me and took off her jacket to reveal a crisp white shirt.

'So – how are the wedding plans going?' she asked, taking a sip of her drink.

'Well, that's partly why I asked you to meet me,' I took a deep breath. 'I've invited Amanda to join us.' I held up my hand as I saw her face drop. 'Please, Janet, Ian and I would be so grateful if you could put your differences aside just for once.' I looked at her. 'She did telephone Mary to apologize for the Christmas disaster. Did you hear from her?'

'I did,' she said stiffly. 'But I told her that I'll never forgive her for the way she blurted out the truth to Ian about his father. Why hurt *him* for heaven's sake? He's always been the biggest victim in all this mess she created.' She frowned at me. 'I can't believe he actually *wants* to invite her to his wedding.'

'I have to confess that it was my idea,' I told her. 'I just want everyone to be happy for us and it doesn't seem right to leave anyone out.'

She took another sip of her sherry then looked up at me. 'I can understand how you feel, of course,' she said. 'And as far as I'm concerned I shall make sure that nothing untoward happens to spoil the day for you. Unfortunately, I can't make any assurances on Amanda's behalf. She could never resist making herself the centre of attention and—'

Her sentence was cut short as a gust of wind heralded the arrival of Amanda. She 'made an entrance' rather than merely arriving, holding the door open just long enough to allow the stiff sea breeze to billow the long red skirt she wore and lift the voluminous sequin scattered scarf that was draped about her shoulders.

'Oh! What a simply *divine* morning!' she enthused, closing the door with a flourish. Then she noticed Janet sitting at the table and her smile disappeared. 'Oh, *Janet*! Elaine didn't mention that you were coming.'

'She didn't tell me *you'd* be here either,' Janet said.

Amanda settled herself at the table, spreading out her various bags of shopping on the floor and the spare chair. 'Do I gather you'd have run a mile rather than come if you had known?' she asked, patting her coiffeur. 'Well it's mutual I can—'

'*Please!*' I held up my hand. 'I'd like the three of us to have a pleasant lunch together so can you two bury the hatchet – just for me?' I looked from one to the other. 'Please?'

Amanda gave me her sweetest smile. 'Of *course*, darling.' She looked across the table at her sister. 'It's the least we can do for darling Elaine, isn't it?'

I could see that Janet was fuming but she gritted her teeth and said, 'Naturally.'

Amanda summoned a waitress and ordered herself a double gin and tonic. 'And how is that sweet little boy of yours?' she asked me.

'He's fine, thank you.'

'How wonderful.' She looked at Janet. 'And your dear little doggie – what's his name – Bimbo?'

Janet swallowed hard. 'You know perfectly well that his name is Brownie and the last time you saw him he was a "*filthy animal*"! There's no need to go over the top, Amanda.'

Amanda turned large sad eyes on me. 'You see, dear? I can't do right for doing wrong.'

'Then perhaps you should—'

'Shall we order?' I pushed a menu towards each of them. This was going to be trickier than I'd thought.

Janet ordered steak and chips and I decided on fish. The waitress looked at Amanda.

'And for you, madam?'

'I'll have a plain mixed salad,' she said. 'On its own with no dressing, thank you.' She handed the menu back. 'Some of us watch our waistline,' she muttered half under her breath. 'We can't all let ourselves go.'

Janet bristled but said nothing.

By the time the meal ended the atmosphere had eased a little. Janet had another sherry with her meal and Amanda drank two more double gins. While both were in a mellow mood I opened my bag and handed them each a wedding invitation.

'We want everyone to be with us on the day,' I told them. 'We want it to be a happy occasion.'

Both sisters agreed that they wanted the same, tucking the invitations into their respective handbags. As we were leaving Janet turned to Amanda and said, 'By the way, did you know that I'm working with Elaine and Mary in their catering business now?'

Clearly taken aback, Amanda stared at her. 'Oh! So you're part of the catering scene now, are you?' She laughed. 'What do you do, cut the sandwiches or put on a black dress and pinny and wait on the customers?'

'Janet makes delicious cakes for us and ices them beautifully,' I put in. 'Actually she's making our wedding cake.' As soon as the words were out of my mouth I knew it was a mistake.

'Well I hope you've taken out insurance against food poisoning.' Amanda quipped with a tinkling laugh.

I tried to lighten the mood by shrugging the comment off. 'I hope you're not referring to the buffet. Mary is doing the rest of the reception food.'

'And of course you don't have to come if you're afraid of getting poisoned,' Janet said as she buttoned up her jacket. She picked up her handbag and kissed me on both cheeks. 'Good luck, my dear,' she whispered. 'And don't say I didn't warn you.' She turned to her sister. 'Goodbye, Amanda. I'll see you at the wedding – if you can bring yourself to take the risk.'

When she'd gone I looked reproachfully at Amanda. Her eyes slid away from mine guiltily.

'Well – you should have told me she was coming,' she muttered.

'Couldn't you *try* to be civil to her?' I asked. 'After all she is your sister and what happened was a very long time ago.'

She adjusted her scarf. 'It's partly habit,' she said, 'I can't resist getting a rise out of her, if you really want to know. She's so bloody tight-arsed.'

'You will behave on the day, won't you? We want you to be there but we don't want any unpleasantness.'

She looked at me. 'I promise to steer well clear of Janet – there, will that do?'

'I suppose it will have to.'

I telephoned to tell Dad the date of the wedding. 'Do you think you could get down for it?' I asked. To my surprise he agreed.

'I can't promise your mother will come with me,' he said. 'She hasn't been at all well, but I'll see if I can persuade her.'

'Mary said that if you were coming she'd be happy to put you up,' I told him. 'We're having the reception at hers. She's doing it all for me as a wedding present.'

'Then we certainly won't expect her to have us there,' he said quickly. 'I'll book into a hotel. Don't worry about it.'

To my utter amazement Mother came with him. They arrived on the day before the wedding and Ian, Jamie and I met them for dinner at their hotel. I was shocked by Mother's appearance. I hadn't seen her since Jamie was a baby. She was a shadow of what she had been then, frail and looking much older than her sixty-two years. We were like strangers, polite to one another, slightly uncomfortable. However she seemed to like Ian and she was nice to Jamie, asking him about his new school and showing great interest in his music. After the meal, when we were sitting in the hotel lounge with our coffee and Mother had gone upstairs to freshen up, Dad told me that she had had two heart attacks.

'That's why I wanted her to come down for your wedding,' he said. 'It's high time she saw what a success you've made of your life.'

I nodded. If only she'd tell me herself that she'd been wrong about me. If only, just once, she could bring herself to show me some affection; but at least she was here and that was a step in the right direction.

I hadn't expected to be nervous on my wedding day. After all Ian and I had been together for some time. We'd made a home and a family life together so why should a ceremony and a piece of paper make any difference? But on the day of the wedding I awoke in my old room at Mary's house with a distinct churning inside. A knock on the door heralded Mary with my breakfast on a tray.

'Good morning, the future Mrs Morton,' she said, settling the tray in front of me as I sat up. I looked at the tray, Porridge, eggs and bacon, toast and marmalade plus a pot of coffee. I gasped.

'Mary! Quite apart from the fact that you shouldn't spoil me like this, I'll never eat that lot. My stomach feels as though butterflies with hobnailed boots are doing a clog dance in there.'

She shook her head. 'Nothing beats hob nailed butterflies better than a good breakfast,' she said. 'Besides, with the wedding being at one o'clock you won't be eating for hours, so get that down you. And as for spoiling you, sure there's no one deserves it more than you.' In the doorway she turned. 'Oh, and don't you dare get up for at least another hour. I want to see you bright-eyed and bushy-tailed at that register office.'

She was right about the breakfast. I felt better after I had made myself eat some of it but I couldn't lie in bed. On my way to the bathroom I glanced out of the window and saw the marquee which filled the top half of the garden. Janet had already arrived and she and Mary were busily popping in and out, for all the world like two nest-building birds. I smiled. I was so lucky to have good friends, a gorgeous future husband and a precious young son.

The ceremony was brief but beautiful. The woman registrar was sensitive and gracious. Neither of us had an attendant, but Jamie performed his ring bearer's ceremony with a grave face, handing up the two rings on their velvet cushion at the given moment. Outside the register office we posed for photographs, Jamie standing proudly in front of us. Then it was back to Mary's for the reception.

She had prepared a sumptuous buffet for us; the table groaning with good things in the centre of which was Janet's cake, beautifully iced with our initials entwined on the top. The speeches were minimal. Ian and I both thanked everyone who had contributed to our special day and my dad said a few words about us both, which brought a lump to my throat. Then to my surprise Jamie stood up.

'I want to say something,' he announced.

I was a little apprehensive, wondering what he might come out with but Ian smiled and squeezed my hand, winking assurance at me.

'I want to say thank you to Ian for being my music teacher and for marrying my mum,' he said in his clear, childish voice. Everyone laughed. He cleared his throat and went on, 'And in case any of you don't know, he's soon going to be my dad – my real dad with a certificate to prove it and everything.' He turned to Ian. 'I just wanted to ask – now that you and Mum are married can I start calling you Dad now, please?' Ian reached out to pat his shoulder and when he said, 'Yes, of course you can.' The two of them received a round of applause.

After the buffet Ian and I circulated the guests whilst a trio of Ian's musician friends played. Throughout the reception I'd been keeping an eye on Amanda. Ever since my first glimpse of her, resplendent in a floating pink dress and white fox fur, a feathered fascinator perched on top of her elaborate hairdo, I hadn't seen her. Ian caught me raking the marquee with anxious eyes and touched my arm.

'I think there's a surprise coming,' he said.

I was about to reply when I spotted Amanda in a corner talking animatedly to one of the double bass players from the Greencliffe Symphony Orchestra. The next moment Ian's friend Harry Turner who was in charge of the music stood up.

'I'd like to introduce you all to Miss Janet Trent,' he said. 'She happens to be the bridegroom's aunt and as well as making that wonderful wedding cake which we've all enjoyed she also happens to be a retired professional singer. Now, with a fond dedication to the happy couple she's going to sing for us.' He nodded to Janet who stepped up onto the dais.

She sang *This is My Lovely Day*, a song from an old musical show called *Bless the Bride*. Her mezzo soprano voice was as clear and beautiful as that of a younger woman and I could see that Ian was deeply moved by her gesture. Mary sidled up beside me.

'She's been rehearsing it for weeks,' she whispered. 'Isn't she the greatest?'

The song was enjoyed by everyone and received rapturous applause but across the marquee I caught a glimpse of Amanda's face, a smile firmly glued to it. She was clapping as heartily as anyone, but her eyes glittered with pure resentment. For once in her life her sister was stealing the limelight.

When Janet's song came to an end Ian slipped an arm around me. 'I've got another surprise,' he said. 'I'm taking you home now.'

I stared at him. 'But all this is going on till midnight,' I told him. 'We have to stay.'

'No, we don't, and you have to pack.' He slipped his hand into an inside pocket and drew out an envelope, handing it to me. Inside it were two Eurostar tickets and a hotel reservation. I looked at the destination, then at him.

'*Paris*?'

He grinned. 'Only for three days but we'll pack everything we can in.'

'Ian! It must have cost a bomb.'

He bent and kissed me. 'It's not every day I get to marry the girl of my dreams, is it?'

Stunned, I looked round at the assembled guests. 'Won't it look odd, our leaving so soon?'

'Not a bit. They all know,' he told me. 'And to their credit they've kept the secret well.'

'What about Jamie?'

'He knows too. Don't worry about him He's going to stay with Janet and Brownie and he can't wait.'

Seven

Paris was wonderful, everything I had always imagined it to be – and more. Our hotel was close to the Arc de Triomphe and in our three days we packed in as much as we could: We window-shopped on the Champs Elysées; ate a delicious lunch on a glamorous boat going down the Seine to marvel at the beautiful bridges. We travelled to the top of the Eiffel Tower and spent a memorable last evening at the *Moulin Rouge* before travelling home the next day with two more days to get Jamie ready for his new school.

He hadn't missed us at all, enjoying his time with Janet and his beloved Brownie. In the car on the way home he asked if he could have a dog of his own.

'I don't know, Jamie. We're out an awful lot. A dog would get bored and lonely,' I explained. His disappointed face tugged at my heart. 'Maybe one day, when we get a bigger house with a proper garden,' I said, knowing full well that I'd be held to the promise.

I waited eagerly for Ian and Jamie to come home on the Thursday afternoon, eager to hear about their first day at their respective new schools. Jamie arrived first. He looked tired but happy as he shrugged off his new satchel and dropped it at the foot of the stairs.

'So, how did it go?'

'Well, I miss Daniel, of course,' he said. 'But I sat next to this great guy called Martin. He plays the trumpet. I think we're going to be friends.'

I smiled at 'great guy' and as I looked at my son I suddenly realized how tall he was getting and knew with a pang of regret that he was growing up. 'You think you're going to be happy there then?' I said.

'Yeah.' He sighed. 'The only thing is I wish we lived nearer. It's on the other side of town from my old school. It's taken me much longer to get home.'

Ian or I had always driven him to school in the mornings till now, but Ian would have to stay at school longer in the evenings to do the following day's preparation. Also Mableton Park, our neck of the woods, was off the school bus route so that would mean public transport. I reflected that in the winter it could be a problem.

'When we look for another house we'll have to bear that in mind,' I told him.

When Ian came home he was full of enthusiasm for his new job. 'There's going to be such a lot to organize this term,' he said. 'There's this new choir to get up and running ready for the Christmas concert. It'll mean lots of rehearsals – some out of school hours, I'm afraid. Then there are the private lessons Jeremy is planning to offer.'

He had kept on his most promising private pupils, ones he could manage at weekends or in the evenings but by the sound of it he would need to put in some evenings at school too in the run up to Christmas. 'I hope you haven't taken on too much,' I said.

He smiled. 'It's not hard work when you love it.'

'But I'm hardly going to see you at this rate.' I stood on tiptoe to kiss him. 'And I hope you love me too.'

Jamie walked in as Ian kissed me and made a disgusted sound. 'Ugh, *gross!*' he muttered as he walked out of the room. Ian looked at me and we both laughed.

'He's growing up,' I said.

Ian nodded. 'I may have a surprise for him on Saturday. We'll see how grown up he is then.'

The surprise turned out to be a new violin. Ian had bought it from a friend who played in the second violin section of the orchestra. He'd been promoted to leader of the section and thought an upgrade on his instrument was called for. Ian showed it to me after Jamie had gone to bed.

'It's a good violin,' he said. 'And he let me have it very reasonably.'

'How much?' I asked tentatively.

He wagged a finger at me. 'Never you mind,' he said. 'I'm paying for it on the never-never, out of my private teaching fees. It's by way of a scholarship present. Janet and George did the same for me when I got into St C's.'

When Jamie saw the new violin his face went bright red. 'Wow! Is it really for me?' he asked incredulously.

Ian nodded. 'You're getting too big for the junior one. Everyone else in your year will have a full sized instrument and we can't have you being odd man out, can we?'

Jamie fingered the violin reverently. 'Can I try it?'

Ian laughed. 'Of course you can. It's yours now. Shall we try one of your pieces or would you rather do some scales.'

Jamie grinned. 'A piece please – the Vivaldi.'

He was a little shaky with the new, larger instrument at first but he soon got used to it. I slipped into the kitchen and left them to it.

The weeks that followed were hectic. Mary and I were busy with a sudden spate of engagement and birthday parties and there was an unusual number of bookings for Christmas weddings. Jamie's travelling arrangements were proving to be a problem. Ian stayed late at school most afternoons and sometimes went back in the evenings. If I was working it was a struggle to be home in time for Jamie's return from school. It became clear that we would have to find another house not so far out of town. We contacted all the estate agents and used up most of the half term break viewing. There was also the business of Ian's adoption of Jamie. We both agreed that it was too important to rush so we decided to shelve it until the Christmas holidays.

Most of the properties the agents suggested were out of the question for one reason or the other. They were either too large or too small; too expensive, or cheap but needing masses of renovation. There was one that stole my heart though, even though the price was too high and it was too large for us.

Beaumont House was an imposing double fronted house in a tree-lined avenue and as well as being about five minutes' walk from the seafront it was only walking distance from St Cecilia's. I fell in love with it on first sight.

'You can't be serious,' Ian said, looking at my wrapt face as we stood in the hall after our tour of the house. 'What do we want with six bedrooms, not to mention the three reception rooms and that barn of a kitchen!'

'In the leaflet it says that it used to be a guesthouse,' I said.

'Exactly!' He frowned at me. 'You're not thinking of going into business as a landlady are you?'

I shook my head. 'I know it's too big and completely unsuitable,' I said. 'But I can dream, can't I?'

'Have you noticed the price?' He held out the leaflet. 'I can't think why they even sent us this one or why we're wasting our time viewing it.'

'Just think of what I could do in that kitchen for *Mary-Mary*,' I muttered. 'And there's room for a big freezer in the utility room. And the third bedroom on the second floor could be made into a second bathroom. We could even let it as a flat and—'

'Stop!' Ian slipped an arm round my shoulders and gave me a squeeze. 'I know it's gorgeous. I'd love to live here too but it's out of the question. Don't worry, darling, we'll find something suitable eventually. We'll just have to keep looking.'

And so the possibility – not that there had ever been one – of buying Beaumont House was firmly removed from my mind. Little could I have foreseen the series of events that were to follow.

It was at the beginning of December that I received Dad's telephone call. I was at Mary's. We were having a morning filling the freezer ready for the coming rush of parties. Mary always liked to work to music so when my mobile began to ring in my coat pocket I didn't hear it at first.

'Elaine, I think that's your phone ringing.' Mary said as she switched off the radio. I retrieved the mobile from my coat pocket and noticed that the caller was Dad. With a feeling of foreboding I pressed the button.

'Dad?'

'Oh, Elaine.' He sounded relieved. 'I was about to give up.'

'Is everything all right?'

'No, love. I had to send for an ambulance for your mother late last night – a severe heart attack.'

'Oh, Dad.' My heart gave a lurch. 'She's in hospital?'

'No.' There was a pause at the other end and even before he told me I knew it was bad news. I heard him clear his throat. 'No love. I'm afraid we never got there. Your mother died in the ambulance on the way there – at three o'clock this morning.'

'Oh, Dad.' I glanced at Mary who was looking inquiringly at me. 'I'll come. I'll drive up there as soon as I can. I'll ring and let you know when I've made arrangements. Dad – are you all right?'

I heard him sigh. 'Yes. I'm all right. It wasn't exactly unexpected but it's still a blow when it happens.'

'I know – oh, Dad, I'm so sorry. I'll be with you as soon as I can. And you must come back with me after the – the....'

'We'll see, love,' he said. 'At the moment I'm not quite thinking straight and there's so much to do.'

'Of course. I understand.'

Mary had guessed correctly what had happened. As I switched off my phone and put it down she crossed the kitchen and put her arms around me. 'I'm so sorry darlin',' she said. 'Just you go. Don't worry about anything here. Janet will help out. I'm sure she'll be glad to.'

I hugged her back. 'Thanks, Mary.' I looked at her. 'I only wish she and I could have had a better relationship. It's Dad I feel for. He'll be all alone now.'

She nodded. 'It's a pity he's so far away. Now, if you want to get off right away just go,' she said. 'I'll have Ian and Jamie here to stay while you're away. I know they could go to Janet but it'll be more convenient for them here.'

I couldn't help smiling at her typically practical turn of mind. 'Thanks, Mary, but I'll wait till they get home this afternoon and we can discuss arrangements then,' I said. 'I'll drive up to Yorkshire in the morning.'

When Dad opened the door to me it was as though he'd aged overnight. Clearly Mother's sudden death had diminished him. His eyes filled with tears as he held out his arms to me. I hugged him tight.

'It's all right, Dad. I'm here now. We'll get through this together,' I said as I kissed his wet cheek.

He nodded. 'It's good to see you, love,' he said huskily.

The funeral was a quiet affair; Mother had made few friends since her marriage. Her doctor came and one or two old teaching colleagues, but apart from them Dad and I were the only mourners. We invited them back to the house afterwards for sandwiches and a glass of wine but they all declined, shaking hands in the church porch

and scurrying away. Dad and I turned up our collars against the driz-
zling afternoon and picked our way across the wet, leaf-strewn
churchyard to where I'd parked the car. As we climbed in gratefully
I looked at Dad.

'Are you all right?'

He nodded. 'You know it's odd, love, but I've got the strangest
feeling that none of this is quite real,' he said. 'I feel I don't really
know who I am or what I'm for any more. All these years I've looked
after your mother and now she's gone. I feel – sort of – cut adrift.'

'Of course you do. It's only natural.' I gave his arm a squeeze. 'But
you still have a life to live, Dad. We've got a lot of talking to do, but
let's get home and have something to eat and drink first.'

Ian and I had discussed Dad's predicament the evening before I
drove up to Yorkshire and he agreed with me that Dad couldn't be
left all that way off on his own. Obviously it would have to be his
decision but we were agreed that the offer to live with us must be
made.

After we'd eaten and washed up Dad looked more relaxed and I
decided to broach the subject of the future. I poured him a whisky
and ginger, his favourite drink and sat down opposite him.

'Dad, I know it's probably too soon to decide but how would you
feel about coming south to live with Ian, Jamie and me?'

He looked up in surprise. 'That's a very generous offer, love, but
you don't want an old codger like me cluttering the place up.'

I laughed. 'Don't talk about yourself like that. What are you – sixty,
isn't it? That's not old nowadays. You're still fit and healthy. You've
got a lot of living to do yet. Have you got any plans?'

He shook his head. 'I haven't even thought about it.'

'Then will you give my suggestion some thought?'

He sighed. 'But that little house of yours – it's too small. You
haven't got room.'

'We've already started looking for somewhere larger, Dad,' I told
him.

'You're sure – you're not just saying that because of me?'

'No. We've outgrown the cottage,' I told him. 'And now that
Jamie's at St Cecilia's and Ian's in a regular teaching job, Mableton
Park is too far out of town for us. We've already started looking at
places.'

He nodded. 'Let me sleep on it,' he said. 'It's true that there's nothing to keep me here. You know what your mother was like; we had no friends or social life to speak of.' He glanced around him. 'And this house will be far too big for me to rattle round in on my own. As a matter of fact I've even had an offer for it already.'

'Dad!' I was horrified. 'Are you telling me that people have been hassling you about the house even before Mother was buried?'

'It's not as bad as it sounds. It was Mr Harrison, the rector, actually,' he said. 'It seems the old rectory is going to be demolished. It's falling to bits and the diocese is looking for a property to buy. As we're not far from the church this house would be ideal.'

'Well, I think they could have waited for a decent interval,' I said.

He shook his head. 'Mr Harrison was just being realistic and it was good of him to think of me, really. Anyone could see this place was going to be too big for me. And the rector and his wife have three school age children so they need the space.'

'Well, as long as you weren't offended. Dad,' I leaned forward and put my hand on his knee, 'I'll have to go home the day after tomorrow. Will you think about coming with me? It needn't be permanent at this stage but I think you could do with a break. What do you say?'

He smiled. 'That'd be lovely, Elaine. Yes, I'd love to come.'

Jamie was delighted to have his granddad to stay but he was full of his stay with Mary. 'It's so much nearer school, Mum. I could walk there in no time. When are we going to move?'

'Soon, I hope,' I told him. 'We just have to find the right house.'

'Well I hope it's somewhere near where Auntie Mary lives,' he said.

Dad was interested in our house hunting and one afternoon as we were passing the end of Wellington Avenue I decided to show him Beaumont House. As we drew up outside I was surprised to see that the 'For Sale' board was still up. Dad stood at the gate and looked at the front of the house.

'Well, I can quite understand why you liked it,' he remarked.

'Would you like to see the inside?' I asked on impulse. When he nodded I took out my mobile and tapped in the estate agent's number. When the receptionist answered I said, 'It's Mrs Morton. My husband and I looked at Beaumont House in Wellington Avenue a few weeks ago and I'd like to view again with my father. Would it be possible now – this afternoon?' The girl asked me to hold on. Moments later she picked up the phone again.

'Mrs Morton, one of our negotiators is actually in the area at the moment. He showed someone round Beaumont House earlier and he still has the keys with him. He could be with you in half an hour. Is that all right?'

I grinned at Dad. 'That will be fine.'

As we waited it crossed my mind that I might have built up my first impression of the house out of all proportion. Maybe when I saw it again I'd be disappointed. I prepared myself mentally for a let-down. But the moment the young man from the agent's unlocked the front door and we walked into the hall my glowing first impressions were reaffirmed. The afternoon sunlight streamed through the long stained glass window on the landing, illuminating the hall with warm pink and pastel green light. I looked at Dad and when he returned my gaze I could see that he shared my view of the house.

We went from room to room and I could tell that Dad was as impressed as me. I looked at the young negotiator.

'The people you showed round earlier,' I said. 'Were they keen?'

He nodded. 'Very. In fact I wouldn't be surprised if they put in an offer very soon. They're thinking of turning it into a retirement home.'

'It would certainly make a superb home for the elderly,' Dad remarked as we got back into the car. 'I wouldn't mind retiring to a place like that myself. And did you see the garden?' He was smiling. 'I'd love to be let loose out there.'

I looked at him. He'd always been a keen gardener but in recent years the demands of Mother's illness had forced him to hand his own garden over to a group of youngsters from the local church who had turned it into allotments. 'Maybe we'd better not mention to Ian that we've been to see Beaumont House,' I suggested. 'It's way out of our price range and anyway it looks very much as though it's about to be sold.'

Dad nodded. 'Just as you please, love.'

But it seemed that Dad had fallen as much under the spell of Beaumont House as I had. After Jamie and Ian had left the following morning he looked at me across the breakfast table. 'I've had an idea, love,' he said. 'How about putting the kettle on again and letting me run it past you, as they say?'

Over mugs of strong tea he laid out his plan. 'Whichever way you look at it I'm going to have to sell the family house,' he said. 'And as I do already have an offer, how would it be if I helped out with the price of Beaumont House and moved into it with you?' Speechless with surprise I stared at him and he seized the opportunity to hurry on, 'That top floor could be turned into a flat without too much work needing to be done. That way I'd be out of your hair. And I'd take over that garden if you wanted me to.' He grinned. 'I could even grow organic fruit and veg for you and Mary to use in your business.'

I laughed. '*Dad*! You've got it all planned out, haven't you? You must have stayed awake all night.'

He smiled. 'Well, not *all* night. Seriously though, I could see how taken you were with the place,' he said. 'I thought it was a cracker too, and you have to admit that it would be the answer to all our problems.'

'You're right there. It would.' Try as I would I couldn't think of any drawbacks off the top of my head. 'We'll have to ask Ian what he thinks when he gets home,' I told him guardedly. 'He doesn't even know we've been back to see it, remember.'

'Of course. But don't forget what that young fellow said yesterday; those other viewers were more than interested, so we shouldn't hang about too long.'

Ian was a little more cautious than I'd been. When we laid out Dad's plan he looked from one to the other and raised an eyebrow.

'Do I get a whiff of conspiracy here?' he asked.

'No!' I protested. 'We were passing the end of Wellington Avenue yesterday and I thought Dad might like to see the house, and—'

He laughed and held up his hand. 'I'm only joking. I think it's a great idea in principal. There are just a few things that need to be thought through, though.'

He pointed out that we'd need to get the vendors to agree to our offer first. Then we'd have to have a survey done to make sure there were no structural problems with the house. He looked at Dad: 'And if we were to agree to your being joint owner we'd need to have a proper legal agreement drawn up. Then there's a little matter of furnishing,' Ian went on. 'How are we going to fill a house that size without making a sizable hole in the bank balance?'

'That's not a problem,' Dad put in. 'There's all the furniture from the house in Yorkshire. I was going to have to sell a lot of it anyway.' He looked at me. 'I know most of it is old fashioned and might not be the kind of thing you'd choose but it's all good stuff and—'

'Dad.' I covered his hand with mine. 'It's a wonderful idea.' I looked at Ian. 'Isn't it?'

He nodded. 'It's very generous of you, Ted. All we have to do now is get the house.'

We discussed our plans for most of the evening, agreeing that the joint purchase of Beaumont House would be the perfect solution to all our problems. Together the three of us decided on the figure we would offer for the house and I was designated to make the telephone call to the agent next morning.

My mouth was dry as I dialled the number. What if the house had already been sold? I steeled myself for disappointment as I listened to the phone ringing out at the other end.

'Haytor and Blake Estate Agents. Derek speaking, how can I help you?'

I swallowed hard. 'Oh, good morning. It's Mrs Morton. I'm ringing to inquire if Beaumont House is still for sale.'

Derek told me that an offer had been made but the vendor had turned it down. The prospective buyers were still considering whether to increase their offer. My spirits rose.

'Is it in order for me to inquire what the offer was?' I asked.

'I'm afraid I'm not at liberty to disclose that information,' he said. 'Were you thinking of making an offer yourself?'

'Well – yes.' I crossed my fingers as I told him the figure that the three of us had decided on.

There was a pause at the other end and I held my breath. 'Well, I can tell you that your offer is a better one than the previous buyer made. I'll telephone the vendor now and ring you back.'

I worked all morning at Mary's with my mobile in my pocket but no call came and it wasn't until I was driving back to the cottage later in the afternoon that the phone began to vibrate in my pocket. I pulled off the road and pulled it out.

'Hello.'

'Elaine, it's Dad.'

'Dad! I'm on my way home. Are you all right?'

'Better than all right! That young Derek from the agent's has just rung. The house is ours, love! The other buyers wouldn't up their offer so they've accepted ours.'

'Oh, *Dad*. That's terrific!' I felt excitement making my heart beat faster.

'I knew you must be on your way but I couldn't wait to tell you,' he went on.

I laughed. 'I'll stop off at the supermarket and get something special for dinner,' I told him. 'And a bottle of something bubbly to celebrate.'

Eight

The work on Beaumont House took a little longer than we antici-pated even though the top floor lent itself well for conversion. Dad chose the medium sized room for his bedroom whilst the largest of the three was made into a living room with a small kitchen area. The smallest room converted nicely into a bathroom, making a compact, self-contained flat. Dad went back up to Yorkshire to see the sale of the house through and as soon as it was completed he arranged for the furniture to be driven down to Greencliffe and put into storage until we moved. In the interim he stayed with Mary.

The day of the move went without a hitch and we were just finishing our takeaway pizza when Mary arrived. She brought a large basket and proceeded to unpack a casserole and one of her famous apple pies.

'You really had no need to be eating that rubbish,' she said, eyeing the remains of the pizza with disdain.

I laughed. 'I wasn't to know you'd be round with offerings,' I said. 'And this was Jamie's choice.'

She shook her head. 'You surely didn't think I'd let you move house without making sure you were properly fed!' She looked around. 'Still, I must say you've made a good start. When do you want Ted to move in?'

'As soon as we've moved his furniture in,' I told her. 'How have the two of you been getting on?'

She smiled. 'Just fine. He's great company. I'm going to miss him when he's gone, but I know he's looking forward to moving into his own little flat. Not to mention licking that garden into shape.'

Dad's furniture arrived two days later and he chose what he wanted for his flat. I'd already made curtains for the top floor dormer windows and when everything was in place he was delighted with it.

'You know you don't have to stay up here by yourself all the time, don't you, Dad,' I reminded him.

'Don't you worry about me, I'll be fine,' he assured me, looking out of the window onto the rambling garden below. 'Anyway, as soon as the spring gets going I intend to be outdoors most of the time.'

The rest of the furniture was distributed around the rest of the house apart from the huge chintz-covered chesterfield that had been in the sitting room at home. Finally I put it in the kitchen and hung Cecily Harding's watercolour painting of St Ives harbour above it to make a tranquil corner.

Jamie had been excited at the prospect of being nearer to his school and only a short walk from Mary's. He liked his new spacious bedroom on the first floor. He would have the first floor bathroom to himself as the room Ian and I were to occupy had its own en-suite. On the ground floor Ian had chosen the smallest of the three rooms to be his studio whilst the room opposite was to be our living room. That just left what had once been the large dining room unfurnished.

In a fit of impulsive enthusiasm I decided to invite everyone to spend Christmas with us at Beaumont House. When I mentioned my plan to Ian he was sceptical.

'Are you sure you want all that work?' he asked. 'Moving the three of us and Ted was a lot of hard work for you. I was going to suggest spending a quiet Christmas on our own.'

I brushed his doubts aside. 'We can't do that. We all went to Mary's last year,' I reminded him. 'It's only fair to return the hospitality, especially now that we have the room to do it.'

'Well, all right if you're sure.' He frowned. 'You say "everyone". Do I take it you're including Amanda?'

'I can hardly leave her out, can I?'

He sighed. 'Don't say you've forgotten how she ruined everything last year. Are you sure you want to risk it?'

I smiled. 'She'll be fine. I think she and I understand one another now,' I told him. 'Anyway, she'd be so hurt of we left her out.'

He shrugged. 'Just as you please,' he said. 'But don't say I didn't warn you.'

It was all arranged. Mary and Janet both accepted my invitation on condition that they were allowed to help with the food. Mary promised to provide home-made Christmas puddings and Janet insisted that she would make and ice a cake.

I was glad of their offers as we were frantically busy at *Mary-Mary* in the run-up to Christmas with parties and weddings. Both Ian and Jamie were busy too with school concerts. Ian introduced his new choir to much acclaim and Jamie played a violin solo in the concert that St Cecilia's put on. Dad and I sat in the front row at both, Dad bursting with pride at his family's achievements.

There had been very little time for Christmas shopping but Ian and I, along with Dad, had discussed the prospect of getting Jamie a puppy. I was adamant that no animal should be left alone for hours on end and Dad happily agreed to take care of the puppy while we were all out, so finally it was decided that Jamie would get his longed-for wish. Janet put us in touch with the woman who had bred Brownie and we learned that she had a litter of puppies which would be ready just before Christmas. Ian and I went along to see them one evening and immediately fell in love with the cute little bundles that tumbled over each other playfully. We decided on a brown and white male pup that looked very much like Brownie, knowing that would be Jamie's choice.

I went round to Ocean Heights to invite Amanda personally. She seemed surprised to see me.

'I've been wondering how you were getting on. I haven't seen you since the wedding,' she said pointedly as she led the way through to her living room.

I explained about my mother's sudden death and how we'd been busy moving house as well as moving Dad down from Yorkshire. 'And so now that we're in we'd like everyone to come and help us housewarm our new home by spending Christmas with us at Beaumont House,' I finished.

'It's in Wellington Avenue, you say?' she said. 'I know that area; very salubrious. But aren't those houses rather big for the three of you?'

'Would have been, yes, but we've converted the top floor of the house as a self contained flat for Dad.'

'Your father is moving in with you?' She looked taken aback. 'Well, that's extremely generous of you. Are you sure poor Ian isn't stretching himself financially?'

I felt a prickle of resentment. 'Not at all,' I said. 'I do contribute to all our expenses myself and anyway, Dad is sharing all the costs with us. He's sold his house in Yorkshire and brought all the furniture down to help furnish the place. We couldn't have done it without him.'

'I see. Well I hope you don't live to regret your decision,' she said, the corners of her mouth drooping disapprovingly. 'Sharing your home with relatives is full of pitfalls.'

'It isn't exactly sharing the house,' I said. 'As I said, Dad has the top floor to himself. He's taking over the garden too, which will be a great help.'

'Oh well, if you say so.' She gave a brittle little laugh. 'Anyway, it's nothing to do with me, is it? Ian must feel he's got his priorities right and I'm sure he gets along *famously* with his new father-in-law – so far.'

I ignored the barb. 'So we'd like you to join us for Christmas,' I said. 'That is if you've no other plans, of course.'

'I've none to speak of – although I've had lots of invitations, of course,' she added hurriedly. She sighed resignedly. 'I suppose Janet will be there.'

'Yes. She's making the Christmas cake,' I told her. 'Mary is making the puddings.'

She raised an eyebrow at me. 'Is that a hint that you want me to contribute too?'

'Not at all, though if you want to....'

'I'll have to think about it,' she said. 'Perhaps a few mince pies. I've a very light hand with pastry. It's my one culinary talent, if I do say so myself.' She looked at me. 'Janet would tell you if she could ever bring herself to pay me a compliment.'

As I drove away from Ocean Heights I felt weighed down by misgivings. Had I had done the right thing in insisting on inviting Amanda to share Christmas with us again? If it all went pear shaped it would be my fault. I'd thought after our last meeting that she and I had built a rapport but today she seemed full of resentment again.

I was determined to make our first Christmas at Beaumont House special. Ian and Jamie helped me decorate the house with evergreens and we bought a large Christmas tree to stand in the hall, dressing it with coloured baubles and lights. On Christmas morning Ian wakened me with a tray of tea and a small parcel wrapped in red holly-sprigged paper. We had decided not to buy each other presents this year as we'd had all the expense of moving, but I had secretly bought him a pair of soft leather driving gloves. Obviously he had ignored our decision too. Berating him, I tore off the paper and found a box containing a pretty silver heart-shaped locket. Inside were photographs of Jamie and Ian. I threw my arms around him.

'Thank you, darling. I love it, but we promised not to.' I reached under my pillow I brought out the gloves, wrapped in Christmassy paper. He laughed.

'The words pot and kettle come to mind!' He tore off the paper. 'Wow, driving gloves! Just what I need. Aren't you clever!'

'We're going to be really happy here,' I told him as we hugged each other. 'I just know it. There's something about this house.'

We'd collected the puppy late the previous evening, after Jamie was in bed and Dad had agreed to have him upstairs in the flat with him until morning. When I went up to the flat with a cup of tea I wasn't really surprised to find the puppy curled up beside him on the bed.

'You're already getting him into bad habits,' I scolded him.

He reached out a hand to fondle the curly little head. 'He missed his mum and his brothers and sisters,' he said. 'I couldn't let him cry himself to sleep, could I?'

'Well, I think it's time he met his new master,' I said. 'So drink up your tea and come down to witness the introductions.'

Creeping into Jamie's room we put the puppy on his bed and then wakened him.

'Happy Christmas, Jamie. Here's someone to see you.'

He sat up, rubbing his eyes and then he caught sight of the puppy rummaging among the pile of presents at the end of his bed. He stared round-eyed at the puppy and then at me.

'Wow! Is he really for me?'

'He's your Christmas present from Ian and me,' I told him. 'He's one of Brownie's great nephews. What are you going to call him?'

Very carefully Jamie reached out to pick up the tiny bundle. The puppy licked him all over his face which made him laugh. 'I think he likes me.' He examined him carefully. 'I'll call him Toffee,' he said, ''Cause he's soft and sweet.'

Toffee helped Jamie to open his other present, tearing up the paper and rolling joyfully in the shreds.

I found that Dad was almost as excited as Jamie. 'We're going to have to train him,' he explained. 'First he needs to know that he has to go out in the garden when he needs a wee, then he'll have to learn how to walk on a collar and lead. After that we might teach him a few tricks.' He looked hopefully at his grandson. 'What do you reckon lad? Would you like me to help?'

'Yes please, Granddad.'

Ian and I left them to it, going back to our room to shower and dress. 'Well, I think you could safely say that that was one present that was a success,' I said.

Ian laughed. 'Who for – Jamie or Ted?'

Mary and Janet arrived together bearing puddings and cake. By the time they appeared I'd laid the table and put the turkey into the oven. Ian had helped me prepare all the vegetables the night before so there wasn't much left to do. We'd decided to eat in the kitchen. There was plenty of room round the big round table that Dad had brought from Yorkshire and the warmth from the Aga made it cosy and welcoming. Mary had brought a lovely table decoration that she'd made herself: holly with plenty of red berries surrounding a fat red candle. It set off the table to perfection. Janet brought crackers and two bottles of champagne and from the boot of the car she pulled out the small basket that Brownie had slept in as a puppy along with a brand new doggie blanket.

'For the newest addition to the family,' she said as she handed them to Jamie.

I made coffee for us all and then Ian set off to collect Amanda. When she arrived I took all three women for a tour of the house. Mary and Janet expressed their delight but Amanda was sceptical.

'I still think it's very large for the three of you, even if your father is sharing it with you,' she said. 'And if you don't mind me asking, why are we eating in the kitchen?'

Janet shot her a warning look but I smiled, determined not to allow myself to be ruffled by her disparaging remarks.

'This is the original dining room,' I said opening the door. 'But as you can see it's not furnished at the moment. That's something we'll get around to eventually.'

Amanda walked into the large room which overlooked the garden. 'Mmm, this is nice,' she said, looking round. 'It needs decorating, of course, but it could be made very pleasant.'

'We had thought of letting it,' I said. 'But that will have to be a last resort. It's lovely having Dad living upstairs but sharing our home with a complete stranger is another matter.'

Christmas lunch went well. The turkey was succulent and Mary's pudding was delicious. Afterwards we all relaxed with our coffee in the living room, except Jamie who played on the floor with Toffee.

'Can I take him for a walk?' he asked.

'Not until he's had all his jabs at the vet's,' Dad told him. 'We don't want him catching anything nasty, do we? Meantime he can play in the garden, once I've made sure all the fences are secure and he can't get out and wander away.'

Everyone took turns to cuddle the puppy except Amanda who recoiled whenever he went near her. 'Why on earth you wanted to saddle yourself with an animal I can't think,' she said to me. 'Bringing dirt and germs into the house.' She looked at Janet. 'Speaking of which, where is your dog today?'

'I didn't bring him because of the puppy,' Janet explained. 'I thought it best not to crowd the poor little thing.'

Jamie looked guilty. 'Oh, poor old Brownie, all on his own on Christmas Day. We'll have to introduce him to Toffee. I bet they'll be really good friends.'

Janet smiled. 'I'm sure they will.'

At four o'clock I went to put the kettle on. Amanda came with me. 'I must go upstairs to powder my nose,' she said. 'Then I'll give you a hand.'

'There's no need to go upstairs,' I called out as she made for the stairs. 'There's a loo down here, Amanda.' But she didn't hear me – or pretended not to, continuing determinedly on her way. I guessed that maybe she wanted to have another sneaky look round.

I was carrying the tray of tea through the hall twenty minutes later when she appeared at the top of the stairs. I looked up. 'Good timing, Amanda. Tea's ready.' But I had hardly uttered the words when she tripped and fell; half rolling, half tumbling down the entire length of the staircase.

The crash and Amanda's cries brought everyone running out into the hall, appalled to find her lying crumpled and white-faced at the foot of the stairs.

'It's my ankle,' she whimpered. 'I think it's broken.'

Mary went to help her up but Ian held her back.

'Better not to move her,' he said. 'She could have other injuries. Someone get a blanket. I'll ring for an ambulance.'

With a cushion under her head and a blanket over her Amanda quickly found her voice, complaining loudly that the stairs were not safe.

'I'm sure that carpet isn't correctly fitted,' she said. 'I must have caught my foot in it.'

Dad wanted to get her a brandy but again Ian shook his head. 'Better not give her anything until the paramedics have checked her,' he warned. 'It might be necessary to give her an anaesthetic.'

The ambulance arrived and the two paramedics confirmed that Amanda had broken her ankle. She was given a pain killing injection and lifted onto a trolley. We all looked at each other. Clearly someone needed to accompany her.

'I'll go,' Mary volunteered. 'You can't leave Jamie, Elaine, and Janet has to get home and see to Brownie.' As she climbed into the ambulance behind a loudly complaining Amanda she turned. 'I'll ring you from the hospital, she said. 'Try not to worry.'

She rang an hour later to tell us that Amanda had a double fracture of her right ankle and that she would have to remain in hospital and undergo surgery to have the bone pinned.

'How is she?' I asked.

'Furious,' Mary told me. 'Complaining about everything she can lay her tongue to. I think the nurses are fed up with her already.'

Amanda's accident put a damper on the rest of Christmas Day. Janet went home to Brownie and Dad stayed to watch the Christmas film with us, after which he declared that he was tired and ready to turn in. Jamie went reluctantly upstairs after we'd put Toffee to bed in his new basket beside the Aga.

'Can't he sleep in my room – please, Mum?' he begged, but I was adamant.

'Not until he's properly trained. We'll put lots of newspaper down for now and we'll think about it again once we've got him clean and dry.'

'He'll be lonely though,' Jamie protested.

I remembered reading somewhere that putting a clock in the basket reminds a puppy of his mother's heartbeat. I found my little travelling clock and tucked it into the blanket and to our relief Toffee settled down happily, tired after his busy day.

Amanda had surgery the following day to pin her badly broken ankle. Ian and I visited her once she had recovered from the effects of the anaesthetic. Propped up in bed she was the picture of suffering.

'The pain is *indescribable*,' she grumbled. 'Nothing they give me comes anywhere near easing it. And the *food*! You wouldn't give it to a pig.' She gave Ian a meaningful look. 'If only I could afford it I'd get them to transfer me to a private hospital where I could get the kind of treatment I'm used to.'

He ignored the hint. 'I'm sure you won't be in here for more than a few days,' he said. 'They don't keep people in hospital for long nowadays.'

'Oh? And where am I to go, pray?' Amanda challenged. 'Back to that high rise flat? I don't think so. How would I ever manage the stairs?'

'There is a lift.'

'Do I really need to remind you that I'm going to be in plaster and on crutches for weeks?' she reminded us.

'Well, once you're in the flat you'll have no need to go out for anything,' Ian said.

'I'll do your shopping for you,' I offered. 'And take you for your hospital appointments.'

'What about the physiotherapy?' she moaned. 'I'm supposed to attend a physio clinic twice a week!' She glared at us. 'Or do you want me to end up a permanent cripple?'

'Don't be melodramatic,' Ian said. 'We'll manage somehow.'

'I'm not going back to Ocean Heights and that's flat!' she declared.

We looked at each other. 'Maybe you can stay with Janet,' Ian ventured.

Amanda let out a loud snort. 'Stay with *Janet*! Not if you paid me a thousand pounds a day!' She shook her head. 'Have that disgusting animal of hers drooling all over me in my helpless condition. I think *not*!' She looked at me out of the corner of her eye. 'I wonder if your father knows how lucky he is to have a doting daughter like you, Elaine, to provide him with a roof over his head in his time of trouble.'

We glanced at each other. Amanda had her own agenda and she was making it abundantly clear. I could see from the look in Ian's eyes that he'd got the message loud and clear too.

'You're *joking*!' Mary stared at me across her kitchen table where we were busy preparing buffet food. 'You're seriously considering having that woman to stay with you at Beaumont House? Have you taken leave of your senses?'

'What else can we do?' I asked. 'She can't go back to the flat.'

'Why not? You said you'd help her and it's only for a few weeks, after all.'

I shrugged. 'You try arguing with Amanda. Once she's made her mind up there's no shifting her.'

'What about Janet. She is her sister.'

'Amanda won't go there. Anyway I think they'd end up killing one another. You know what they're like.'

'So it's down to you. Where would you put her anyway?'

'She suggested that she might have the dining room. I reminded her that it isn't furnished and she said she'd bring her own furniture from the flat.'

'Which sounds suspiciously as though she has no intention of going back there.'

I sighed. 'Looks very much like it, doesn't it?'

'Oh, Elaine; just when you've found your dream house and settled in so nicely.'

'I think she resents the fact that we've given Dad a home,' I said. 'I've told her he shared all the costs with us but she still feels she's entitled to the same treatment.'

'The cheek! Ian doesn't owe her anything. She'll drive the pair of you barmy!' Mary's eyes narrowed. 'You don't think she chucked herself down the stairs on purpose, do you?'

I shook my head. 'I don't think even Amanda would be that

devious. It was a lucky break – if you'll pardon the pun. But she'd have found a way to get what she wanted in the end somehow.'

In spite of her disability Amanda managed to make arrangements for her furniture to be moved from Ocean Heights to Beaumont House. There was more than enough to turn what had been the dining room into a bedsit for her. She very graciously informed us that we could arrange for the decorating to be done at a later date after her ankle had mended. I tentatively brought up the subject of rent.

'Obviously you won't have the same self contained facilities you had at Ocean Heights so maybe half of what you paid there....'

She fixed me with a hard stare. 'Let me get this right – you're expecting to take *rent* from me?'

In spite of my sinking heart I stood my ground. 'Naturally. We were going to rent the room out anyway, to cover our overheads, and I'm going to have to take on a cleaner for the extra work. Ian and I don't earn a fortune.'

'Do you take rent from your father?'

'No, because Dad is part owner of the house. He paid for the renovations and he gave us a lot of the furniture.'

She shrugged. 'I've always thought that blood is thicker than water. I think it's outrageous that my own son is expecting his mother to pay him rent,' she said.

'It's not long since you were worrying that he might be stretching himself financially,' I daringly reminded her. I didn't remind her of her warning that sharing a house with relatives was full of pitfalls, though I was sorely tempted to.

She turned away. 'Oh well, if you insist I suppose I shall have to try and eke out my meagre income.'

I asked Ian to have a word with her but to my annoyance he agreed to let her stay rent free on a temporary basis.

'You know it won't be temporary,' I told him. 'Once she digs her heels in she'll stay on for nothing. You know she will.'

He sighed. 'Oh don't worry, I'll thrash it out with her again later,' he said dismissively. 'I've got too much to think about at the moment to face up to a battle with Amanda.'

She moved in a week later to much moaning and complaining and kept me running after her for the rest of the week. Finally Ian insisted that we put an ad in the local paper for a daily cleaning woman.

'You'll be making yourself ill,' he said. 'What with your job, the house and Jamie and I; not to mention keeping an eye on your dad and the dog.'

A week later we'd had three replies. One was a blonde girl with a very short skirt and lots of make-up who was under the impression that Beaumont House was still a guesthouse and she could expect tips at the end of the week. Once she knew it was a strictly domestic environment she lost interest. The second applicant was an elderly woman who looked too frail to lift a broom never mind sweep with one. The third arrived to be interviewed on Saturday morning. She was what you might call flamboyant. Her hair was an unlikely crimson and when she spoke it was with a strong Cockney accent. I put her age at around sixty and once I'd taken in the scarlet coat and black miniskirt revealing knobbly knees, I doubted whether she would be any more suitable than the other two.

'They call me Cleo,' she told me as she settled herself at the kitchen table, 'Although me real name – the one on me insurance card is Betty – Betty Mott. But Cleo was me stage name an' it's what I likes best to be called.'

'I see. So you're an actress then – er – Cleo?' I asked doubtfully.

She laughed. 'Bless you, no. I used to be half of a magic act. We used to top the bill in all the number one variety shows. Trouble is there ain't no call for variety shows any more and there's no work on the telly either for the likes of The Great Zadoc and Cleo.'

'Was that the name of your act?'

'S'right,' she said. 'We done the usual magic tricks – y'know, sawing me in half an' the disappearing cabinet, then, when work started to dry up we introduced more exotic stuff: fire eating, weight lifting, bed o'nails.'

'Bed of nails?'

'Yeah. Bert, that was Zadoc's real name, used to lie on it and I used to sit on his belly.'

I winced. 'Didn't it hurt?'

'No. I never felt a thing!' She laughed. 'Can't speak for Bert, mind!'

We laughed together and I decided that I liked her. She was thin and wiry but she looked strong and she had a good sense of humour which I decided would be called for with Amanda around. I explained our unorthodox situation. She nodded sympathetically.

''Avin' the mother-in-law to live with you ain't no joke. You can't tell me nuthin about it,' she said. 'I had the mother-in-law from hell – God rest the old battleaxe!'

'Oh, well I'm sure you and Mrs Trent will get along fine,' I said quickly. 'She used to be on the stage too, so you'll have something in common. My father has the top floor flat and he likes to do his own cleaning so you don't have to worry about him.'

We arranged terms and she promised to start the following Monday at nine sharp. 'You'll find me a good time keeper,' she said as I showed her out. 'Never been late for a show yet.'

As I watched her tottering down the drive, the muscles in her stringy legs bulging, I congratulated myself. 'I think she'll do,' I told myself. 'I think she'll do very well.'

Nine

By early March Dad had made a good start on clearing the jungle-like mass of undergrowth from the garden. He unearthed an overgrown lawn and flower beds in which spring bulbs were trying hard to raise their new green shoots. Massive bonfires burned at the bottom of the garden every day and Dad came in late each afternoon filthy but blissfully happy, his face streaked with soot as he climbed the stairs with Toffee at his heels, to take a shower and cook his evening meal.

Jamie's Christmas puppy was growing into a nice little dog and Dad was doing a really good job in getting him trained. Although Toffee relied on Dad for company all day he was always waiting, tail wagging in anticipation when Jamie came home from school; eager to share his tea and to curl up at the end of his bed at bed time. I'd long since given up the battle on that score. Everything would have been fine – if it hadn't been for Amanda, as I told Mary as we worked together in her kitchen one morning in early April.

'I thought she and Cleo would get along fine with them both of them having been in the same business.'

'But they don't?' Mary gave me a 'why aren't I surprised?' look.

I sighed. 'Amanda complains that Cleo is over familiar. But worse than that, she objects to being put in the same category as a magician's assistant.'

'But surely it's all show business?'

'Not according to Amanda. She tells me that she is what is called a "legitimate" actress.'

'And Cleo is, what – illegitimate?'

I shrugged. 'Don't ask me. It's almost three months now since

Amanda moved in and so far she's shown no desire to move out or to pay us any rent.'

'Have you spoken to her about it?'

'I have hinted. Her response is to point out how inconvenient it is for her, living on the ground floor at Beaumont House with a shared kitchen and having to struggle upstairs to the first floor bathroom. She makes it sound as though she's doing us a favour by putting up with all the hardship.'

'But surely it's not that hard for her to get upstairs now, is it? Her ankle must be almost back to normal.'

'Not to hear her talk. She insists that she still finds the stairs a problem, yet she's always in the first floor bathroom first thing in the morning when Jamie's trying to get ready for school.'

'Ask her to wait till the morning rush is over.'

'I have. It makes no difference. She's always in the kitchen too, getting under my feet, making her own meals when I'm trying to get ours. I've suggested that I cook for all of us but she objects to what she refers to as my "outlandish cuisine".' I sighed. 'And then of course there's Dad.'

'Ted?' Mary's eyebrows shot up. 'Bless his heart, what can he possibly have done?'

'It's just that he will tease her. He sees right through her, that's the trouble, and he never could bear boasting. He knows she exaggerates the success of her stage career and he tries to take her down a peg. It infuriates her. I've asked him not to do it but it seems he can't resist it. The more she rises to the bait, the more he does it.'

Mary tried unsuccessfully to stifle a giggle. 'I can't say I blame him,' she said. 'The way she goes on you'd think she was Vivienne Leigh and Dame Sybil Thorndike rolled into one.'

'It's not funny, Mary,' I told her. 'You don't have to live with it and try to keep the peace. I've taken her to all her hospital appointments and physio sessions yet I've never had a single word of thanks from her.'

'What about Ian? Won't he have a word? After all, she is his mother and it must affect him too.'

'No, it doesn't. He's so full of his school work and his teaching. The minute he gets home he shuts himself in the studio. If he's not teaching he's recording work for school or preparing lessons. Then, when Jamie gets home he's helping him with his practice and they're shut up together for hours. I hardly get to see either of them these days.'

'How's the adoption going, by the way?'

I felt tears of angry frustration pricking my eyelids. 'Slowly,' I said. 'Like the rest of my life, it seems to be on hold.'

Mary stopped what she was doing and crossed the kitchen to put an arm around my shoulders. 'I'm sorry, darlin',' she said. 'Sorry I laughed too. I can see it's not funny. It's really getting to you, isn't it? You know, you can't go on like this or you'll make yourself ill.' I dashed away the tears impatiently as she handed me a tissue. 'Stop what you're doing,' she said. 'We need a break so I'll put the kettle on and you can moan as much as you like. Get it all off your chest.'

Ten minutes later we were seated at the table with coffee and chocolate biscuits; Mary's remedy for all ills.

'When we moved into Beaumont House I thought you and I would be able to use the kitchen there,' I said. 'I know we'd have to have had it approved just as we did yours, but it would have been so useful. On days when I needed to be at home I could still have worked and we'd have had double the freezer space. Now Amanda clearly considers it half hers to use whenever she feels like it.'

'Mmm, that is a problem.' Mary looked at me thoughtfully. 'I'm still intrigued at this so-called "outlandish cuisine" of yours,' she said. 'What can you be cooking that's so bizarre?'

'Nothing. It's just that she won't touch anything with a sauce,' I told her. 'Or even anything that involves a recipe. Nothing wrong with plain cooking, she says. Her idea of an exotic dish is spag bol!'

'That'll be all those years of staying in cheap theatrical digs,' she said. 'Mutton stew with boiled cabbage and watery mash.'

I laughed in spite of myself. 'Don't ever say that in front of her. Amanda Trent only stayed in the very best five star hotels!' I took a sip of my coffee. 'When I went to see her when I first became pregnant I thought we'd established a sort of rapport. I still think there's another side to her somewhere. I'm just not sure I can be bothered looking for it any more.'

Mary laid a hand on my arm. 'Let me have a word with Janet,' she offered. 'After all, she is Amanda's sister. Meantime, I've been thinking, business is a bit slack this time of year. If you fancy getting out of the house a bit more why don't we do a leaflet drop around town? I think the personal touch is better than an ad in the paper. I'll get some flyers done on the computer; you can help me design something artistic and then we can target places we haven't tried before.'

Mary's idea cheered me up. As I drove home I thought of places we hadn't previously targeted. Maybe the local schools. They often arranged functions – speech days for instance. We could even offer them special terms. Then there was the local library. They were having a refurbishment at the moment. Maybe they were planning some kind of reopening event.

At home I went upstairs to change. Looking out of the window I saw Dad busy down in the garden. He'd given the newly discovered lawn its first mowing and was trimming the edges. In the flower beds the daffodils and crocuses were blooming and the forsythia was a mass of bright yellow stars. At the bottom of the garden, fringing the vegetable patch Dad had discovered some ancient fruit trees.

'It's too late to prune them,' he told me. 'But I'll spray them now and have a good go at them in the autumn. There's apple and plum and a cherry too,' he added delightedly. 'You'll have plenty of fruit to freeze for the winter.'

He looked like a new man since he'd been with us. The hollows in his cheeks had filled out and his eyes were bright and clear. He was already tanned from working in the early spring sunshine. Looking after Mother had taken its toll on him; I could see that now and it made me feel guilty that I hadn't been there for him earlier. I wondered why Ian seemed oblivious to the fact that Amanda was spoiling our new life together. He owed her nothing. All her life she'd put herself first. I'd spoken to him about it several times but every time I raised the subject he waved it aside. Why couldn't he see that the longer he continued to brush the problem under the carpet, the worse it was going to get? Amanda was becoming a fixture. Why couldn't he see what it was doing to me – to *us*?

I spent the afternoon designing what I thought was an eye-catching leaflet and Mary ran off a few dozen on our firm's computer. She had made a list too and when she mentioned the idea to Janet she volunteered to join us. Our tour of prospective new clients helped to take my mind off the problems at home and I quite enjoyed myself.

The three of us had decided to split up and meet again to discuss our progress over lunch.

I found the library particularly interested in our service.

'You couldn't have come at a better time, actually,' Maureen Jones, the chief librarian told me. 'We're planning the reopening to coincide with an author event. The author has roots in this part of the country and his newest book is actually set here so his publisher has asked if we'd launch it here. He's an international best seller so naturally we're excited,' she enthused. 'It's an honour. He's always number one on our waiting lists and it couldn't have come at a more opportune time.'

'That sounds fascinating.' I took out my notebook. 'What's the date?' I asked. 'And the author's name?'

'It's planned for the 10th of May and the author's name is Jake Kenning,' she told me. 'He writes detective fiction. I daresay you've heard of him. A couple of his books have been adapted for TV. We're planning to invite the mayor and town councillors to take a buffet lunch first,' she went on. 'Then Mr Kenning will cut the ribbon and declare the newly refurbished library open. He's agreed to give us a talk about his career afterwards and sign books for his many fans.'

I made a note on my pad. 'Would you like us to send you some sample menus and prices?' I asked.

She nodded. 'Yes please. They'll have to be okayed by the powers that be, of course. I don't have the final say on it.'

'Of course. I'll email them to you if you like.' I took down the email address and details of how many people were to be catered for.

When I told Mary and Janet over lunch Janet beamed with delight. 'Jake Kenning! He's one of my favourite authors. He's brilliant.' She looked at Mary and me. 'Don't tell me you've never heard of him!'

Mary shook her head. 'I'm not a great one for novels. My favourite bedtime reading is usually the latest cookery book.'

Janet laughed. 'Mary! You're incorrigible!' She looked at me. 'Surely you know his work, Elaine.'

I frowned, trying to rack my brain. 'I don't really get much time for reading,' I confessed. 'Though I do like detective plays on TV.'

'Then you must have seen *The Mourning Rose*? It was on just before Christmas.'

The title jogged my memory. Ian and I had both enjoyed the two-

parter screened a few months ago. 'Oh yes, we did see that. It was very good.' I was glad to be able to say I knew the author's work, even if it was only a TV adaptation.

That afternoon Mary and I set about compiling and costing three menus for the event. When we were satisfied I emailed them to the library before setting off for home.

I heard raised voices the moment I opened the porch door and I hesitated, standing back for a moment.

'I won't have it, do you hear me?' It was Amanda's voice, loud and strident. 'I can't spend all day with the curtains drawn. I can't live like a goldfish either. You have to stop gawping at me through the window.'

'I wasn't gawping at you!' Dad returned indignantly. 'I was trying to alert you to the fact that it was raining and you had some washing out.'

'That's another thing. Why were you ogling my underwear?'

I heard Dad's low chuckle. 'Ogling? Did you say *ogling*, woman? Why would I want to do anything of the kind?'

Amanda's voice rose at least an octave and a half. 'Because you're an old *pervert*, that's why!'

I decided it was time to intervene. Stepping through the front door I found them facing each other in the hall. Dad looked annoyed and slightly bemused but Amanda's face was scarlet with fury. She turned to me.

'No use complaining to you,' she said. 'You'll obviously take *his* side!'

I looked at Dad. 'What's the problem?'

He shrugged and spread his hands. 'You'd better ask her,' he said. 'She's just accused me of being a pervert because I tapped on her window to let her know it was raining.'

Amanda laughed mirthlessly. 'Oh yes! It sounds so *innocent* the way he puts it. The fact is, every time he passes my window he stares in at me. I've no privacy at all.'

'I'm sure it's not intentional,' I offered.

'*There*! I said you'd take his side.' Toffee who had been sitting by Dad's feet suddenly jumped up at Amanda's skirt. She aimed a kick at him. 'Get off me, you filthy creature!'

Toffee let out a yelp and Dad bent to pick him up. He turned to her, his patience clearly exhausted. 'There's no need to take it out on the dog,' he said. 'If you really want to know, I think there's something seriously wrong with you. You're utterly self obsessed and paranoid about just about everything. If you ask me you've got a highly inflated opinion of your own importance.' He gave me an apologetic look and turned to walk up the stairs.

I looked at Amanda. 'Maybe we'd better go inside and make you some tea,' I suggested. 'You need to calm down.'

Without a word she led the way into her room. I looked around. The bed was unmade although it was late afternoon. The table was littered with magazines and papers and there were used cups and plates everywhere.

'Hasn't Cleo been in here today?' I asked.

She turned to me, pulling herself up to her full height and staring me straight in the face. 'No. I've dismissed her.'

'You've *what*?

'I told her that her services are no longer required,' she said haughtily. 'She was impertinent.'

'But you had no right,' I told her. 'You are not her employer.'

'She was downright insolent. I won't be spoken to like that.'

'Like what? What did she say?'

'First of all she had the effrontery to suggest that she and I were the same age! Then she said we had a mutual acquaintance. As if I'd stoop so low as to consort with anyone *she's* worked with!'

I let the age question go. Amanda had always been cagey about her age but Janet had no such inhibition so I knew exactly how old Amanda was. The 'mutual acquaintance' was something else.

'I hardly think that's a sacking offence. You had no right to dismiss her, Amanda. She's a good worker. Who is going to do the cleaning now – are you?'

She bridled. '*Me*? Of course not. You'll have to find someone else.'

'I certainly will not find anyone else,' I told her, trying hard to contain my exasperation. 'I shall have to go round to Cleo's this evening, apologize and ask her to come back. If she agrees I'll tell her not to touch your room in future. You can do as Dad does and clean it yourself.'

She began to splutter more protestations but I walked out and closed the door firmly. I didn't trust myself to stay any longer. This time she had really overstepped the mark.

After supper I went round to the address Cleo had given me. I'd mentioned the debacle between Amanda and Dad to Ian when Jamie had gone off to do his homework, but as usual he only listened with half an ear.

'You know what she's like,' he said dismissively. 'It's a storm in a teacup. I'm sure you'll handle it with your usual diplomacy.'

I found Verbena Street without too much trouble. It was in the oldest part of the town and consisted of small terraced houses. The door of number six was painted bright blue. I rapped the clown's head knocker three times and a moment later Cleo opened the door.

'Oh, Mrs M.' She held the door open. 'Please come in. I'm ever so pleased you've come.'

'Thank you, Cleo. I'm sure you know why I'm here.'

'I think I can guess.' As I stepped inside she said, 'I'll slip through and put the kettle on. I'm sure you can drink a cup of tea.'

The front door led straight into the living room and I saw that the walls were decorated with photographs of many of Cleo's show business friends as well as she and her partner, the Great Zadoc. The younger Cleo looked extremely pretty in her glamorous spangled costume and The Great Zadoc (Bert) looked handsome in full evening dress whilst in another shot he was dressed in a leopardskin leotard, clearly about to recline on his bed of nails. Cleo came back into the room and saw me looking at the photographs.

'That's us in our heyday,' she said, pointing to a shot of the two of them taking a bow; Bert kissing her hand. 'I was only sixteen in that one. It was when we played the London Palladium,' she told me proudly. 'We was on telly that time, Bert'n'me – Sunday Night at the London Palladium. It was all the rage in the sixties. You wouldn't remember.'

I took the cup she handed me. 'You must miss that life.'

She smiled wistfully. 'I do, of course, but all good things 'ave to come to an end, don't they? Poor Bert passed on several years ago now an' I couldn't carry on by meself. We all 'as to move on, don't we?'

'Cleo, I owe you an apology. Mrs Trent had no right to dismiss you and I'm here to apologize on her behalf. Naturally I don't want to lose you, so if you can overlook….'

She was shaking her head. 'Don't give it another thought. I don't want to lose me job anyway.'

'In future you must leave Mrs Trent's room,' I told her. 'I've told her she must do her own cleaning from now on. My father does it so why shouldn't she? And if it means she won't be arguing with you any more....'

'It were nuthin' really,' she said. 'I just thought she'd enjoy a chinwag about old times. I keep in touch with some of me old mates from showbiz days, y'see, and the other day I 'ad a phone call; turns out this feller used to know her. What a coincidence, I thought, so I told 'er. I thought she'd be chuffed.'

I was intrigued. 'But she wasn't.'

Cleo puffed out her cheeks. 'Blimey! You can say that again. Went orf like a bleedin' fire cracker, she did – if you'll pardon my French.'

'So – who was this person?' I asked.

Cleo refilled our cups. 'Haydn Jenkins, 'is name is. Welsh feller; used to be stage manager at the Wichhaven Empire.'

'Wichhaven?'

She nodded. 'It's a little town up north – Cumbria – near the lakes. Seems that Amanda Trent was in a company that done a summer season up there.' She gave me a sly wink. 'Between you'n'me I reckon they 'ad a bit of a thing goin'.'

I began to see why Amanda was reluctant to be reminded. Cleo went on. 'Haydn was ever so pleased to get news of 'er. He was married at the time but he and 'is wife split up years ago and 'e's retired now o'course. He hinted that he'd like to meet up with 'is old flame again.'

I bit back a smile. 'Did you tell her that?'

'Yeah.' Cleo shook her head. 'That's when she kicked orf. Really blew'er top, she did. Made out she'd never 'eard of 'im; called me a liar and a troublemaker.'

'I'm sorry about that, Cleo. She had no right to speak to you like that, but maybe it would be best if you didn't mention the past to her again.' I looked at her. 'You will come back and work for me again?'

She smiled. 'Be 'appy to, Mrs M.'

'See you tomorrow then.'

'Right'y'are.' She grinned happily. 'See you tomorrer.'

*

Maureen Jones emailed Mary to accept our best buffet menu for the author event at the library. Mary rang me, delighted to report that Councillor Langley had given us a good recommendation, remembering that we had catered for both his daughters' weddings. This, it seemed, had clinched the deal. 'Three of the other people we canvassed have booked us too,' she went on. 'One wedding and two birthday parties – all for next month, and the high school emailed to ask for our brochure, so our hard work paid off.'

'That's great news, Mary. It was a good idea of yours.'

'By the way, I had a word with Janet on your behalf after you'd gone home,' Mary went on. 'She was sympathetic and said she'd be happy to take Amanda off your hands for a few days' break – if she's willing to go. But she doesn't feel that either of them would want to make it permanent.'

'I know the feeling,' I said wryly. I went on to tell her about the row I'd walked into the previous day between Dad and Amanda and my trip to Cleo's to pour oil on troubled waters. She was sympathetic.

'I don't know what the answer is, love,' she said. 'But at least we have plenty of work coming up now to take your mind off things at home.'

It seemed ungracious to point out that I'd rather have had a happy home life than lots of work lined up that would distance me even more from my marriage and family.

On the day of the library's reopening Mary and I arrived early. Maureen Jones met us, opening the staff entrance for us in a state of suppressed excitement and speaking in breathless, hushed tones as though we were fellow conspirators.

She was already attired for the event in a pale pink twin set and tweed skirt; her grey hair freshly set in a bouffant style and sprayed to the consistency of candyfloss. She led us upstairs and into the new staff room where we began to lay out our buffet on the two long tables that had been provided. There was a well equipped kitchen adjoining the staff room and we unloaded the crates of fruit juice, white wine and champagne, putting them into the fridge to keep cool, uncorking the red wine and leaving it to 'breathe'. By the time we had filled trays with wine glasses and champagne flutes the first of the councillors had begun to arrive. We poured the wine and circulated. Glancing at Maureen I noticed that she was flushed and even more agitated than before as she glanced repeatedly at her watch.

'Is everything all right,' I asked quietly as I passed.

She sipped her wine nervously. 'I thought he'd be here by now,' she whispered. 'Our guest of honour, I mean. He said twelve sharp and it's already half past. We're supposed to be holding the opening ceremony at two. At this rate there won't be time to eat your lovely buffet lunch before the opening ceremony.' She glanced round the room. 'I don't know what to do about it or to say to the councillors. They must be wondering what's happening.'

I followed her gaze. The councillors: eight men and six women, along with their respective partners, seemed totally unfazed, chatting among themselves and sipping wine quite happily. 'I wouldn't worry,' I said. 'They look quite content at the moment. I'll go round and refill their glasses again, shall I?'

At that moment Maureen's mobile vibrated in her skirt pocket, making her squeak nervously. 'Oooh!' She fished it out and pressed the button. She looked at the display and flushed an even deeper pink. 'It's *him!*' she hissed at me. 'Oh my God. I hope nothing's wrong!' She turned away into a corner of the room. '*Hello,*' she squeaked into the phone. 'Mr Kenning – is everything all right – only we've been.... Oh! Yes, I know the traffic gets very bad at this.... I see. You're driving into town now? *Directions?* Yes, of course. Where exactly are you? Right – when you cross the bridge turn left – no, no, *right* at the traffic lights and....' She continued to give him directions. When she'd finished she snapped her phone shut and looked at me with relief. 'He's been stuck in traffic but he'll be here in about five minutes. I wonder – would you be kind enough to do me a favour and go downstairs to meet him while I explain the delay?'

'Of course. I'll go now.' I slipped into the kitchen and took off the miniscule white muslin apron I wore over my black dress. Mary, who was opening a new bottle of wine looked at me. 'Where are you going?'

'Maureen has asked me to go down and greet the guest of honour,' I told her. 'Seems he's been stuck in traffic.'

'Well, thank God he's arriving at last,' Mary said. 'If that lot in there get much more of this down them they'll all be too drunk to care one way or the other!'

I ran down the stairs and out through the staff entrance. The main doors were still sealed with the brightly coloured ribbon that was to be cut later. The library was tucked away in a quiet tree-lined street close to the municipal gardens. Hardly any traffic passed this way. I waited for a few minutes, hoping that Maureen's directions had been less confusing to Jake Kenning than they had to me. I'd been waiting about five minutes when a car drove slowly round the corner. It was a black BMW, discreet and understated, not the kind of car I'd been expecting at all. I'd visualized a best-selling author driving a sleek silver Mercedes or a flamboyant Lamborghini. Surely this couldn't be him. But the car drew to a halt outside the main library entrance some distance from where I was standing. The driver got out and looked around him uncertainly.

From my vantage point a few yards away I took in his appearance with interest. He wore a very expensive looking suit: dark grey with a faint pinstripe, set off by a gleaming white shirt and plain blue tie. His dark hair was attractively frosted with silver. I took in the fact that he was possibly a few pounds overweight, but decided that he was tall enough to carry it. He reached inside the car for his briefcase then closed the door and locked the car with a beep of his remote control key. I took a deep breath and began to walk towards him, putting on my best, 'happy-to-meet-you' smile and holding out my hand.

'Mr Kenning – how do you do? I'm so sorry you've had such a difficult journey. I hope—' The smile froze on my face. Subconsciously I'd already sensed something vaguely familiar about him the moment he'd turned towards me, but now the tilt of his head and the way he walked stopped the words in my throat.

His eyes widened. 'I don't believe this,' he said. 'Elaine of all people! What a surprise.'

Surprise was the understatement of the century. He took my cold hand in a warm grip and held it fast. 'How lovely to see you. I'd have known you anywhere. You haven't changed a bit!' He was laughing delightedly, his eyes crinkling at the corners; those blue eyes that I remembered so well.

He frowned as he took in my stunned expression. 'You look stunned! Am I a horrible, ghastly shock?'

Inside my head it was like the fast rewinding of a tape. *Zoom!* Back went the years – back to college, to Cecily Harding's cottage in Cornwall, to that first all enveloping love that later turned to desolation, heartbreak and despair.

I tried to speak but it all felt so surreal. All that came out was a husky whisper. '*Chris!*'

Ten

It felt like an eternity that I stood there, gaping like an idiot. The shock of seeing Chris again was still reverberating through my body when he said, 'Right – so are you the official welcoming committee?'

I hurriedly pulled myself together. 'N-no, I'm half of the catering firm actually. Miss Jones, the librarian asked me to come down and meet you.'

'I see.'

I disengaged my hand from his and cleared my throat. 'I think we should get back upstairs,' I said. 'They're all waiting for you.'

'Of course.' As I turned away he caught my hand again. 'Elaine – we must catch up later. It really is good to see you.'

I felt my colour rise. 'Yes – yes. It's this way,' I stammered.

Maureen was waiting by the door and as she greeted Chris effusively and hurried him off towards the waiting councillors, I made my escape to the kitchen.

Mary took one look at me. 'My God! What's happened? You look as though you've seen a ghost!'

'I have.' I closed the door. 'It's Jake Kenning – he turned out to be Chris.'

She shook her head. 'Chris? Chris who?'

'Chris Harding.'

Just for a moment she looked blank, then her eyes widened and her hand shot to her mouth. 'That wretched waste of space who dumped you – Jamie's—'

'*Yes!*' I couldn't bear to let her say it. 'Mary, what shall I do?'

She frowned. 'Do? Nothing! All that was over years ago when you were both kids. You made your choice back then. It's in the past; dead and buried.' She peered at me. '*Isn't* it? My God, Elaine, don't say—'

'Yes of *course* it's in the past,' I said hurriedly. 'It was just a shock, seeing him again after all this time. It's embarrassing, being here and meeting him like this.'

'What did he say?'

At that moment the door opened and Maureen's flushed face appeared round it. 'We're ready to eat now.' She simpered, 'Oh, he so *nice*, isn't he – Mr Kenning? So *natural*. Not a bit stuck up or grand. I think today is going to be a great success.'

To my relief there was no more time for discussion. We took the hot food out of the microwave and added the dishes to the buffet table. The guests helped themselves whilst Mary and I circulated with our bottles of wine, replenishing glasses. When I paused to refill Chris's glass he smiled at me and lowered his head.

'Will you be attending the talk later?'

I shook my head. 'We'll be clearing up here and taking all our equipment away.'

'But I must see you. Maybe we could meet for a drink later.' He caught my wrist as I turned away. 'Do say yes, Elaine.'

I swallowed hard, horrified at the way my heart was reacting. Mary had been right; what Chris and I had shared had been nothing more than a teenage romance. It had been over years ago. But even while I was trying to convince myself I knew I was in denial. There was the one massive secret that Chris didn't – never *could* know. Why, oh why did he have to come back like this? It wasn't fair.

He was looking at me. 'Maybe tomorrow if not this evening. I'm going to be around for a day or two, looking up old friends. A bit of a nostalgia trip. Meet me for lunch tomorrow?'

I glanced around and saw Mary watching me out of the corner of her eye. 'I can't,' I said quickly. 'I – we're busy.'

'A drink then – later on this evening?'

'*No!*' Suddenly I realized how bizarre my behaviour must seem. 'There's an awful lot to do,' I finished lamely.

He laughed. 'Elaine! What are you afraid of? I'm still the same person. I just thought it might be fun to catch up on all that's happened to each of us.' He put his hand in his pocket and pressed a card into my hand. 'My number's on there,' he said quietly. 'Give me a ring if you change your mind.'

I slipped the card into my apron pocket and turned quickly away. He was looking up old friends, he said. 'A bit of a nostalgia trip', that was all. I was nothing more than an old friend to him, so why was I getting in such a state about having a drink with him?

In the kitchen Mary looked at me. 'Well, he certainly looks prosperous enough,' she said. 'I hardly remember him at all – only saw him a few times at college.' She took in my flushed face and asked, 'I saw him chatting you up. He wasn't trying to proposition you, was he?'

I made myself laugh. '*Mary!* Of course not. As if!'

She raised a cynical eyebrow. 'Methinks the lady doth protest too much,' she said.

I grabbed a fresh plate of scampi out of the microwave and began stabbing cocktail sticks into them. 'There's a lady out there who'll be protesting too much if you don't uncork another couple of bottles,' I told her. 'And is the champagne chilled enough? The opening ceremony is in fifteen minutes. I can hear the rest of the library staff arriving downstairs already.'

'All right – all right, little Miss Efficiency,' Mary said with a grin. 'But his lordship in there obviously thinks he's a celebrity and God's gift, so don't let yourself get carried away.'

Trays of champagne flutes were already lined up on the reception desk down in the library and fifteen minutes later everyone trooped downstairs for the opening ceremony whilst Mary and I went into the library and prepared to open the champagne. There was a queue of people outside and a cheer went up as Maureen appeared with Jake Kenning and handed him the scissors with which he was to perform the opening ceremony. The local press was there in force and after Chris had made the official opening speech the crowd surged inside for their complimentary glass of champagne. They milled round Chris, cameras flashed and reporters jostled for his attention.

As everyone took their seats in anticipation of the promised talk Mary and I loaded the used glasses onto trays and made our discreet exit upstairs.

'Thank God that's over,' I said as we began to pack everything away and dispose of the detritus.

'What, the opening ceremony or being in close proximity to your ex?' Mary asked.

'I wish you'd stop making those innuendos,' I said. 'If I hadn't told you Jake Kenning was really Chris Harding you have been none the wiser.'

'One look at your face was enough to tell me something was up,' Mary said. 'You came back up here all of a do-dah.'

'I did *not*. It was a shock, that's all.'

'Okay, have it your way.' She began clearing the left over food from the serving dishes. 'Does that pup of yours eat sausage rolls?'

'No he does not!' I said, too sharply. 'We don't want him growing into an elephant, do we?'

Mary said nothing but the look she gave me said it all.

We drove back to her house in silence to stack her industrial dish washer and throw the tablecloths into the washing machine. When I had my coat on ready to leave she grabbed me and gave me a huge hug.

'Today has been difficult for you, hasn't it, darlin'?'

I felt tears string the corners of my eyes. 'I'm sorry, Mary. I know I've been a bit of a cow.'

She shook her head. "Course you haven't. I'm sorry too. I shouldn't have teased you. I meant it when I said that your relationship with Chris was dead and buried though. It's much too late to be changing anything now, love. You made your decision – right or wrong – a long time ago and I think you know that you have to stick with it. I'd hate to see any of you get hurt now.' She tipped up my chin to look into my eyes. 'You and Jamie and Ian are the closest I'll ever have to family. You mean the world to me.'

'I know.' I swallowed the lump in my throat. 'I know you're right too.' I kissed her cheek. 'See you soon, Mary. And thanks – for everything.'

At home I went straight upstairs to change. As I opened the linen basket to throw my soiled apron in something slipped out of the pocket and fell onto the floor. I picked it up. It was Chris's card. I put my foot on the pedal of the bin but something wouldn't let me drop the card inside. Instead, I opened my handbag and pushed it into the mirror pocket. Just a souvenir, I told myself, refusing to let myself think of the other possibilities.

That evening Ian and Jamie were attending a concert rehearsal together at St Cecilia's so as soon as I had changed I went down to the kitchen to start preparing our evening meal early. To my dismay Amanda joined me in the kitchen and I noticed that although her unwashed lunch dishes were in the sink she was making no attempt at washing them up. She began to talk but I carried on peeling vegetables, only half listening to what she was saying.

'So – what do you think of the idea?' she asked suddenly.

I looked at her. 'Think of what idea?'

She gave an exaggerated sigh. 'There. I knew you weren't listening.' She took a deep breath and spoke slowly and clearly as though I were deaf or childish, 'I – asked you – what you thought – of having an en-suite – installed in my room. There's plenty of space for it.'

Stressed by the day's shocking happenings, her rudeness grated my already shredded nerves. 'Absolutely not!' I snapped.

She stared at me defiantly. 'And why not, may I ask?'

'Amanda, staying here was only supposed to be a temporary measure to help you until your ankle healed,' I said with as much patience as I could manage. 'You've done nothing but stir up trouble ever since you arrived. First you insult my father then you have the cheek to sack the cleaner, now you calmly suggest that we install an en-suite for you.'

'You're the one who is always complaining that I'm using the bathroom when your son needs it.'

'You've got all day. You could always wait for half an hour.'

'Why should I be the one who has to wait?' she demanded. 'If I had my own en-suite—'

'Are you going to pay for it?'

She bridled. 'It's *your* house! Anyway, look at the money that was spent on your father's flat!'

I sighed. 'Amanda, I've told you a dozen times. Dad is part owner of this house and he paid for the conversion of his own flat.'

'So you say!'

'What does that mean?'

'When I asked him he refused to discuss it.'

'I don't blame him. Why should he discuss his personal finances with you? And apart from everything else he's done to help us, Dad makes a huge contribution by tending the garden.'

She bristled. 'Perhaps you'd like me to scrub the floors. You've already deprived me of a cleaner for my room.'

'You sacked the cleaner,' I reminded her. 'You were extremely rude to her. The only way I could persuade her to come back was to promise that you and she needn't cross paths again.'

For a moment she was silent then she looked at me. 'Elaine – I thought once that you and I were friends,' she said. 'You came to see me once and we had a heart-to-heart, remember? I really believed we understood one another.'

I returned her look. 'So did I, Amanda, but it seems I was wrong.'

'Why do you hate me?' she whined. 'What have I done to make you dislike me so much?'

'I don't hate you, Amanda. I just wish you could try not to be so selfish; to consider others more.'

She gave a little shrug. 'As a matter of fact Janet has asked me to go and stay with her for a while. I refused, but maybe you'd like me to go.'

'You must do as you like,' I said, turning away. 'You always do anyway, don't you?'

She walked out, shutting the kitchen door behind her sharply as she went. I slipped the pie I had made into the oven and sat down at the table, my heart heavy. I'd hoped so much that life here at Beaumont House would be happy but now I wished we were back in the little cottage in Mableton Park. It was cramped and inconvenient but we were happy there, the three of us. Since we'd moved in here everyone seemed to have separate lives, except Amanda who insisted on encroaching on everyone else's. It was as though we were slowly moving apart and there was nothing I could do to stop it.

My attention was caught by Cecily Harding's painting of St Ives Harbour, which I'd hung on the wall where I could see it when I was cooking. A pang of nostalgia hit me and I longed to see the place again. But it wouldn't be the same. It never could.

Ian and Jamie rushed in from school, ate the meal I had cooked without any obvious enjoyment, went upstairs to get ready and hurried off out again, with a perfunctory, 'See you later'. I was left with an empty space and the washing up.

As I dried the dishes and put them away my thoughts were still on St Ives and, inevitably, Chris. It would be nice to meet again and reminisce. A drink, he had said. What harm would it do? The alternative was an evening alone in front of the TV. I opened my bag and took out the card. Mary's words echoed warningly in my head but I pushed them aside. I was a grown-up, married woman with my own business, not a silly teenage girl any more. I had my head screwed on the right way, as Dad used to say. It would be interesting to hear how Chris had made his mark and become Jake Kenning, best-selling novelist.

I laid the card on the table and took out my phone. As I tapped in the number part of me hoped his phone would be switched off. It would be a sign. If it went straight to voicemail I'd switch off without leaving a message. The tone rang out several times. Clearly he was not going to pick up. Partly relieved – partly disappointed, I was about to give up when his voice suddenly cut in.

'Hello – Elaine. Sorry, I was in the shower – didn't hear the phone.'

My heart began to hammer against my ribs. What on earth was I doing?

'Oh – Chris. I just – I thought—'

'You've changed your mind?' he said eagerly. 'You'll meet for a drink after all?'

He sounded so pleased that my fears were allayed a little. 'Well if you're not – if it's—'

'It's *fine*. I couldn't come to Greencliffe and not meet you and catch up,' He sounded delighted. 'Look, have you got a favourite place or would you like to come here? I'm staying out of town a bit; the Meadwell Country Club. Mainly because I can be incognito here. Do you know it?'

I did know it and 'incognito' sounded fine to me. 'I know it,' I told him. 'At least, I've driven past. It's far too expensive for the likes of us.'

He laughed. 'It's not that posh. Meet me in the bar then – say in an hour?'

'I'll be there.'

I snapped my phone shut and waited for my heart to stop thumping. What was I doing? *Nothing*, I insisted. Meeting an old flame – long since doused – for a chat and an exchange of news. That was all. *That was all*!

Eleven

Chris was waiting when I walked into the bar at the Meadwell Club. He was wearing jeans and a roll-neck sweater. Immediately I felt over dressed. It had taken me three different changes before I decided what to wear. Finally I'd chosen a plain black dress and my highest heels. I wanted to present the image of a mature, sophisticated woman, even though I didn't feel like one. Inside I was still that young girl from Yorkshire, starry-eyed and naive. Something inside me had regressed ten years the moment I set eyes on Chris again, but I wouldn't admit that, even to myself.

When I walked in he stood up and stepped forward to kiss me on both cheeks. 'Elaine, hi! What can I get you?'

'Just a plain tonic water, please,' I said. 'I'm driving, remember.'

'Oh come on. One small measure of gin in it won't send you over the limit.'

I shrugged. 'Okay then.'

The barman poured my gin and tonic and Chris picked up his half finished whisky and soda and looked at me. 'Shall we find a quiet corner?'

The lounge was almost empty and Chris carried the drinks to a table in the far corner. When we were seated he looked at me.

'So – what made you change your mind?'

The question immediately put me on a back foot. To my horror I felt my colour rise. 'Curiosity,' I said with sudden inspiration. 'I just had to know how you made that dream of yours come true.'

He laughed. 'The answer to that is – with great difficulty, though heartbreak, disappointment and sheer tenacity come into it in generous measures too.'

'You had faith in yourself,' I said, taking a sip of my drink. 'You always did.'

He nodded. 'You could say that, though at times my confidence took some severe knocks.'

I smiled, feeling myself beginning to relax as the alcohol in my drink calmed my nerves. 'So what's the story?'

'Are you sure you know what you're asking?' he laughed. 'Writing's a lonely business. Once you start a writer talking about himself you could be in for a long night.'

'I'll take that risk.' I settled back in the comfortable chair. 'Do you still live in St Ives?'

'No.' Chris sipped his whisky. 'I stuck it out at the cottage for a couple of years, working my socks off and getting through the money at an alarming rate. It took me six months to write the first book and I sent it off, fully expecting it to be the hit of the century. It came back with a scathing note damning it to hell and back in seven short words. Predictable plot. One-dimensional characters. Repetitive and flimsy.'

'Ouch!'

'Exactly. But by the time I received that one back I'd almost finished another. I sent that off and after months of waiting I got a slightly more encouraging rejection. It was then that I decided that I ought to have an agent.'

'Sounds like a good move.'

'You'd think so, wouldn't you? Trouble is it's a catch twenty-two situation. No agent worth his salt wants to take on a writer with no successes, but you can't get any measurable success without a good agent.'

'So what did you do?'

'By this time the money had run out. I was living on beans on toast and finding it hard to pay the bills. I sold the cottage and moved to London. I found a job in the accounts department of an engineering firm.'

'So your grandmother was right when she insisted you study accountancy.'

'Yes, though I didn't stay on at college to qualify as you know, so the salary wasn't great. I rented a top floor flat in Hackney where I burned the midnight oil writing my third opus.'

'And that one found success?'

'Not immediately. I sent it to an agent. He was an unknown guy who was just starting up so I guessed that he'd be looking for clients. He'd previously worked for a major publishing house so he knew what he was talking about. He wrote and asked me to go and see him. At that time he was still working from home – didn't even have an office. In fact his flat wasn't much better than mine. He said he could see a lot of potential in my book. He pointed out the places where it failed but he liked the plot and he had lots of suggestions for improving it. He said he was willing to work with me on a re-write as long as I could take criticism.'

'What happened?'

'When the book was finally finished to his satisfaction – and it took a while, with me working evenings and weekends – he sold it to a major publisher for an advance that nearly made my eyes pop out.' He smiled. 'And the rest, as they say, is history. There have been six more books since then; all of them best sellers, here and abroad.'

'Congratulations.'

'Mike, my agent has to take a lot of the credit. I couldn't have done it without him. He is wholly responsible for my success.'

'You were lucky to find him.'

'Yes, but by the same token, he was lucky to find me. I'm responsible for his success too. He now has an office in Mayfair and a client list to die for.'

'And I take it you moved out of your flat in Hackney.'

He grinned. 'What do you think? I've got a nice little pad in Kensington now: the penthouse in a fashionable block on the High Street.' He tossed back the last of his drink. 'There's a little villa just outside Sorrento too, with a fantastic view of Vesuvius. It's my bolt hole.'

'What a wonderful success story, Chris,' I said a little wistfully. 'By the way, how did you come by your pen name?'

'That was Mike's doing too. He thought that Christopher Harding sounded more like a civil servant than a crime novelist.'

'He sounds as though he has his ear to the ground.'

'He certainly has.' He lifted his glass. 'Here's to Mike Nolan. May his client list never grow less – as long as I'm still top of it!' He looked at my glass. 'Another of those?'

I shook my head. 'No, better not. You go ahead though.'

He called the waiter over and ordered another whisky and soda. Although this Chris was very different to the restless, frustrated boy I'd fallen in love with all those years ago there were still traces of the youthful charisma I remembered. His looks had changed of course; he was heavier and more mature. He carried the aura that comes with success.

He looked at me. 'Your turn now. Come on, what have you been up to all this time?'

I shrugged. 'Nothing much. You already know I'm half of a catering firm. Mary and I have done very well.' I looked at him. 'You remember Mary Sullivan; my landlady when I was at college?'

'Ah, yes.'

'When we both qualified we went into business together.'

'Well if the buffet lunch today is anything to go by I'm not surprised. It was delicious.' He looked at me, glass halfway to his lips. 'So – did you marry?'

I nodded. 'Yes. Ian is a musician. He's teaching at one of the town's largest schools and he has a list of private pupils too.'

'Good for him. Kids?'

I'd known this was inevitable so I was prepared. 'I have a son, Jamie. He's gifted musically too.'

'Great! What a talented family.'

Was he being the slightest bit patronizing? 'What about you?' I asked quickly. 'You haven't mentioned a wife.'

He paused. 'I was married – for a while.'

I held my breath. 'Children?'

He shook his head. 'No, thank goodness. Kids would really have messed things up. It was one of those crazy things; a bit wild. Sometimes I think she was just after the reflected glory of being married to a successful author. From my point of view it was more passion – lust if you like – than love. It burned too brightly and just....' He shrugged. 'Fizzled out. Splitting up was the best thing we could have done.'

'Who for?' I asked, suddenly glimpsing the old single-minded Chris under the veneer.

'For both of us. We were making each other unhappy. Where's the sense in hanging on to that?'

'Where indeed?' I stood up and reached for my coat. 'Well, it's been lovely, Chris, catching up like this, but I have to go now.'

He looked taken aback. 'Already? That's a shame. I'll walk you out to the car park.'

In the late spring dusk the air was redolent with nostalgic scents, wallflowers and cherry blossom. Suddenly I was reminded of Cornwall and Cecily – memories that had lain buried for so long. I shivered slightly and Chris took my coat and wrapped it round my shoulders.

'It's chilly. Can't have you catching cold.'

'I expect you'll be gone by the weekend.' The moment I said it I wished I could take the words back. It sounded as though I was hinting at another meeting. Embarrassed, I added hurriedly, 'Your agent must have promotional dates lined up for you.'

Although it was almost dark I could hear the smile in his voice. 'As a matter of fact the world is my oyster at the moment. I'm between books, and my next publication date isn't till September.'

I forced a laugh. 'Lucky you! You should take advantage and fly off to that villa of yours in Sorrento.'

He sighed. 'I would – if it wasn't so lonely.'

My heart gave an uncomfortable jerk. I sensed that he was looking intently at me and I refused to meet his eyes. 'I have a confession to make,' I told him lightly. 'I've never read any of your books. I did see The TV adaptation of *The Mourning Rose* last winter, though. Ian and I enjoyed it very much.'

Suddenly he took my shoulders and turned me towards him. 'Come to Sorrento with me.'

I stared up at him, stunned at the suggestion. 'What an idea!' I made myself laugh. 'Surely you can't be lonely when you're busy writing.'

'You've no idea.' I was acutely aware of his hands, firm on my shoulders. 'I haven't told anyone this, least of all Mike, but I'm suffering from what is known as writers' block at the moment.'

'No new ideas?'

'Not even the ghost of one. Try as I may my mind is like the bottom of a pit.'

'Sorrento will work wonders for your imagination, surely?'

'I don't think so. The trouble is that when you shut yourself off in a study and write day after day there comes a time when you stop actually *living*. The mind just – dries up.' He shook his head. 'But why am I burdening you with my problems? Just come over to Italy, Elaine – for a holiday.'

'I take it the invitation includes my husband and son?' I asked.

He hesitated. 'No. I'm inviting *you*, Elaine – for a break. I'm sure you deserve one. There are orange trees in the garden and you can read all my books, sitting in the sunshine by the pool. How does that sound?'

'Idyllic, but I'm not free to do as I like. I have my business commitments as well as the family.' I laughed and shook my head. 'But why am I justifying myself? The idea is preposterous, Chris and you know it.'

'I don't see why in this day and age. Surely married women aren't shackled to the kitchen sink any more.' His hands dropped to his sides. 'Sorry. Of course it's a preposterous idea. Forgive me, it was just wishful thinking.' He touched my cheek with one fingertip. 'I can't tell you how wonderful it's been, seeing you again, Elaine. I'd have known you anywhere, except that you're lovelier than ever.'

'I'm sure that's not true, but it's been great seeing you too, Chris.' I fumbled in my bag for my keys and began to open the car door. Suddenly I was aware of a tension between us and I couldn't get away fast enough. I turned to him 'Goodbye, Chris and thank yo—' He drew me close and kissed me on both cheeks as he had when we met. Then suddenly his lips were on mine. I pulled away.

'Chris – *no!*'

He let me go abruptly. 'I know – It wasn't fair. I'm sorry.'

'You've just spoiled a pleasant evening.' I was aware that my voice was shaking.

'Don't say that. Please say you'll see me again, Elaine.'

'I can't!' I got into the car and started the engine. He bent down to the window. 'Please! There's so much more I want to say.'

'No, Chris. I shouldn't have come this evening. It was a mistake.'

'Then why did you?'

It was the one question I couldn't answer. I let in the clutch and pressed my foot down hard on the accelerator, driving the car forward towards the exit much too fast. In the mirror I could see him standing there, his arms spread in a helpless gesture. As I turned onto the road and began to drive towards home bitter tears of regret and self-disgust ran down my cheeks. What had I done? Oh God, what had I done?

To my relief the house was quiet when I got in. I ran upstairs to change. Taking a quick shower as though to wash the guilty feelings of the evening away. Ian and Jamie arrived ten minutes after I'd finished. In the kitchen I gave Jamie hot chocolate and biscuits.

'How was the rehearsal?'

'Fine,' he said, looking up at me, his top lip brown with chocolate stain. 'I'm playing a solo – *Dance of the Blessed Spirits*.'

'That's good. But straight up to bed with you as soon as you've finished your chocolate,' I told him. 'Or you'll never get up for school in the morning.'

'Where's Toffee?' he asked, looking round.

'I expect Granddad took him up to the flat,' I said. 'So that he wouldn't get lonely.'

'Lonely? But you've been here, haven't you, Mum?'

As he spoke Ian came into the kitchen. He smiled at me. 'Did you go round to Mary's for a cooking session?'

I nodded. 'That's right. Do you want some chocolate?'

'Yes please.'

I escaped gratefully to the scullery to refill the kettle, my cheeks crimson with guilt. It was the first time I had ever lied to Ian. And I promised myself it would be the last.

Twelve

I lay awake well into the small hours, asking myself, why had I gone
to see Chris? In a way it had been curiosity, but there had been something else too. Had I been hoping to lay a ghost? Maybe. Instead I'd
reopened what for me was unfinished business. There was no denying
that Chris was Jamie's father. Was it right that they were unaware of one
another? It was a question I hadn't asked myself for years. Had Mary
been right all those years ago when she had said that Chris had a right
to know he had a son? But Ian was his father now – had been for almost
half his life. Ian was the only male role model Jamie had ever known;
his mentor, music teacher and soon to be adoptive father. Nothing –
nothing must be allowed to disrupt that. And nothing *would*, I promised
myself, turning over and punching the pillow for the hundredth time.

Ian stirred beside me. 'Are you all right, darling?' he asked
sleepily, sliding an arm across my waist.

'I'm fine. Go back to sleep,' I told him. 'A bad dream, that's all.'
And right at that moment that was what it felt like – a bad dream.

In the cold light of morning everything looked different. The
morning rush over, Ian and Jamie gone, I sat down at the table for
another cup of coffee and thought hard about the previous evening.
I told myself I was foolish to worry about it. Chris would be gone
in a few days' time. He would soon have a new idea for a book and
would forget all about our meeting again. He knew nothing about
Jamie. They need never even meet. All I had to do was sit tight and
wait for the problem to go away. Writing came first in Chris's life.
Once he started working on a new idea I would be forgotten. I
pushed away the memory of his lips on mine. The kiss had been
brief. I'd pushed him away. But at the back on my mind I couldn't

deny that it had stirred up memories; memories of joy and laughter, of first love and later the pain of heartbreak and despair. It was like a potent wine or an addictive drug: once taken, yearned for forever.

Dad opened the kitchen door, jolting me out of my reverie.

'Morning, love.' Toffee was trotting at his heels and ran over to greet me.

'Morning, Dad – morning, Toffee.' As I fondled the little dog's ears I glanced up at the square of blue sky I could see outside the window. 'Looks as though it's going to be a fine day.' I could see that he was already dressed for the garden in his old corduroy trousers and an open-necked shirt.

He nodded. 'I thought I'd go and buy some bedding plants this morning,' he said. 'Time to get planted up ready for summer.' He looked down at Toffee. 'I'll take young feller-me-lad here with me. Better than leaving him here.' He raised an inquiring eyebrow at me. 'I take it you'll be going round to Mary's?'

'Yes.' I looked at my watch. 'I'd better get going or she'll be wondering where I've got to. Toffee will be perfectly okay here for an hour you know, Dad. You mustn't spoil him. He has to learn to be by himself sometimes.'

He pulled a face. 'That's just it,' he said. 'He wouldn't be by himself, would he? She'll be here.' He nodded towards the hall.

'Amanda, you mean?'

'I do – wouldn't trust her with a feather duster, never mind an animal.'

'I'm sure she wouldn't purposely hurt him, Dad.'

'Are you? I wouldn't bet on it. She's got a vindictive streak, that one. Anyway, better safe than sorry.'

'Well, just as you please.' I got up and began to clear the table. 'Want to eat with us this evening, Dad? I'm going to put a casserole in the crock pot before I go out.'

He shook his head. 'No, lass. I told you when we started out that I'd keep to my own quarters and I mean it. You've got a right to your own privacy. It's good of you to have me here.'

'Not at all, it's half your house! Well, you know you're always welcome so if you change your mind....'

In the doorway he looked back with a wistful grin. 'Casserole did you say? Would that be anything like hotpot?'

I laughed. 'Not a million miles off.'

'In that case I wouldn't object if you were to save me a portion.'

I was quiet as we worked together in Mary's kitchen that morning.
She was quick to pick up on my mood.

'Are you all right, Elaine?'

I looked up. 'Of course.'

'You're very quiet. Something worrying you?'

'No.'

'Not still thinking about yesterday?'

'Yesterday? Why should I be thinking about yesterday?'

Mary nodded. 'That means you are. Put him out of your mind,
Elaine.'

'Chris, you mean? I already have.'

'Well, I hope you mean it.' She picked up the diary. 'We've got a
busy month ahead. Maybe it's time we arranged a holiday rota.'

I thought of Chris's invitation to go to Italy with him and felt my
heart miss a beat. 'Mine will have to coincide with the school holidays as usual,' I said.

'That's what I thought. It's good that we have Janet to help now.'
She looked up. 'She's coming in later with some new recipes she's
found. Honey glazed pork loin and some rather super sounding
dressings – some yummy vegetarian dishes too.'

'We're lucky to have her. Did I tell you she's offered to have
Amanda for a while?'

'No. That's good. Is she going – Amanda, I mean?'

I sighed. 'I doubt it. The latest is that she wants us to install an en-
suite for her – at our expense of course.'

'She's got one hell of a cheek. What does Ian say?'

'I haven't had time to discuss it with him yet. He was out all last
evening rehearsing for this inter-schools end-of-year concert.
Amanda was waiting for me when I got in yesterday afternoon. I
hardly had time to take my coat off before she started.'

Mary was immediately sympathetic. 'Oh, poor love. And here I
was accusing you of day dreaming over you-know-who.'

'I hardly slept last night,' I added. 'Sorry if I've been a bit preoccupied.'

'Who could blame you?'

The back door opened and Janet looked in. 'Only me. I've brought those recipes. Is this a good time?'

'Couldn't be better,' Mary said. 'We're just about ready for a coffee break, aren't we, Elaine?'

I nodded and went through to fill the kettle at the sink. As I plugged it in my phone rang. I fished it out of my pocket and looked at the display. I froze and quickly switched it off. How did Chris get my number? Then I remembered. When I rang him last night it would have come up on his phone. How could I have been so stupid?

Driving home at lunchtime Chris's attempt to call me niggled at the back of my mind. There was only one thing to do – ring him back. If I didn't he'd ring again, most likely at an even more inopportune moment. I pulled off the road and took out my phone, feeling part annoyed, part guilty. How dare he put me in this impossible position?

He answered the call almost immediately. 'Elaine! You rang back. Thanks.'

'I was at work when you rang,' I said, a little breathlessly. 'What is it, Chris – what do you want?'

'To apologize for – last night.'

'Apologize?'

'Don't pretend you don't know what I'm talking about, Elaine. Look, seeing you again affected me far more than I expected it to. It shook me but it answered a lot of questions for me too.'

'What questions?'

'I'd really like to explain.'

'So – I'm listening.' Although I was trying hard to sound cool my voice was shaking. I swallowed hard, telling myself I was being stupid and ridiculous. Chris and I had a student affair at college – years ago. It was ancient history, except that my – *our* – son would always be there to remind me.

'I can't, not on the phone. Please meet me again, Elaine. I promise not to let my feelings run away with me next time.'

'I don't know. I'm really busy. Mary and I are booked solid – every evening this week,' I added untruthfully.

'What about lunch.'

'Lunch – when?'

'Now. I could meet you any place you like.'

'Oh!' I was momentarily taken aback. I had nothing to go home for. Ian and Jamie both ate lunch at school. I'd left a casserole in the slow cooker for this evening. What excuse could I make? Sensing my hesitation Chris broke in.

'Please, Elaine. Spend an hour with me – for old times' sake. And to let me make up to you for my unforgivable behaviour.'

'Oh – all right then.' You're going to regret this, a small inner voice warned. 'I'm in the car,' I said. 'I could come to the Meadwell again if you like.'

'Great! See you in the bar in – what – fifteen minutes?'

He was waiting in the bar again. This time he wore expensively cut chinos and a black silk shirt. Manicured and well groomed, he looked every inch the best-selling author. The moment I walked in he rose to greet me and asked what I'd like to drink. I shook my head.

'Nothing, thanks. I'm driving.'

'Have a mineral water then – and maybe a glass of wine with your lunch.'

I shrugged. 'Well, maybe a small one.'

The restaurant was almost empty and when the waiter had taken our orders he reached across the table and touched my hand. 'Elaine, again, I can't tell you how sorry I am. You were right when you said that I'd spoiled the evening.'

I shook my head. 'Shall we just forget it?' I picked up my glass of mineral water. 'Here's to your next book.' I remembered what he'd said about the inspiration drying up and added quickly, 'When you get a new idea, which I'm sure will be soon.'

He touched his glass to mine and smiled. 'I hope you're right.'

The meal was delicious but I felt so uncomfortable that I hardly tasted it. As soon as it was decently permissible I would make my excuses and leave, I promised myself. But even as we ate I was conscious of Chris's eyes on me, and as we spoke I became painfully aware of familiar gestures and facial expressions – familiar not only because they resurrected memories but because, disturbingly, I had had seen the same mannerisms in Jamie.

I refused a dessert and Chris waved the menu away too, asking for coffee to be served out on the terrace. We moved out to where the half glazed sun terrace looked out onto a golf course and a wonderful rolling Dorset view. Sitting side by side with the tray of coffee on a low table in front of us, I poured the coffee.

'You mentioned the answers to some questions.'

'Ah yes.' He glanced at me. 'Promise you won't get upset and leave.'

My heart gave a painful lurch. 'Okay, I promise to hear you out.' I lifted my coffee cup and looked at him over the rim. 'Go on.'

'Last night – seeing you again made so many things clear to me,' he said. 'My restlessness, my failed marriage. I thought I was over you long ago but it's not true. What we had was something special. I was a fool, giving you up the way I did. It wasn't because I didn't love you. It was just that I didn't want to spoil your life with my selfish ambition; an ambition that was so tenuous. When I came into Gran's money I knew it was my chance to try to make my dream come true. Maybe the only chance I'd ever get. If I hadn't seized the opportunity I'd always have wondered if I could have made it work, but I felt at the time that I had to go it alone.' He emptied his coffee cup in one draught. 'Believe me, those first months down in Cornwall were hell; the loneliest, most miserable I've ever spent. I missed Gran of course, but I missed you far more. Every bone in my body ached for you, Elaine. You'll never know how much.'

Inwardly I was shaken. He couldn't know the agony I went through; the months of fear and indecision about the child I was carrying – his child. But I was determined not to let him know. 'It was all worthwhile for you though, wasn't it?' I pointed out, trying hard not to sound cynical. 'What ever sacrifices you made paid off. Look at you now.'

'Nothing is worth losing the love of your life.' His fingers crept towards mine but I drew my hand away and made myself laugh.

'I do believe I can hear an author talking.'

He shook his head. 'I'm sincere, Elaine. Please believe me.' He paused then looked at me hesitantly. 'I suppose it's a hell of a nerve to ask what you felt when you saw me again.'

'Yes, it is,' I said, feeling my colour rise. 'I'm married, Chris – happily married.' How much more of this was he going to put me through?

'That's not what I asked you.'

I took a deep breath. 'You ask what I felt. Right. I felt surprise and later pleasure at your success. It was good to know that the heartache you caused me hadn't been for nothing.'

As soon as the words were out of my mouth I wished I could take them back. He was on it at once, reaching for my hand and grasping it determinedly.

'Heartache. Did I really hurt you that badly, Elaine? I'm so sorry. If I could choose to have that time back again I'd—'

'But you can't,' I interrupted. 'It's all in the past and that's where it has to stay.'

He gave me a long, lingering look. 'Can I ask you something?'

'Of course.'

'How long did it take you to find this – Ian, did you say his name is?'

'Not long,' I said briskly.

He winced. 'I walked right into that one, didn't I?' He leaned in closer. 'Or dare I ask: could it possibly have been on the rebound?'

'That's an extremely arrogant question.'

'I know. I'm sorry.' He helped himself to another cup of coffee from the pot and added cream thoughtfully. 'I wish I could read you, Elaine,' he said at last. 'I could be wrong but you seem to me very much on the defensive. It makes me think I must have made you suffer even more than you're admitting.'

He was getting so close to the truth that it was all I could do not to get up and run. It was on the tip of my tongue to pour out to him exactly what he had done to me; the aching heartbreak when he told me it was over and then the dread and despair I felt when I knew I was pregnant – *the fact that he had a son*. I leaned forward to refill my own cup and found the pot empty. Somehow it seemed to sum up our whole relationship. He noticed the last of the dregs running into my cup and said quickly.

'Oh, I've taken all the coffee. I'll order another pot.'

As he raised his hand to summon a waiter I said, 'No, it doesn't matter. I have to go anyway.' I stood up. 'Thank you for lunch, Chris. I expect you'll be going back to London any day now. It's been nice to meet again.'

He was on his feet. 'Don't go – not like this.'

'I have to.'

'There's so much more I want to say.'

'I think you've said it all. It's just nostalgia, Chris. We'd all like to go back and change things we did in the past, but if we really had the chance we'd probably do exactly the same again. What we had was just a youthful crush. It was all over years ago. Let it go.'

He walked out to the car park with me in silence and when we arrived at my car he said. 'I think you're in denial. What we had was no youthful crush and you know it.'

'Nevertheless, it's been over for a long time.'

'Has it?' He held my shoulders lightly and looked deep into my eyes. 'Prove it.'

'How?'

'Come over to Italy and spend a few days at the villa. I won't pressure you in any way and if you still feel nothing at the end of it I promise I'll stay out of your life for ever.'

I stared at him. 'You have to be joking!'

'Why?'

'I've told you. I'm happily married. I have family commitments, not to mention a business to run.'

'You have to have holidays – time off.'

'Yes – to spend with my family.'

His hands tightened on my shoulders. 'A few days, Elaine. That's all I ask. Let me try to make up to you for my selfishness in the past. Do it to prove to yourself and me that we're over one another if you like. Give us both the chance to put what we once had to rest now and for all time.'

'As far as I'm concerned there's nothing to prove.' I took out my keys and began to unlock the car. 'Anyway, what you suggest is out of the question.'

He grasped my hand. 'But you want to come – you know you do. I can see it in your eyes.'

I turned to him, my cheeks flaming and my heart thudding with anger. 'You think you can click your fingers and get anything you want,' I said. 'You chose your ambition over me years ago and now that you're successful you think that even though I'm married I'll drop everything and run off into the sunset with you like – like something out of one of your books!'

He was smiling. 'Oh dear, you really *haven't* read any of them, have you? I don't write romances, Elaine – and I don't do happy endings.'

'And there's to be no happy ending for this story either, so just let it go!' I opened the car door and slid into the driving seat. As I switched on the ignition and put the car into first gear he stood back, but as the car began to move forward he called out.

'I won't give up, Elaine. If you don't come we'll never know our true feelings or what might have been. I'll ring or text you.'

'Please *don't*!' I called through the open widow. But even as I said it I knew he would.

At home I put the car away and went through to the kitchen. Taking the lid off the slow cooker I saw that the casserole was done to a turn. I ladled a portion into a bowl and took it upstairs for Dad. He was out – possibly still in the garden so I put it on his tiny worktop with a scribbled note and went back downstairs to peel potatoes for the evening meal. It wasn't long before I was joined by Amanda.

'You will no doubt be happy to know that I'm going to spend a few days with Janet,' she said.

I looked up. 'I'm glad you're going to have a break, Amanda. A change of scene will do you good.'

'Yes, won't it?' She shot me a triumphant smile. 'And by the time I get back my en-suite will be finished.'

I turned to her. 'We've already discussed this and I thought I'd made it clear that installing an en-suite wasn't an option.'

'Maybe *you* did,' she said smugly. 'Luckily Ian thought otherwise.'

Stunned, I dropped the potato peeler. 'Ian? I'm sure that's not true. He hasn't mentioned it to me.'

'Well he has to me.' She folded her arms. 'My son seems to have inherited my understanding nature. *He* could see how difficult it was for me, climbing those stairs several times a day.'

Inwardly I fumed. Ian hadn't even mentioned the matter to me, let alone discussed it. Why did he feel he owed Amanda anything? She'd never treated him like a son in the past but now that she was older she expected him to behave like a grateful, adoring son.

'Clearly the two of you have the whole thing sewn up,' I said. 'I can't think why you're even bothering to mention it to me.'

She shrugged. 'I quite thought you'd know about it, Elaine,' she said. 'But now that you mention it, has it occurred to you that Ian might keep things from you because of your over-the-top reaction to everything nowadays?'

I spun round, a sharp comment on my lips but she had already gone; mistress of the sharp exit line as always.

Throughout the meal I managed, with great difficulty, to remain quiet about Amanda's revelation but as soon as Jamie had gone upstairs to do his homework I brought the subject up.

'There's something I need to talk to you about, Ian,' I said as I brought in the coffee.

He looked at his watch. 'Can it wait till later? I've got a pupil arriving in about ten minutes.'

'No, it can't wait,' I snapped. 'Every time I try to talk to you lately you're rushing off somewhere.'

'I can't help it, Elaine. I can't turn down lucrative work, can I? The bills here are much higher than they were at Mableton Park.'

'I know that and I do contribute as much as I can, Ian.'

'Of course you do. I'm not saying—'

'Which is why I think you might have paid me the courtesy of discussing it with me before you promised Amanda that we'd install an en-suite for her.'

He sighed and passed a hand across his forehead. 'Oh God, she's told you?'

'Yes – and not before time!'

'I was going to tell you.'

'*Tell* – not ask – not discuss?'

'She's been nagging me about it for ages,' he said. 'Complaining that it hurts her ankle to have to go upstairs every time she wants to use the bathroom.'

'I'm sure I don't need to remind you that staying here was only supposed to be a temporary measure anyway.'

He frowned. 'I get the feeling that she's hard up but too proud to admit it.'

'She's not too proud to make demands on us though, is she?' I looked at him. 'You've just mentioned that the bills are higher here so how do you think we're going to pay for an en-suite?'

'It would be an investment,' he said. 'It would allow us to ask a higher rent if we let the room out.'

'That's if Amanda ever leaves it,' I pointed out. 'And the more comfortable we make her the less likely that is to happen.'

He sighed. 'You can be very hard sometimes, Elaine.'

'*Hard*?' I stared at him. 'When it comes to *hard* I think Amanda has the monopoly! Have you really forgotten the way she's treated you over the years? Have you forgotten the bombshell she dropped on you the Christmas before last? I don't—'

The sound of the doorbell interrupted me. Ian stood up. 'I'm sorry, Elaine but that'll be my pupil. We'll talk about this later.'

I washed up and went through to the living room to switch on the TV; flicking through the listings I searched for some mindless entertainment that would relax me and calm my shredded nerves. I'd just settled myself on the sofa when the door opened and Jamie came in carrying his violin, Toffee at his heels.

'Mind if I turn the telly off, Mum?' he said. 'I need to practice and Ian's teaching in the studio.'

I stood up. 'No, that's fine. I was going up to have a bath anyway. You carry on.'

'And could you take Toff up to Granddad, please? The violin always makes him howl.'

'All right.' I scooped up the little dog and carried him upstairs with me. On the landing the bathroom door was locked. I rattled the handle knowing there was only one person who could be inside. 'Amanda! Are you going to be long?'

Her voice was shrill with irritation as she called, 'Damn it, Elaine, I've only just got into the bath. Can't you use your en-suite? Really, some people don't know when they're well off!'

'I wanted a *bath*, not a shower!'

'Well I'm in here now so you'll have to wait, won't you?'

As I turned I saw Dad at the turn of the staircase. 'You can come up and use my bathroom if you like.'

I shook my head. 'It's all right, Dad. I've gone off the idea now anyway.'

'I was just coming down to say thanks for the hotpot. It was just the ticket.'

'Good. I'm glad you enjoyed it. I was coming up to you with Toffee anyway. Jamie says the violin makes him howl.'

He laughed and took the little dog from my arms. 'We can't all be music lovers, can we, Toff?' He ruffled the dog's head. 'You sound a bit down, love,' he said looking up at me. 'Are you all right?'

'Not really.' I shrugged, ashamed of the tears that thickened my voice. 'It's just that I don't seem to have anywhere to go in my own home. Ian's busy in the studio with a pupil. Jamie's practising in the living room and now Amanda's hogging the bathroom. I might as well call it a day and go to bed.'

'Come up to the flat and chat to me,' he invited. 'Just till Ian's finished. I hardly seem to see anything of you these days.'

Dad made coffee and we chatted for a while. I told him about Amanda's plans for an en-suite and Ian's weakness in going along with it.

'Why don't you talk to Janet about it?' Dad suggested. 'She seems like a reasonable woman and she's very fond of Ian. The last thing she'll want is to see pressure put on the two of you.'

'She has invited Amanda to stay for a few days,' I told him. 'But to be honest I don't think she's any keener to have her on a permanent basis than we are.'

'Can't she go back to the flat she had before?'

'To be honest, Dad, I don't think she can afford it. I don't know for sure but I think she had a man friend who used to help her out financially.'

Dad grinned. 'And he decided he'd had enough?'

I shrugged. 'Something like that.'

'Well, I can't say I blame him.' Dad reached out to pat my arm. 'Don't look so worried, love. It'll all work out in the end, you'll see. Ian's a lovely lad and he thinks the world of you.'

'Does he? Sometimes I feel just a bit taken for granted.'

He sighed and gave me a rueful smile. 'I'm afraid that happens in all marriages after a bit. 'Specially when you both lead such busy lives. Look, why don't you have a holiday, just the three for you? I'm here to hold the fort as they say.'

I felt my spirits lift at the idea. It was just what we all needed.

'Maybe that's just what we need. I'll talk to Ian about it. Thanks, Dad.'

Downstairs Ian's pupil had gone but I could hear Jamie practising his concert piece in the studio, accompanied by Ian on the piano. I went through to the kitchen to put the kettle on. Time Jamie went to bed. It was a school day tomorrow. I went back to the hall and tapped on the studio door, putting my head round it.

'Cocoa and biscuits in the kitchen,' I said. 'I think you've both had enough for one day, don't you?'

When they came through I saw that Jamie was looking round the kitchen. Guessing what he was looking for I said, 'Toff's up with Granddad. You might as well leave him there now.' I looked at Ian. 'I was talking to Dad earlier and he suggested that we all have a holiday. It's only a few weeks till the end of term and....' I stopped, seeing his frown. 'What? Don't you like the idea?'

'We can't really afford a holiday this year.'

'But surely we could have a week,' I argued. 'It doesn't have to be expensive.'

'I'm not going anywhere I can't take Toffee,' Jamie protested.

'Well, maybe a caravan. In Cornwall or somewhere.'

'We see the sea all the time,' Jamie said. 'It's boring. If I went anywhere I'd rather go to Egypt.'

I laughed. 'In your dreams!'

'Anyway, there's the—' I saw Ian shoot Jamie a restraining look and he stopped speaking and hid his face in his cup. I looked from one to the other.

'There's the *what*? What's going on?'

They exchanged glances then Ian said, 'It's not set in stone or anything but there's a music summer school in Cardiff in August. I've been meaning to talk to you about it but somehow there hasn't been a minute lately.'

'Summer school?' I looked at Jamie and saw that his face had turned pink.

'It'll be super, Mum,' he said eagerly. 'Lots of workshops and several famous musicians will be there – giving master classes and lecturing.'

'I see, and you can take Toffee there, can you?' I asked pointedly. 'Won't he spend the whole time howling?'

Jamie looked a little shamefaced. 'Well, no, but we thought....'

'Who's this "*we*"?' I swallowed my resentment and looked at the clock. 'We'll talk about it tomorrow,' I said briskly. 'High time you were in bed now, Jamie. You go up, and make sure you clean your teeth. I'll be up to say goodnight soon.'

When he was safely out of earshot I looked at Ian. 'I suppose you would *eventually* have got around to telling me about this summer school,' I said, trying not to sound sarcastic.

'Of course I would. Anyway, it's not for ages yet.'

'So is it free? I only ask because you keep mentioning how hard up we are?' Trying hard to stop my hands from shaking I stood up and began to clear the table.

'No, it's not free but it isn't expensive either,' Ian answered tetchily. 'As a matter of fact I've been asked to tutor one of the workshops so I get in at a cheaper rate.'

'For something that isn't set in stone, as you put it, you seem to have things remarkably well planned out.' I looked at him. 'I don't suppose it's even worth asking if *I'm* included.'

'Well no. Anyway you'd be bored.'

'It would be nice to have been given the option.'

Ian frowned. 'This is just what Jamie needs, Elaine; the chance to mix with other young musicians; to get some insight into music as a profession. I'd have thought you'd be only too happy for him to go. You surely don't want to stand in the way of his music!'

My anger broke through. '*Stand in the way*? Is that how you see me, Ian? I'm his mother. I've always recognized that my son has talent, ever since he was old enough to reach the piano keyboard, so don't tell me I'm standing in his way!' I abandoned the tray of used dishes and flung out of the kitchen, slamming the door behind me.

Ian didn't come to bed for some time but although I pretended to be asleep I was still wide awake – still fuming. It seemed I counted for nothing any more. I wasn't so much 'taken for granted' as 'walked all over'. I didn't remember until much later that for the first time since we married I'd referred to Jamie as '*my son*'.

At some time in the small hours I must have fallen asleep but I was awake again long before the alarm went off. As I shifted my position Ian said,

'Are you awake?'

'Yes.'

'Look....' He slipped an arm round me. 'I'm sorry about last night – the summer school and all that. I know I should have told – *talked* to you about it when I first heard.'

'It doesn't matter,' I muttered without turning over. 'Obviously it's all planned now and despite what you seem to think I don't want to spoil things for Jamie. Anyway, I'd have to be here to take care of Toffee and the house.'

'Your father seems to have taken a shine to the dog,' Ian said. 'And he's more than capable of acting as caretaker for a few days, so I've been thinking; why don't you have a few days away yourself somewhere while we're away?'

'On my own? What fun!'

'You must have someone you could team up with,' he went on. 'The break from all of us would do you good – recharge your batteries. You've been under a lot of pressure and working hard lately.'

I turned to look at him. 'Is that another way of saying I've been downright bad tempered and you'd be grateful to get me out of your hair for a few days?'

He grinned, the familiar grin that had always melted my heart. This time it merely irritated me. 'Of course. What else?'

Suddenly I made up my mind. 'Okay,' I said, slipping out of bed and pulling on my dressing gown. 'Maybe I'll take you up on that.'

Thirteen

The first text message arrived as I was washing up the breakfast dishes.

Thought any more about Sorrento? Please come!

I quickly deleted it and slipped the phone into my handbag. The second came just as I drove into Mary's drive.

I'll be there for a couple of weeks in July – 10th to the 25th. Please say you'll join me for a few days at least.

I closed the phone and sat thinking about it. Ian had unwittingly offered me this chance on a plate. He was so completely wrapped up in his music that he had little time for me at all these days and now he planned to take Jamie to this music summer school. Did he know or even care where his indifference might push me? He owed me something. *Not this though*, a small inner voice argued. But did I owe it to myself to lay Chris's ghost once and for all?

There was little doubt that Chris had more in mind than a platonic weekend. And would I be able to resist his persuasive charm against a background of warm sun, orange trees and fragrant bougainvillea? On the other hand – did I really want to? There was no doubt that seeing him again had awakened all sorts of half forgotten emotions and desires and however much I might deny it, I was tempted.

As we worked I brought up the subject of holidays with Mary.

'You asked me to think about holiday dates,' I said. 'Have you made any plans yourself?'

She shook her head. 'As a matter of fact your dad mentioned a really nice coach holiday to the Scottish Highlands in September.'

I looked at her. 'Dad?'

To my surprise she blushed. 'Yes. We thought we might go together. I haven't had anyone to share a holiday with for years and of course, since your mother's illness, he hasn't really had a break either.' She looked at me. 'You've no objections, have you?'

'Me? No, of course not,' I said hurriedly. 'It's just that I didn't realize you and he had been seeing one another.'

'We haven't exactly been *seeing* each other,' she said defensively. 'Not in the way you mean anyway. We've been out for a drink a couple of times. We're old friends, aren't we? We've always got along together as you know.'

I laughed. 'Mary! You don't have to justify yourself. I think it's great that you and Dad are going out together. I just wish one of you had mentioned it that's all. We could all have had a meal together.'

She shook her head. 'Come off it, girl. It's no big deal; just a couple of lonely old codgers teaming up.'

'Not so much of the old codgers. You're both in your prime! I think it's lovely. September, you say. So would it be okay for me to have a few days – say four or five in the middle of July?'

Mary dried her hands and fetched the diary from the office. 'That'll be fine,' she said, making a note. She looked up at me as she closed the book. 'Are you sure you wouldn't like longer?'

I shook my head. 'Ian is taking Jamie to a music summer school in Cardiff in August and he's suggested that I take myself off on my own for a few days; recharge the batteries as he puts it.'

'Sensible man. So where are you heading?'

'I haven't really decided but I quite fancy Italy.'

'*Italy*! On your own?'

'Yes. Nothing wrong with that, is there?' It was my turn to be defensive.

'No, of course not if you fancy it. But I'd have thought you'd need at least ten days for Italy,' she said.

'No. Four or five will be plenty,' I heard myself saying. What was I thinking about? And if I gave in to this mad idea where would I be this time next year? I asked myself. Everything depended on those five days in July.

I was talking to Jamie in the kitchen later that afternoon as I prepared our evening meal when to my horror the text tone on my phone sounded again. Jamie snatched up my phone from the table.

'I'll get it, Mum, your hands are wet,' he said. 'Want me to read it out to you?'

'It's all right. I'll get it.' I snatched it from him but the phone slipped through my wet fingers and skittered under the table. I scrambled for it but Toffee got to it first, running round the kitchen with it in his mouth, delighted at this new game. Eventually Jamie, helpless with laughter managed to rescue it from him. To my horror he immediately opened the phone and pressed 'options' to read the message.

'It says, Would you like a hundred free minutes on your phone?' he said.

Weak with relief I took the phone from him, switched it off and put it into my pocket. 'I think you'd better take Toffee for his walk before tea,' I said. 'He looks as though he could do with using up some energy.'

He was hardly out of the door when another text arrived.

Can you meet me tomorrow? I have to go back to London on Sunday.

We had a wedding booked for the following day. I was going to be busy all day. I didn't see how I could. I was torn between relief, disappointment and fury with Chris for what he was putting me through. Alone in the kitchen I decided to risk it and ring him.

'Elaine! How lovely.' He sounded pleased, which irritated me.

'You must stop texting me,' I told him. 'I'm turning my phone off after this call. We have a wedding on tomorrow. I'll be busy all day. I can't possibly meet you.'

'But you have to.'

'No, I *don't*. This has to stop, Chris.'

'Don't be angry. I just need to know if you've made a decision – about Sorrento.'

I hesitated. 'I'm – still thinking about it.'

'That means you haven't ruled it out.'

'I *said* I'm still thinking about it.'

'All the more reason why we should meet before I go back to London. My agent rang to say he's had an offer from the BBC to serialize my last book.'

'Oh, congratulations.'

'So I have to go up and talk terms. Meet me after this wedding thing is over. It can't last all day surely.'

'It will. We're catering for the reception and then the dance afterwards.'

'Oh, for heaven's *sake*! This evening then? Please say you'll come, Elaine, if it's only for a few minutes. The Meadwell – later – come when you can. I'll be waiting.' He rang off before I could reply.

As the three of us sat together at our evening meal I brought up the subject of holidays.

'I've booked five days off in July,' I said. 'I thought I might go to Italy for a short break.'

Ian looked up in surprise. 'Oh! But the music summer school is in August.'

'I know that, but I have to fit in with Mary's holiday schedule.'

He frowned. 'I thought she and your dad were going to Scotland in September.'

I looked up in surprise. 'How did you know about that? I only found out myself this morning.'

He looked a little shamefaced. 'Ted mentioned it to me a couple of weeks ago,' he said. 'He thought you might disapprove and he was waiting for the right moment to tell you.'

'Am I such an ogre?' I shook my head. 'Why is it that no one tells me anything any more? I'm kept completely in the dark about everything. First there's Amanda's en-suite, then this music summer school, now Mary and Dad's holiday arrangements.'

Ian sighed. 'To be honest, you do go off the deep end about things lately,' he said. 'I think you're really tired, Elaine. A little break will do you good.'

'It'll get me out of your way for a few days, you mean?' I snapped. 'Okay, I'll go ahead and book it, shall I?' Without waiting for his reply I stood up and began to clear the table. My nerves had been on edge ever since I saw Chris again, that much was true but that was only a few days ago. Surely I hadn't been difficult to live with for that long? Ian really sounded as though he'd be glad to get rid of me.

While I washed up Ian made coffee. Without turning round I asked, 'What are your plans for this evening?'

'There's a concert rehearsal,' he told me. 'Once Jamie has finished his homework we'll be off to that, but we should be back by nine.'

'Well I hope you will,' I said stiffly. 'That's late enough for Jamie.'

'It is Saturday tomorrow,' he reminded me.

I hung up the tea towel and turned to him. 'I have to go to Mary's to put the finishing touches to the preparations for the wedding tomorrow,' I lied. 'I've no idea what time I'll be back so will you give Jamie a drink and make sure he gets off to bed and doesn't stay awake reading for too long?'

'Of course I will.'

'Thanks. I'll go and get ready then.'

As I changed I was suddenly appalled at the ease with which I had lied to Ian. All my life I'd despised liars yet now the lies were tripping off my tongue without a moment's guilt. The realization came as a shock and as I put on my make-up before the mirror I paused to take a long hard look at my reflection. Seeing Chris again seemed to have brought out the worst in me. *So why had I agreed yet again to meet him?* It was like running headlong towards an abyss with my eyes shut. My stomach churned and I knew a moment's panic as I felt my self control slipping away. Then I took a deep breath and reminded myself that Chris was, after all, Jamie's father. Whether he was aware of it or not we had created a child together. It was natural that I would feel a connection to him. I was an adult; married to a man I loved and the mother of a son I would die for. Spending time with Chris in Italy was necessary to put things in perspective for me, I told myself, to lay the past to rest once and for all.

He was waiting for me as usual but this time the lounge bar of the Meadwell Club was busy. His hand closed around my upper arm as he said,

'We can't talk in here. Come up to my room.' Seeing my hesitation he added quickly. 'No strings, Elaine. All I'm after is a modicum of privacy.'

'Of course.' I followed him into the lift, my heart bumping against my ribs as we walked along the corridor together. As he slipped the key into the lock and opened the door I was relieved to see that it was a suite. The room we entered was furnished with two comfortable armchairs, a settee, a low table and TV. An open door to my right revealed a bedroom and en-suite bathroom. As he switched on the light and crossed the room to close the window I stood awkwardly by the door. He turned and saw me.

'For heaven's sake, Elaine, you look like a scared rabbit!'

'Don't be absurd.' I took off my coat and sat down on the settee. 'I haven't got long,' I said looking at my watch. 'I have to be back for nine.'

He frowned. 'Nine? What are you – a slave?'

'I'm a wife and mother,' I told him. 'It carries responsibilities.'

'Surely you're entitled to some time of your own?'

'Why are we here, Chris?' I asked. 'Just what is this really all about?'

'You know what it's about. I want you to come to Sorrento, to the villa for a few days.'

'For what exactly?'

'For old times' sake, I suppose.' He threw out his hands helplessly. 'Does it have to be *for* anything? We're a couple of adults – old friends. Old *flames* if you like. Is it wrong to want to spend some time together?'

'No.'

He looked at me. 'So what's the problem?'

I shrugged helplessly.

'So – are you coming?'

I sat for a moment looking down at my hands.

He laughed. 'You're hidebound by convention, is that it?'

'No.'

'Would you like some coffee, or a drink?' Without waiting for my reply he lifted the telephone and asked for room service, ordering a pot of coffee and two brandies, as he replaced the receiver he turned to smile at me.

'Perhaps a brandy will help to relax you.' He joined me on the settee. 'Why can't you be honest with me, Elaine? Just what are you afraid of? Can't you trust me or could it be that you don't trust yourself?'

I stood up. 'If you want the truth, I wish I hadn't met you again, Chris. I think it would be madness to spend time together in Italy. I've made up my mind. I'm not coming. In fact this evening must be the last time we see one another. You have to promise not to get in touch again. I—' I was interrupted by a knock on the door. Chris got up to open it and took the tray of drinks. Coming back into the room he put the tray down on the table.

'At least help me drink this before you go,' he said with a wry smile at me.

In silence I poured the coffee while Chris took up the two brandy glasses and handed one to me. 'What shall we drink to?' he asked as he raised his glass. 'From where I'm sitting it looks as if there isn't much left to toast.'

I swallowed my brandy and felt its warmth course through my veins making me instantly calmer. 'We can drink to your success,' I said. 'You have everything going for you; a new TV contract in the offing and I'm sure you'll soon get over that writers' block thing and be on the way to a new book.'

For a long moment he looked at me then he put his glass down and sat back on the settee beside me. 'Look, time to put the cards on the table. We both know that this is more than two old friends taking some time out, don't we?'

I nodded.

He touched my hand. 'I wish you knew just how much I'd give to be able to turn back the clock,' he said softly. 'I should never have sent you away. Believe me I've suffered for it ever since.'

Something inside me tightened. 'You don't mean that. Look at the success you've made of your writing. You were right to be single minded.'

'No, I wasn't. Deep down I think I knew it even then. I'd give anything to have that time back again. I realize now that with you beside me I could have been a better writer – probably made it in half the time. Seeing you now, mature and sophisticated, even lovelier than before, makes me realize what I've missed out on. Meeting again, it's as though fate is offering us a second chance. We can't just turn our backs on it.'

'You're wrong,' I argued. 'Things always seem rosy looking back. You might see our meeting again as a second chance but for me it's too late – *way* too late.'

'How do you know until you give it a chance?' he said urgently. 'Right away from here – just you and me. Time to discover the truth – what we might have had, and could have again.'

'It's not what I want, Chris. I'm happy with what I have.'

'You *think* you are, but how can you know for sure?'

'It's not just me I'm thinking of. So many other people would be hurt.'

'Sometimes we have to think of ourselves. When was the last time you put yourself first, Elaine?'

I stood up. 'I can't listen to any more.'

He stood to face me. '*Elaine*! Stop panicking. It only proves to me that you feel the same as I do. You're in denial. Admit it!' He pulled me to him and kissed me hard. Shocked, I resisted but he held me even closer until at last I felt as though the years had slipped away and we were back in those first heady days of first love. My mouth softened under his and my body relaxed against him.

'Darling, Elaine,' he whispered against my hair. 'I never stopped loving you. It's the truth and I believe you feel the same.' He drew back his head to look down at me. 'Say you'll come to Italy – please! Just tell me the date and I'll send you your plane ticket. If it doesn't work out you can come home and no harm done. If it does....'

'If it does?' I looked into his eyes.

'Let's take it a step at a time,' he said. 'Just for now say you'll come. We owe it to ourselves – to each other.'

Amanda left for her break with Janet the following week and the builders moved in to install her en-suite. It was surprising the difference her absence made to the atmosphere in the house. In spite of the noise and mess the builders made the atmosphere was much calmer and less tense. I found myself wishing that the break could last for more than a week, but when Janet looked in at Mary's a couple of days later it was clear that she'd already had enough.

'I wouldn't mind but she takes over,' she complained as the three of us shared a coffee break. 'She has an absolute genius for being in the wrong place at the wrong time. It's almost as though she does it on purpose.'

'Like hogging the bathroom when you're dying for a nice long soak?' I suggested.

Janet nodded. 'Or preparing one of her complicated meals in the kitchen when you want to prepare your supper,' she said. 'And why is it that she uses every pan you possess and yet never seems to feel the need to wash them up afterwards?'

I would have laughed except that I was already guessing with dismay that Janet's invitation was not likely to be a regular event.

'Unfortunately she's not likely to change at her age,' I mused.

Janet laughed. 'You can say that again!' She looked at me. 'I hear you're going away for a few days shortly,' she said. 'Do you need any help with the boys while you're away?'

I found myself blushing; feeling as guilty as though I was abandoning them. 'I'm sure they'll manage for five days,' I said. 'Ian and Jamie are going to Cardiff for a music summer school in August but the dates didn't fit in with our schedule or I'd have taken my break at the same time.'

Janet looked at Mary. 'Oh, that's a shame. Surely you and I could manage on our own for a few days, couldn't we?'

'I've already booked,' I said hastily, feeling my cheeks redden. 'But thanks for offering, Janet.'

'How is the building work going?' Mary asked.

We talked about Amanda's en-suite for a few minutes but my mind was already on the approaching five days in Italy. As the time grew closer I found myself becoming more and more nervous and doubtful about it. I'd tried to fool myself into believing that I needed to go to lay the ghost of my relationship with Chris to rest once and for all, but in my heart I knew it wasn't as simple as that. As yet he had no idea that Jamie was his son. Was I going to tell him or not? Ian's adoption of Jamie was still going through. The legal proceedings took time and as yet there had been no notification of a court hearing, but it couldn't be that far off. When we'd first applied and completed all the necessary forms we had discovered that if the biological father was absent and could not be found his agreement to the adoption was not necessary. It hadn't been a problem at the time but now things were different. Now that I was in touch with Jamie's father again was I breaking the law by not saying so? I pushed it all to the back of my mind, telling myself there was no need to do anything about it yet. But two days before school broke up for the summer holidays – and three days before I was due to fly to Italy – Ian received a letter. He looked up at me across the breakfast table with a delighted grin.

'We've got a date for the adoption hearing,' He said, making my heart turn a somersault. 'It's September 1st. We'll get it in just before we go back to school. That's great, isn't it?' He looked across the table at Jamie who beamed back.

'Hey, wicked!'

They both looked at me.

'That's great,' I tried hard to sound enthusiastic. It seemed we'd arrived at a crossroads.

'It says to expect a further visit from a social worker before that date,' Ian went on.

My heart sank. What questions would we be asked that we hadn't already answered? If I were to be asked the crucial one, how would I answer it?

Since Amanda had been back from her visit with Janet she had done nothing but find fault. To begin with she'd been pleased with her new en-suite facilities then she had decided that it cut down her living space more than she'd expected. She complained that her furniture looked cramped and the en-suite cubicle, which was in the corner nearest the kitchen, was in the wrong place. We explained that it was necessary to choose this location because of the plumbing but she refused to see the logic of this. She couldn't get used to the controls. To begin with the shower was too powerful then it was too hot – too cold. She even accused me of deliberately turning on the kitchen taps to disrupt her morning toilette. It seemed that every time I walked through the hall her door would open and I would hear her directing a newly thought-up complaint at me. I began to hear her shrilly protesting voice in my sleep.

On the evening before my departure the inter-schools concert was to take place. I'd been packing, trying to decide what to take and how many clothes I would need for five days. At breakfast Jamie was all nerves and excitement.

'You won't sit in the front row, Mum, will you?'

I looked up. 'Why not?'

'I'll see you and it'll put me off.'

'Oh! Thanks a lot.'

'No – you know what I mean.'

'Would you like me to wear a bag over my head?'

Ian came through to the kitchen zipping up his briefcase. Catching the gist of the conversation he said. 'Come on, Elaine, you know what he means. Having a close family member with their eyes boring into you is really distracting.'

Hurt, I stood up and began to clear the table. 'Perhaps it would be better if I didn't come at all,' Immediately, I regretted the remark as I saw the look on Jamie's face.

'Oh, Mum, I didn't mean I didn't want you to come at all.'

Ian shot me a reproving look. 'Of course Mum's coming. Come on Jamie, I'll drop you off but we'd better get going or we'll both be late.'

Regretting my bad mood I decided to go after them. Dumping the tray of breakfast dishes on the draining board I went through to the hall. Amanda was standing by the open doorway reading a letter she'd just received from the postman.

'Have they gone?' I asked her.

She looked up distractedly. 'Gone – who?'

'Ian and Jamie. I wanted to....' At that moment Toffee came racing down the stairs, heading straight for the open door. I called out, 'Amanda! Quick – Toffee!' She looked vaguely at me then at the dog. '*The door*, Amanda!' I screamed. 'Stop him!' But it was too late. Toffee's paws skittered on the wooden floor as he paused briefly in the doorway then in an instant he was through it, leaving Amanda gazing open-mouthed at me.

'Oh, for heaven's sake! Why couldn't you close the—' Before I could finish my sentence there was a screech of brakes in the road outside followed by a heart-stopping yelp of pain.

'What's happened?' Dad stood on the stairs looking at me as I stood transfixed with horror. Recovering, I pushed past a stunned Amanda and rushed out of the house. A small red car had stopped at the kerbside and a young woman was bending over Toffee's small body as he lay ominously still in the road. As I ran out, my heart in my mouth, the driver looked up at me, her face white.

'Is it your dog? I'm so sorry. He just ran straight under my wheels. I didn't have a hope of not hitting him.'

Without answering I bent down. Dad was at my side now, on his knees, his hand on Toffee's chest.

'He's alive,' he said, looking at me. 'But that hind leg looks broken to me and he may have internal injuries.' He looked up at the driver. 'Did you actually run over him?'

She shook her head. 'I don't think so. He sort of bounced off my front wheel. Oh dear, I'm so sorry. Can I help – take you to a vet or something?'

Dad looked at me. 'Get me a blanket or something to wrap him in. I'll take him. You go inside. I'll ring you as soon as I know anything.'

I pulled off my cardigan. 'Here, wrap him in this.'

I watched helplessly as they drove off together then went back into the house. Amanda stood where I had left her in the hall, the letter still in her hand. She looked at me.

'Is it dead?'

I felt anger writhing inside me like a venomous snake. 'This is all *your* fault, you stupid old cow!' I yelled at her. 'Why couldn't you shut the door when I asked you? And for your information Toffee is Jamie's dog – not an *it*! If he's not dead it's no thanks to you.'

'Don't take that tone with me....' she broke off and took a step backwards, seeing the look on my face.

'Get out!' I hissed at her. 'Get out before I – I do something I'll regret!'

As she scuttled into her room and closed the door Cleo came through from the kitchen and took my arm. 'Come through and let me make you a strong cuppa, love,' she said. 'You've had a nasty shock.'

Suddenly a dam broke somewhere inside me. I felt as though I was being punished. I'd lashed out at Amanda but really it was my fault. I'd been sharp with Jamie and bitchy to Ian this morning and I'd been planning to betray them both. Now this had happened. What kind of person was I turning into? At that moment I hated myself. Tears welled up and poured down my cheeks. Italy was out of the question now. I couldn't possibly leave Jamie when his beloved dog had been run over. What on earth would he do if Toffee died?

'There, there, love.' Cleo put her arms round me and hugged me. 'Don't worry. He might be all right. Come and sit down. Let's hope for the best – yeah?'

Fourteen

Cleo made me a strong cup of tea, generously laced with brandy from a bottle she found in the pantry. It tasted vile but I drank it down quickly and felt better for it. Half an hour went by without a phone call from Dad at the vet's. I went upstairs and sent Chris a text.

Unable to join you due to a family crisis. Please do not reply – E.

Ten minutes later as I was coming downstairs the telephone in the hall rang. I snatched up the receiver. 'Dad?'

'Yes, it's me, and don't worry, it's good news,' he said, putting my mind instantly at ease. 'The vet has X-rayed Toffee and there are no internal injuries, thank God. But he's badly shocked, poor little chap and his hind leg is broken in two places. The vet is setting it this afternoon and they'll keep him in overnight under sedation to give the leg a chance.'

'Oh, thank goodness!' Suddenly I remembered Jamie and the concert. 'We can't let Jamie know, Dad,' I said. 'We'll have to keep it from him somehow, at least until the concert is over. He's going to be devastated.'

'I know. Don't worry, leave it with me. I'll think of something.'

'Was the girl all right?' I asked. 'The driver of the car.'

'Poor girl, she was so upset,' Dad said. 'She's insisting on paying the vet's fee.'

'Oh no!' I said determinedly. 'Someone else is going to be paying that; the person who's really responsible.'

I spent the afternoon unpacking and putting my clothes away. Deep inside I felt nothing but relief. I'd never quite believed I would go to Italy anyway and now I couldn't help feeling that I'd been held back from the brink of something disastrous. Fate had stepped in and stopped me from making the biggest mistake of my life.

When Jamie and Ian came home that afternoon Jamie immediately began looking round for Toffee. Dad was ready with a white lie.

'I let your Auntie Janet take him home for the afternoon,' he said. 'Poor old Brownie has been a bit off colour and she thought Toffee might cheer him up.'

Jamie appeared to be satisfied and went off to get ready for the concert. The four of us, Dad, Mary, Janet and I, chose seats halfway back in the hall and settled down to wait for the concert to begin. About five minutes before the start my phone beeped. I fished for it in my bag and saw that it was a text from Chris. I glanced at it surreptitiously.

Bitterly disappointed. Decided to return to London next week. Come up for the weekend? Please say yes. C.

'Everything okay?' Dad was looking at me.

I nodded. 'It's fine.' I switched the phone off feeling slightly apprehensive. Clearly Chris wasn't going to let it go.

The concert began and for a while the events of the day were forgotten. We were entranced. Ian's new choir was enchanting and received a standing ovation and Jamie's solo went without a hitch. Ian played a piano solo, his own arrangement of the second movement of Rachmaninov's *Second Piano Concerto*. It was so brilliant and I was so proud of him that I felt tears pricking the corners of my eyes.

Dad and I said goodbye to Mary and Janet in the car park and waited for Ian and Jamie to emerge. In the car on the way home Jamie was still hyped up on adrenaline and couldn't keep still.

'Did it really go okay, Mum? Did you like it? What about you, Granddad? Was I okay?'

'Everyone loved it,' I told him. 'And I was very proud of you – the proudest mum in the audience.'

Dad reiterated my approval but the moment we arrived home Jamie's first thought was for Toffee.

'He's been all on his own all evening. Where is he? I'll take him for a little walk.'

Dad and I exchanged glances. There was no putting it off any longer. I opened my mouth but Dad held up his hand.

'Jamie, lad. Your mum and I have a bit of bad news to tell you. When I told you he was with Auntie Janet this afternoon it wasn't quite true. I'm afraid there was an accident this morning. The front door had been left open and Toff got out. Before we could stop him he ran out into the road and—'

'*Oh no!*' Jamie's eyes were huge and tear-filled. 'Granddad – he isn't – isn't *dead*, is he?'

'No, no! He was hurt, though, and he has to stay at the vet's just for tonight. One of his back legs is broken and the vet had to fix it. Apart from that he's all right. You and I will go and pick him up tomorrow morning, eh? We'll have to take great care of him for a few weeks, but I bet he'll cheer up when he sees you.'

'Are you sure he's all right, Granddad? You're not just saying that?' I could see that he was trying very hard not to cry.

'I promise you, Jamie,' Dad said gently. 'He's fine. He'll be as good as new in a few weeks' time, you'll see.'

Jamie swallowed hard. 'I want to know exactly what happened. Will you tell me?'

Dad looked at me. 'Come on, lad. You've had a busy day. Go up now and I'll come up when you're in bed and tell you all about it.'

'Okay.' Jamie threw his arms around my neck. ''Night, Mum. Thanks for coming to the concert and for taking care of Toffee.' He looked into my eyes. 'He will be okay, won't he?'

'He'll be fine, I promise,' I told him, swallowing the lump in my throat. 'And now you'll have all the summer holidays to spend with him, helping to get his leg better.'

When they gone Ian looked at me. 'What really happened?'

I sighed. 'Amanda had a letter in the post that she couldn't wait to read, apparently. She was standing reading it at the open door and Toffee ran downstairs and straight out into the road before I could stop him.'

He sighed. 'You were right; it really isn't working, is it, having her here? We're going to have to do something about it.'

I felt like telling him he'd taken long enough to realize it but instead I sighed. 'I don't know that there's anything we can do now.' I looked at him. 'I'm not going to Italy,' I told him. 'I've cancelled. I couldn't go and leave Jamie after what's happened.'

He frowned. 'Oh, Elaine, what a pity. You really needed that break.'

I shrugged. 'It can't be helped,' I said, guilt making me abrupt. 'It doesn't matter. I'll go some other time.'

'Maybe you and I could get off somewhere on our own,' Ian said. 'Just lately we don't seem to have had much time for each other, what with one thing and another.' He reached for my hand. 'What we need is a second honeymoon.'

Before I could think of a reply there was a tap on the door. It opened immediately and Amanda looked round it.

'I'm not intruding, am I?'

I felt my eyebrows rise. It was so unlike Amanda to be considerate. I hadn't seen her since that morning when I'd lashed out at her and I felt slightly uncomfortable.

'No, it's fine,' Ian said. 'What can we do for you?'

'I couldn't go to bed without inquiring about the dog,' she said, with a glance in my direction. 'Is it ...' she glanced at me. 'Is *he* all right?'

'He's being kept at the vet's overnight,' Ian told her. 'His leg is broken, but he'll make a full recovery.'

'Oh, well that's good.' Uninvited, she came into the room and sat down. 'I'm sorry. I know it was my fault. Obviously, I'll pay the vet's bill.'

I could hardly believe my ears. 'I owe you an apology, Amanda,' I said. 'I was very rude to you this morning.'

She shook her head. 'You were upset. Forget it.'

She remained seated and into the awkward silence that followed I asked, 'Would you like a drink? Coffee –chocolate?'

'You haven't got a brandy, have you?'

Ian and I looked at each other. 'I think there's a drop left in the bottle in the pantry,' I said. 'Will you have a look, Ian? Cleo made me a cup of tea after the accident and she put some in it, so I'm not sure how much is left.'

'Wouldn't put it past her to be knocking it back herself!' Amanda glanced at me and bit her lip. 'But there, perhaps I'm being unduly suspicious.'

Ian found a small glassful left in the bottle and poured it for Amanda who knocked it back in one swallow. She gave an appreciative nod then looked at us. 'I've got some news.'

'Good news, I hope,' I said. 'We could do with some.'

'That letter I had this morning,' she began. 'It was from someone I used to know when I was in the theatre. He works in TV now. Seems that the BBC is planning a new soap for BBC Radio Four and there's a part in it that would suit me. It would be at least six months' work. He's put my name forward but I'll have to audition, of course. They're being held in London next week and he wants me to go up.' She gave a coy little smile. 'He's offered to meet me from the train and take me to lunch first.'

'How exciting,' I said.

Ian looked doubtful. 'Are you sure you're up to it after all this time?'

She bridled. '*Up to it*? I'm not in my dotage yet, thank you very much, Ian, and I have worked for the BBC before, remember.'

'Not for some time.'

'Actresses of my age and experience are hard to find. Anyway, time will tell, won't it?'

'So you're definitely going to try for it?'

'Of course I am! Apart from anything else the money will come in very handy.' She looked from one to the other of us. 'I'd be able to pay you proper rent for instance.'

'But surely if you'd be working in London you'd have to live there?' I put in.

'Not necessarily. The train service from here is very good.'

'The travelling would be tiring for you though,' Ian said. 'Much better if you could get a flat close to the studios.'

Amanda raised an eyebrow. 'If I didn't know you better I might think you were hoping to get rid of me.' There was a moment's silence as we looked at one another then Amanda said ingenuously, 'Don't think I haven't appreciated your letting me stay here rent free.'

Ian cleared his throat. 'Does this friend of yours have a name?'

'Yes, it's Haydn,' Amanda said. 'Haydn Jenkins.'

The name rang a bell but it wasn't until much later that I remembered where I'd heard it before. Haydn Jenkins was the 'old flame' that Cleo had put in touch with Amanda again. She'd been angry at the time, probably because she thought he was still a humble stage manager in the provinces, but now that his career had progressed and he had some clout she clearly saw him in a different light.

With all the preoccupation of the inter-schools concert and Toffee's accident the impending visit from a social worker had completely escaped my mind, so when we received a letter on the morning after the concert informing us that Rosemary Saunders would be visiting at three o'clock one week from the following Monday it came as a shock. Ian remarked that it couldn't have come at a better time. Now that school had broken up he would be free to be interviewed with me. As for me, it opened up a whole new set of problems.

Dad took Jamie to the vet's to collect Toffee and they came back, Jamie carrying his pet tenderly in his arms. The little dog still looked slightly woozy from the sedation and hobbled round uncomfortably with his damaged leg in plaster. Jamie fussed over him like a mother hen.

'He'll have to stay here in the kitchen with his basket all day,' he told me. 'He's not allowed to run upstairs or jump onto the furniture or up and down steps. I can take him for gentle little walks and round the garden but that's all for the time being. He's got to go back to the vet in ten days' time to have his stitches out.' He looked at me. 'He can still sleep in my room though, can't he, Mum? I can carry him up at bedtime.'

'Of course you can.' Obviously Jamie was going to be fully occupied for most of the summer. I reflected that it was a good job we hadn't booked a holiday.

Working with Mary that morning I was quiet, preoccupied with thoughts of the social worker's visit. Predictably, Mary noticed.

'What's up? You're not worrying about that little dog, are you? I'm sure Jamie won't let anything happen to him.'

I looked at her. My mind was in turmoil. I had to talk to someone. I knew Mary would be furious with me but I was prepared for that, desperate as I was for some sensible advice.

'I've got a problem, Mary,' I said.

She laughed. 'Haven't we all?'

'A big one,' I went on. 'One that could well ruin my life – Ian's and Jamie's too. I don't know what to do.'

Her face changed immediately and she put aside what she was doing. 'Right,' she said. 'First things first; let's get the kettle on then you can tell me about it.'

When I confessed that I'd been seeing Chris ever since the library opening she was even angrier than I had expected.

'My God, Elaine, what were you thinking about? You realize what you're risking, don't you?'

'Of course I do. That's why I'm so worried.'

'What on earth made you want to start seeing him again? I thought it was over years ago.'

'It was – it *is*. It was him. He said letting me go was the worst mistake he'd ever made. He kept ringing and texting, begging me to meet him and – I don't know, things just got out of hand.'

'Right.' She reached for my hand. 'Let just get one thing out of the way; have you slept with him?'

'*No!*' I shook my head.

'So – at these secret meetings nothing happened?'

'Most of them took place in public places.'

'Most?' She cocked an inquiring eyebrow at me.

'We went to his room once.' I glanced up at her. 'Nothing happened, except – kisses.'

Mary threw up her hands. 'My God, Elaine! Are you mad? And what about this trip to Italy? What kind of message do you think you gave out by agreeing to go?'

'I know what you're thinking.'

'So *why*?'

I shook my head. 'I suppose I was in denial.'

'In denial! Running head first into a brick wall, more like! I can't believe you can have been so naive! You must have been only too aware of what would happen – what he obviously *intended*?'

'But it didn't happen, did it? I didn't go.'

'Only by sheer chance.' She paused. 'What is it, Elaine? What's wrong? Aren't you happy with Ian? Don't you love him any more?'

'Of course I do!'

'Then why…?'

'I don't *know*! Maybe it was just remembering the way Chris and I used to be – the fact that he's Jamie's father.' I shook my head help-lessly. 'Just lately Ian and I seem to have drifted apart. He's so totally preoccupied with his music that I seem to have taken second place. Then Chris came along and he – well – *wanted* me.' I looked at her. 'That sounds feeble and shallow, doesn't it?'

'Yes it bloody well does,' she said brutally. 'Not a bit like you at all; though, having said that, we're all human I suppose. All marriages drift a bit at times. Life gets in the way. It sounds to me as though you and Ian need to start working on your marriage a bit harder. Why don't you try to get away together? Spend some time reminding yourselves how much in love you still are.'

'He's been suggesting just that and I know you're both right.'

'Do you think he suspects?'

'No.'

'So what's the problem? Be strong. Tell Chris to take a running jump.'

'If only it were that easy.' I sighed. 'The adoption thing has come up again. We've been allocated a date for the hearing now.'

'Why should that make a difference?'

'When we first began the proceedings and filled in all the necessary forms I had no idea where Chris was, which meant that his agreement to the adoption wasn't necessary. But now I do know where he is. And we're getting a visit from a social worker the week after next. What do I tell her?'

'Nothing,' Mary said firmly. 'Chris hasn't a clue about Jamie so it really comes to the same thing as him being absent, doesn't it?'

'But is that honest? And supposing it came out? Could I be accused of perjury?'

'I don't see how it could come out – unless….' Mary was silent for a moment. 'You're not thinking of telling Chris he's Jamie's father, are you?'

'Maybe I should now that he's back on the scene?'

'Are you going to discuss this with Ian?'

'How can I, Mary? He'd insist that we did it together and I wouldn't put it past Chris to tell him we'd been seeing each other.'

'So – what's the alternative?'

'He – Chris – wants me to meet him in London next week, when he gets back from Italy. I think I've got to go – tell him I can't see him any more and ask him to grant his permission for the adoption.'

'And if he refuses to give it unless you keep up the relationship? God, Elaine, you're playing with fire!'

When Rosemary Saunders arrived she wasn't what I expected at all. A kindly grey-haired lady in her early fifties, she put Ian and me at our ease at once.

'This is only a formality,' she said as the three of us sat down together. 'Just to check that nothing has changed since you first put in your application.' She looked expectantly from one to the other of us. 'I take it nothing has?'

Ian shook his head vigorously. 'Not at all. We can't wait to be a proper family, can we, darling?'

'No.'

'And your son?' Mrs Saunders consulted her notes then looked up at us. 'Where is Jamie by the way? Will he be joining us?'

'He's out walking his dog,' I told her. 'Unfortunately the dog was involved in an accident last week and he has one leg in plaster. Jamie is taking great care of him.'

She smiled. 'I'm glad to hear it. He's happy then at the prospect of Ian becoming his adoptive father?'

'Absolutely. He can't wait,' Ian told her proudly.

At that moment Jamie came in with Toffee. Mrs Saunders paused to ask about Toffee's leg and Jamie gravely gave her all the details.

'I expect you're looking forward to having Ian as your dad,' she said, 'and having Morton as your legal name.'

Jamie nodded enthusiastically. 'It'll be wicked!' He looked at me. 'Can I take Toff upstairs now, Mum?'

I nodded. 'It's fine. Off you go.'

I made tea and Mrs Saunders drank a cup. I got the impression that she was no pushover in spite of her motherly appearance. As she sat sipping her tea she took in every aspect of her surroundings and asked numerous questions about our family life, particularly Ian and Jamie's mutual love of music. The front doorbell rang and Ian looked up.

'I'm sorry but I'm afraid that will be one of my pupils,' he said. 'Do you need me for anything else?'

She shook her head. 'No. I think I have all I need, Ian, thank you.'

As Ian left the room she made no attempt to leave herself. There was something about her direct grey eyes that unnerved me slightly. I put my hand on the teapot and asked if she would like another cup of tea.

She smiled. 'Thank you.' I was aware of her watching me as I poured and when I handed her the cup she said. 'Mrs Morton, I get the feeling that there is something you want to tell me.'

Her perception took my breath away. I paused. 'Well – you asked if anything had changed,' I said.

'Yes?' She eyed me over the rim of her cup.

'When – when we first filled in the adoption forms, Jamie's biological father could not be traced. Recently I have – quite accidentally – discovered his whereabouts.'

She replaced her cup on the table. 'Ah – that does rather change things.'

My heart sank. 'Does it mean that he now has to give his permission?'

'Agreement,' she corrected. 'I take it you and Ian have discussed this?'

'No. Ian doesn't know.'

She frowned. 'I don't follow. You say you've discovered Jamie's father's whereabouts?'

'He changed his name some time ago,' I explained. 'It was quite by chance that we met again. You see, the problem is that he doesn't know that he fathered a son. Our relationship ended before I knew I was pregnant.'

'I see.'

'So, do you think he should be made aware of the fact now?'

She frowned. 'It might be advisable to put him in the picture – just in case of complications later.'

'Complications?'

'How many other people know about this?'

'Only three: my husband, my father and my business partner.'

'They know his new name, and that you've found him again?'

'No. It's – been difficult,' I told her. 'My business partner knows about it,' I added hurriedly. 'But she would never—'

'You can never be absolutely sure. Circumstances change.' She looked at me. 'What is it you're worrying about, Elaine? Are you afraid he might want to assume his role as a father – become part of your son's life?'

I felt a chill clutch my heart. 'To tell you the truth I have no idea,' I confessed. 'He's a very different person from the man I once knew. We were just students then. He has a busy and successful career now, so probably not.'

'Mmm, it's difficult.' She paused for a moment. 'As you say that he has changed his name it's understandable that so far he has been untraceable, but now that you've renewed your acquaintance it alters things.'

'Is it possible to leave things as they are? After all, he's still completely unaware that he's Jamie's father.'

'But there will always be a possibility that he could find out,' she said. 'That could make life very difficult for you. Could you live with that likelihood? Then there is Jamie himself to consider. As he grows to manhood he might want to know who his biological father is.'

I shook my head. It was even more complicated than I had envisaged. 'Will this delay things?' I asked. 'Can the hearing still go ahead on September 1st?'

'It rather depends on what you decide to do,' she said. 'You will need to contact me by the end of next week. I'm afraid I can't wait any longer than that for your decision.'

'I understand.' I decided to throw myself on her mercy. 'Please, what do you advise?'

She began to collect her briefcase and handbag together. 'I advise you to talk to your husband. I really feel that whatever you decide must be mutual.' She took a notebook from her briefcase and jotted down a number. 'This is my mobile number,' she said, tearing out the page and handing it to me. 'I won't do anything about the hearing until I hear from you.' She stood up and held out her hand. 'Goodbye – and good luck, Mrs Morton.'

'Goodbye and thank you.' I saw Mrs Saunders out and went back to the kitchen. I knew she was right; I owed it to Ian to tell him about Chris and talk through what we should do – and the sooner, the better.

Fifteen

I sent Chris a text to say that I would visit him at his London flat on the following Friday, arriving some time during the morning. He replied saying that he would put a key to his flat in the post for me as he might be delayed until late afternoon. Having burned my bridges I steeled myself to talk to Ian – something I looked forward to with dread.

I chose a time when I knew we would not be interrupted, after Jamie was in bed. Ian had a late pupil and came through to the kitchen as I was making a bedtime drink. He looked happy and relaxed and my heart sank at the thought of what I was about to tell him.

'I need to talk to you, Ian,' I said as I carried the tray through to the breakfast room. 'There's something I have to tell you – something important.'

He looked at me. 'That sounds ominous. What's wrong?'

'You remember when Mary and I catered for the opening of the new library?'

'Yes.'

'The opening ceremony was done by the author, Jake Kenning.'

He shrugged. 'If you say so. Where is this leading, Elaine?'

'Jake Kenning turned out to be Chris Harding,' I told him. 'Jamie's biological father.'

For a moment he looked stunned. 'You never mentioned it. So – did he recognize you? What happened?'

'I met him once or twice for a drink. I should have told you. I wish I had.'

He held up his hand. 'Wait a minute. You say you met him? Just what are you trying to tell me?'

'He asked me to meet him that day at the library,' I told him. 'I never meant for it to go on....'

'But it did?'

'He was very insistent. I saw him three times altogether.'

'Are you saying you've been having an affair?'

'No!'

'Then what? Why did you keep on seeing him if it wasn't...?'

'I wish I *knew*, Ian.' I shook my head. 'I suppose it had something to do with the fact that we once shared something but I promise you, nothing happened.'

He paused for a moment. 'You say you shared something – like Jamie for instance. I can't get my head round this, Elaine. You've told him that he has a son and he wants—'

'No, *no!*' The hurt expression on his face tore at my heart. How could I have been so stupid, so cruel and naive? Suddenly I knew that if I lost Ian I'd have lost everything. And even worse – so would Jamie. 'Chris has never been a part of Jamie's life. You know that,' I reminded him. 'I regret seeing him again. I know it was wrong. I should have told you.'

'So why are you telling me now? Are you saying that you still have feelings for him – that it isn't over between you?'

'Of course I'm not.'

'*Then what?*' He got up and began to pace the room. 'For God's sake, Elaine, why don't you just come out with it? What's going on?'

'I want to tell you the truth, Ian; all of it. It wasn't an affair. I told you, nothing happened, but ...' I licked my dry lips. 'I admit that it could have gone further. He invited me to go and stay at his villa in Italy.'

He swung round. 'Your break in Italy! You were planning to spend it with him?'

'But I didn't go, Ian.'

'You didn't go because of Toffee's accident. If it hadn't been for that....'

'That only brought me to my senses. I think I must have been a little crazy even to have contemplated it. I'm not making excuses but – we haven't been very close for some time; ever since you took up the teaching post. You seem so wrapped up in your music.'

'Oh, I see, so now it's my fault, is it?'

'Of course not. You're my world, Ian, you and Jamie; though lately it seems as though even Jamie's putting music first too. I seem to be slipping further and further into the background.'

'That's rubbish and you know it!'

'Do I? All I really know at this moment is that I must have been mad to put everything I have in jeopardy. I'm sorry.'

'So am I.'

'That's not all though, Ian,' I went on. 'The trouble is that Chris suddenly putting in an appearance again affects the adoption. Now that I know that he is no longer untraceable it means that one of the facts we entered on the original forms is no longer applicable.'

'Oh.' Taken aback, he sat down. 'So what happens now?'

'I talked to Mrs Saunders, the social worker about it. Her advice is that Chris should be told about Jamie.'

'That's it then, isn't it?' He ran a hand through his hair. 'The adoption won't be possible.'

'Why not?'

'He won't agree to give up his son. Why should he?'

'He's a complete stranger to Jamie.' I reached out a hand to him. 'Jamie is more your son than his,' I told him. 'You've been a father to him ever since he was five years old. When I see Chris I'll make it clear that this is what we all want.'

He looked up at me sharply. '*You* will? Shouldn't that be *me*?'

'I'd rather do this on my own, Ian.'

'Why? Is there something else you're not telling me?'

'I promise I've told you everything, Ian. But I feel this is something I have to do myself.'

He paused for a long moment. 'Tell me the truth; if it hadn't been for the adoption problem would you have told me about this?'

I took a deep breath. 'You want me to be completely honest?'

'Naturally.'

I looked into his eyes. 'I might not have found the courage,' I said. 'I already knew I'd made a bad mistake. I might just have let it go at that.'

He sighed. 'Well, thanks for being truthful – even if it does hurt.'

'I'm sorry, Ian,' I said. '*So* sorry, and I do love you.' I reached out my hands to him but he turned away.

'So when are you planning to see – Harding, or whatever he calls himself?' He turned towards me and the look in his eyes made me cringe. 'I take it you've already arranged a meeting.'

'Next Friday.'

'And how can I be sure you'll come back? How do I know you won't let him talk you round again?'

'I won't. I'm asking you to trust me, Ian.'

He laughed. '*Trust* you? That's good in view of what you've just told me.'

'Surely the fact that I told you—'

'You said yourself that you only told me because it was unavoidable.' I opened my mouth to speak but he held up his hand. 'Let's get it straight. You go up to London on Friday and meet him – drop the bombshell that he has a son and ask for his agreement to the adoption then – providing that he agrees, you come home again. Have I got that right?'

'Yes.'

'It all sounds a bit naive to me; foolishly optimistic to say the least.'

I looked at him. 'Ian – if you can't feel the same about me I understand. If you can't trust me any more, do you want to do something about it? Do you want to cancel the adoption application? Do you want me out of your life?'

To my dismay I saw his eyes fill with tears. 'How can you ask me a question like that?'

'It would break my heart but …' I went to him, hands outstretched. 'I'd understand how you felt if you—'

'*Understand how I felt*? You say you understand after asking a question like that!' He walked to the door. 'You haven't got the faintest idea what you've done to me.'

'Ian – please….'

He turned, holding up his hand. '*No* – I don't think I can take any more of this tonight, Elaine. I'll see you in the morning. Goodnight.'

I was dismayed when I went upstairs to find that Ian had taken his things and moved into the spare room. He remained there for the rest of the week. During the day he was closeted in the studio for most of the day, only emerging for meals and to go out to pupils he taught in their own homes. Luckily Jamie was too preoccupied with nursing Toffee to notice anything amiss but Dad noticed and commented on it on Thursday evening when I was preparing the following day's meals ready for my absence.

'Everything all right between you and Ian?' he asked, his kindly face concerned.

'Fine,' I told him a little too brightly. I turned to him. 'Dad, are you sure you're all right about looking after Jamie for the day tomorrow?'

He looked at me. 'When wasn't I all right about spending time with my grandson?'

'I know, but….'

'There *is* something wrong, isn't there?' he insisted.

I shook my head. 'It's just a tiff. We'll get over it.'

'Anything I should know about?'

I paused then, on impulse, I decided to confide in him. 'There's a hitch with the adoption,' I began. 'Jamie's real father has surfaced again after all these years. That's why I'm going up to London tomorrow – to see him and ask for his agreement.'

Dad looked shocked. 'No wonder Ian looks so stressed. He's resurfaced? How?'

'It's complicated. He turned up at one of the functions Mary and I catered for and we met again.'

'I see. Is Ian going to London with you?'

'No. I think I should do this alone.'

He frowned. 'But you told me this lad didn't even know you were expecting.'

'He didn't, but now things are different. I'll have to tell him about Jamie.'

'And you think he won't be curious – won't want to know his son?'

I swallowed hard. 'That's a risk I'm going to have to take.'

He covered my hand with his. 'Elaine, love – what if he doesn't agree to the adoption?'

'I don't know, Dad. I've just got to hope for the best.'

'And what about Jamie – have you considered him? Don't you think that he might want to have the opportunity of meeting his biological father – at least having the choice; if not now then one day in the future?'

I groaned. 'Oh, please, Dad; don't make this any more difficult than it is.'

'Well, far be it from me to interfere but if you don't tell him now and later it all comes out I'm afraid you could have trouble on your hands. He might never trust you again.'

He left me to mull over that thought and I sat down at the table, my mind in turmoil as I wondered what to do. The situation just seemed to get worse and worse.

That night after Jamie was in bed I went up to see him. I tapped on the door and put my head round it. 'Can I come in?'

''Course.' He was sitting up in bed reading. Toffee, lying comfortably in his basket beside the bed looked up and wagged his tail. I sat on the edge of the bed.

'There's something I want to talk to you about.'

He put his book down. 'What's up, Mum?'

'Nothing's up, it's just something I want to ask your opinion on, Jamie.'

'Okay.'

'Once, a long time ago you asked me about your father – your real father. Do you remember?'

'Yes. You said he didn't know about me and you didn't know where he was.'

'That's right. Well, what would you think if I told you I knew where to find him?'

He frowned. 'But Ian's going to be my dad now.'

'Yes, but if you knew where to find your real dad, what would you want to do about it?'

He thought about it for a long time then looked up at me. 'Do you really know where to find him then?'

'Yes.' I held my breath.

He considered for a moment. 'I'd still want Ian to be my dad.' He said at last. 'He's the only dad I've ever wanted.'

'But wouldn't you be a little bit curious? Wouldn't you want to know what kind of person he was – what he looked like – what he did for a living?'

He shrugged. 'Maybe.'

'Wouldn't you want to meet him?'

The silence in the room was broken only by Toffee's tail as it wagged against the side of the basket. Finally Jamie looked up at me. 'He doesn't seem real though. He's like someone on the telly or the films. He might as well be an alien from outer space.' He sighed. 'No, Ian's the only dad who feels real. I *know* Ian.'

'And you wouldn't like the chance to meet him – even if it's only out of curiosity?'

He shrugged. 'Not specially.'

'You're sure?'

'Yeah.' He put his book down on the bedside table and snuggled under the duvet. 'Anyway, it's all going to happen soon isn't it – the adoption? And once Ian's my official dad that'll be it.' He grinned. 'I can't wait.'

I tucked him in. 'All right then, if you're sure. I just thought I'd ask you.'

He smiled up at me. 'Thanks. 'Night, Mum.'

I bent to kiss his forehead. 'Night-night.' I patted Toffee's head. 'Night-night, Toff.'

As I switched off the light and closed the bedroom door I heaved a sigh of relief. I had no idea what I would have said to Ian if Jamie had said he wanted to meet Chris. It would have complicated matters even more, especially as Ian still wasn't speaking to me except when it was absolutely necessary.

Ian wasn't about when I left the house next morning. He'd left early, not saying where he was going. I explained to Cleo what I'd left for lunch and was just going through the hall when Amanda opened her door and emerged. She looked her glamorous best in a rose pink dress and fur stole, a hat made of pink and black feathers perched on top of her newly set hair.

'Oh! Is it today you're going up to town?' she asked, feigning surprise. 'What luck. Can I beg a lift to the station?'

I stared at her. 'You're going today? I thought it was next week.'

'It was but they've brought it forward.' She took my arm. 'Isn't it fun? We can travel up together and have a lovely chat.'

My heart sank. The last person I needed for company was Amanda but it seemed there was no getting out of it.

'What did you say you were going up for?' she asked as she settled herself in the passenger seat.

'I'm just having lunch with … friends,' I told her.

'How nice. At what restaurant?'

'At … their flat in Kensington.'

'That's nice. I expect you'll be hitting the shops afterwards.'

'I daresay.' I kept my eyes firmly on the road.

'If Haydn wasn't meeting me I could have joined you,' she said. 'But what with the auditions and then lunch I'm going to be busy all day.' She sighed. 'It's going to be such fun reminiscing about old times.'

Thank goodness, I muttered under my breath. All I needed was Amanda hanging around, today of all days.

The key to Chris's flat and the E-card for the building had arrived on Wednesday and were now safely stowed at the bottom of my handbag. They were accompanied by a slip of paper with the address written on it. It seemed that 138 Mallory Court was the penthouse of a large block in Kensington High Street. It shouldn't be hard to find.

We alighted from the train at Waterloo Station and as we walked along the platform I could feel Amanda's excitement coming off her in waves.

'Are you looking forward to seeing your friend again?' I asked as her eyes raked the crowd of people waiting at the barrier. 'Are you nervous about the audition?'

She looked at me. 'Old hands like me don't get nervous,' she said. 'But I admit it will be nice to see Haydn again.'

'I thought you were angry when Cleo mentioned that she knew him.'

She bridled. 'It was none of her business,' she said. 'You don't go passing on information about people without asking them first. That was what annoyed me.'

We'd reached the barrier now and so far Amanda had shown no sign of recognition for any of the people standing there. I was beginning to wonder what I would do if the renowned Haydn didn't show up when suddenly a stocky little man stepped forward. He was bald but the lack of hair on his head was more than made up for by a full beard of shaggy grey whiskers. He smiled and held out his hands.

'Well, well, if it isn't little Mandy Trent. I'd have known you anywhere!' He grasped her in a bear like hug and kissed her noisily on both cheeks, knocking the feathered confection on her head over one eye. I glanced at her scarlet face.

'I'll go now then, Amanda,' I said. 'Good luck with the audition and maybe I'll see you on the way home.'

'Oh – er – yes.' Hastily pushing the hat back into place she attempted to introduce me. 'Haydn – this is my s – my – er – nephew's wife.'

Haydn smiled and held out a plump hand. 'Pleased to meet you – er....'

'Elaine,' I supplied. 'Well, I'd better be going; nice to meet you too, Mr Jenkins. 'Bye.' I couldn't help smiling to myself as I headed for the Underground. Clearly the years hadn't been as kind to Haydn as Amanda had expected.

I spotted Mallory Court as soon as I walked out of the Underground station. Crossing the road I stood at the imposing main entrance. Inside the double glass doors was an entrance lobby with the numbers and occupants of the flats displayed. I checked that the occupant of number 138 was in fact Jake Kenning and inserted the E-card in the entrance door. It opened for me and I went through into the rather grand main hallway to the lift.

Soaring silently skywards I contemplated the day in front of me. With Amanda chatting away on the journey I'd had no time to think about what I was going to say to Chris. Anyway all I could think of at the moment was Ian. The silence between us was getting to me. I'd tried once or twice to talk to him but received no response. How could I blame him after the bombshell I had dropped on him? Would he ever forgive me? Would things ever be the same between us again?

I got out of the lift and let myself into number 138. I'd expected it to be opulent and it was. The entrance hall was square with a black and white tiled floor. Off it led several rooms with opaque glass doors. The one to the main living room stood open and I walked in and looked around. Furnished in a minimalist style everything seemed to be black and white – white walls, black leather sofas and ebonized wood and smoked glass tables and chairs. The rugs on the wood block floor were black and white with geometric designs. The whole place had an art deco feel about it and I guessed that Chris had engaged the services of an interior designer. I allowed myself the indulgence of having a look round the flat. There were two bedrooms, both with en-suite bathrooms, and the most amazing kitchen I had ever seen. It looked like something from a sci-fi movie with its gleaming high-tech equipment and I wondered just how much cooking was ever done in it. On the worktop was a note addressed to me.

Elaine – Welcome to my humble pad (humble indeed!) *Help yourself to lunch. There's plenty of food in the fridge. I hope to be with you later. Can't wait to see you. Love C.*

I took off my coat and went into the hall to hang it up in what I thought was a cupboard. It turned out to be a small study. One wall was equipped with a desk-cum-worktop on which stood a computer. Obviously Chris worked here when he was in London. The rest of the workspace and the floor were littered with paper, some of it screwed up into balls, and I remembered what he had said about having writers' block. I wondered if he had a secretary to take care of his correspondence and clear up after him. Clearly if he had she hadn't been here for some time.

Back in the kitchen I looked inside the cavernous refrigerator. There was plenty of salad and I found bread and a tin of pâté from which I made myself a hasty lunch. As I ate I wondered just how long Chris would be. The longer I waited the more nervous about the coming interview I became.

I was washing up my plate and cup when there was a ring at the doorbell. I hesitated. Maybe I should ignore it, although it could be Chris arriving earlier than expected. Had he sent me his only key?

I opened the door to find an elderly lady standing outside. She was small and thin and wore a blue twinset and a string of pearls; her elegantly coiffured hair was rinsed in a shade that matched her twinset.

'Oh!' She affected surprise at seeing me but I wasn't convinced. I'd spotted her downstairs in the lobby when I first arrived and seen her eyeing me curiously. 'I'm so sorry to disturb you, my dear but Mr Kenning borrowed my copy of *War and Peace* a while ago and I rather wondered if he might have forgotten.' She simpered at me. 'I'd so like to read it again – one – er – forgets….' She peered past me into the hallway.

'I'm afraid he's not here at the moment,' I told her. 'I'll pass on the message to him when he—'

'Oh dear, how very remiss of me,' she broke in. 'I should have introduced myself. I'm Lydia French from number 134, downstairs. Mr Kenning and I are *great* friends – such a joy, having a best-selling author right on one's doorstep.' She peered inquiringly at me. 'You must be another of his *sisters*. So nice to come from a large family, I always think. I was an only child myself. It's very lonely being an only child.' As she spoke she was edging past me into the flat. 'If I could just look on his bookshelf I needn't bother him again.'

'Well, I don't know….'

'Oh, I assure you he wouldn't mind. As I said, we're the greatest of friends.'

Clearly she wasn't going anywhere without her book. I closed the door behind her. 'I'll help you look,' I said.

But once inside the flat she seemed to forget all about the book. With a glance towards the kitchen she said, 'I wonder – would you think it an imposition if I asked if I could have a glass of water?'

'No, of course not.'

'I do get so dehydrated, you see. It's the wretched medication I'm on.' She trotted behind me into the kitchen where I took a glass from the shelf and filled it from the tap. As I handed it to her she hesitated,

'Oh – you wouldn't have any bottled water, would you? I never quite trust the tap water in London.'

I poured the water down the sink and opened the fridge. There were several unopened bottles of spring water stored in a door shelf. I took one out and handed it to her. She peered at it.

'This is sparkling, dear. Is there a still one? All those bubbles play havoc with my digestion.'

I looked again and found a bottle of still spring water. I watched, fascinated, as she opened it and downed almost half straight from the bottle. 'Right, shall we look for your…?'

'So where do you come in the family, dear?' she said, extracting a lace hanky from her sleeve and dabbing her lips.

I was taken aback but decided to play along. 'The family – oh, about halfway.' I was beginning to wonder what kind of yarn Chris had been spinning her though I couldn't blame him. She was so inquisitive and had the cheek of the devil. She and Amanda were two of a kind. She was nodding.

'I see, so no doubt you'll know his wife.'

I swallowed hard. 'Naturally.'

'Such a shame about their divorce,' she said, shaking her head. 'I don't hold with it myself and I found it particularly upsetting with things the way they were at the time.'

'What things?'

She stared at me in surprise. 'Well, with dear Frances being in the family way. I couldn't understand how he could let her go.' She glanced at me sideways. 'Unless of course….'

'Unless what?'

She gave her shoulders a little shake. 'Well, it's not for me to say but I couldn't help wondering if the child was, well, you know….'

'Shall we go and look for your book now, Mrs French?'

'It's Miss, dear. I never married. Not that I wasn't asked – many times but I looked after dear Mummy and Daddy until they both died and after that it was….'

'*War and Peace?*'

'Pardon, dear?'

'Your book. I think you said it was *War and Peace*. Shall we go and see if we can find it now?'

She took a couple of steps and then stopped. 'So, I daresay you keep in touch with dear Frances.'

'Not really.'

'But you must know if she had the baby.'

'I'm afraid I don't.'

'How sad. I don't understand these modern marriages. No one really *commits* any more, do they?' She glanced at me, the glint in her blue eyes as sharp as glass. 'Will you be staying overnight?'

'No, I'm going back later this afternoon.'

'Going home – to – where would that be?'

'Miss French, I have things to do so shall we get your book now?'

The smile left her face and her expression hardened. 'I hope I'm a good neighbour, Miss – Kenning. I do my best to help in whatever way I can. I assure you my only interest is for the welfare of my fellow tenants. And I've just remembered that it was someone else I lent the book to. Not Mr Kenning at all. I'm sorry to have troubled you.'

'That's quite all right.' I opened the door for her but as she passed through she delivered her parting shot.

'Do give my regards to your *other sisters* when you see them.' The blue eyes narrowed. 'Odd how *different* you all look, isn't it?'

After she had gone I sat down to digest what she had said. She was a nosy old gossip of course, but probably just lonely. Clearly she'd witnessed young women arriving at the flat, passed off by Chris as his 'sisters'. And why had he never mentioned that his ex-wife had been pregnant when they split up?

I wandered into the study again and stared at all the discarded paper, evidence of Chris's frustration. I picked up some of the crumpled balls and put them into the waste paper basket then I spotted a folder on his desk. Opening the cover I saw that he'd made jottings of ideas he'd had. At the top of the page in capital letters he had written, RENEWED AQUAINTANCE followed by OLD AFFAIR. Under this was a series of titles: NEVER LOOK BACK. THE SWEET SCENT OF BURNING. I read on, my eyes widening. He'd outlined a plot idea and as I read my heart quickened. It was our story, from our student meeting and relationship – the parting and meeting again years later. Further on there was blackmail and murder. Anger rose in my chest like a pain. I felt sick. After all the trauma I'd put myself through, after my stupidity in believing every word he said, all the time he had simply been using what we'd had as material for a sleazy detective story. I felt used and humiliated.

Hurrying through to the hall I began to put on my coat; my only desire to get home as quickly as I could and try my best to salvage what I could of my marriage. But I had the door half open when I suddenly remembered what I had come for. Chris was still Jamie's father. I couldn't leave without making him aware of the fact. Somehow I had to get him to agree to Jamie's adoption. Slowly I unbuttoned my coat and settled down to wait, my heart heavy in my chest.

It was almost an hour later when I heard his key in the lock. I stood up, bracing myself, wishing with all my heart that I could fast-forward time so that the coming interview was over, and I was on the train and heading for home.

'Darling! It's wonderful to see you at last.' He threw his coat down and came towards me, arms outstretched but I put out my hands to ward him off.

'Chris, we have to talk,' I began, my mouth dry. 'I must catch the six o'clock train home so there isn't much time.'

He shook his head. 'But I thought you were staying for the weekend, to make up for not being able to make it to Sorrento. What's wrong? You look stressed. Look, have a drink, you'll feel better.' He went to the drinks table by the window.

'No, Chris. Nothing to drink for me. What I have to say needs a clear head.'

He looked put out. 'Oh. Well, I'm having one anyway.' He poured himself a stiff whisky and sat down, glancing up at me. 'Come and sit down.' He patted the sofa beside him. 'Whatever's wrong I'm sure we can easily straighten it out.'

I stayed where I was. 'This has to be the last time we meet, Chris,' I said. 'I think I went a bit crazy for a while but it has to stop now. I've come to my senses and I know now what I want.'

'Oh, you've got cold feet.'

'I said – I know what I want.'

He smiled calmly. 'And that is?'

'My marriage means too much to me to throw it away. I love Ian. He knows I've been seeing you again and he's already hurt enough.'

'Does hurting *me* not matter then?'

It was my turn to smile. 'I think you'll survive very well, Chris. One of your *sisters* will help you forget.'

He frowned. 'What the hell are you talking about?'

'I met a fellow tenant of yours earlier. She seems surprised that you have so many sisters, none of whom look like you.'

His brow cleared. 'Oh, old Leery Lydia from downstairs. You don't want to take any notice of her.' He put down his glass and stood up to face me. 'All that was before we met up again, Elaine. You didn't expect me to live like a monk after my marriage ended, did you?' He laughed. 'Don't tell me you were jealous. Is that what this is all about?'

'No, it isn't. I have something important to tell you, Chris so you'd better sit down again. It's serious, something that could have a big impact on all our lives.'

He sighed. 'Okay, let's have it.' He sat down again, crossing his legs and looking up at me with a sardonic smile.

I sat down in the chair opposite and took a deep breath. 'After we split up all those years ago; after you decided that you wanted to go it alone I discovered that I was pregnant. You have a son, Chris. My son, Jamie, he's yours.'

If I'd expected him to be shocked or surprised I was wrong. He looked at me, his face a mask. 'If that's true why didn't you get in touch with me at the time?'

'If it's *true*! Do you really think I'd have come here today if it wasn't?'

He spread his hands. 'How do I know what women do or why? It could be that, seeing that I'd made a success of my life you saw an opportunity to cash in on behalf of your kid.'

I felt as though all the breath had been dashed from my body. 'How *dare* you say that to me?'

'I'm not saying that's what you *thought* – just that it's a possibility. After all, you must want something from me, if not why are you here? It obviously isn't for the pleasure of my company – more's the pity.'

Suddenly I saw him for what he was – for what the years and his success had made him. The Chris sitting in front of me wasn't the same person I'd known all those years ago. Jamie's words came back to me: *He might as well be an alien from outer space.* He'd been right.

'I'll tell you what I want from you,' I said as calmly as I could. 'My husband, Ian wants to adopt Jamie as his own son. He's been a father to him since he was very young. Now he wants to make it legal. Unfortunately, I need his biological father to agree.'

'Oh, is that all?'

'You mean you'll give it – your agreement?' I held my breath.

'If you want – as long as it isn't going to get into the papers.'

At that moment I came close to hating him. 'Are you sure you don't want a DNA test?'

He shrugged, the cynicism lost on him. 'I'm prepared to take your word for it,' he said casually, his back to me as he refilled his whisky glass.

'And you're not going to turn up suddenly, demanding to see your son?' I'd reached the stage where I wouldn't have put anything past him.

'Do you honestly think I've got nothing better to do?'

'Considering you're not even interested in your legitimate child – no.'

He turned to look at me. 'I see Lydia's been spreading the poison. Well, good luck to her. Look, Elaine, I've never been interested in kids; never wanted any. I told Frances that before we were married but she went ahead and let herself get pregnant. She broke the deal we made.'

'You make it sound like breach of contract.'

'Well, it was.'

'So now you have two children you've never met.'

'I suppose so. I offered to do the right thing by Frances,' he went on. 'I promised to support her and the child – provided they both stayed out of my life.'

'Big of you!'

He shrugged. 'She had been warned. As it happens she chose to forego my support.'

'So you're letting her struggle alone?'

'Her choice. Anyway, her parents are loaded. No doubt they'll see she's okay and probably find some chinless wonder to offload her on eventually.'

'You're all heart, aren't you Chris? I can't help wondering what Cecily would have made of you.'

'Cecily?'

'Your grandmother – the one who brought you up and educated you. Remember her?'

He was clearly taken aback. 'I think she'd have been proud of my success.'

'Maybe, but not of the man you've let yourself become.' I glanced at my watch and gathered up my coat and bag. 'I'll have to go now.' I looked at him. 'You'll sign the form that you'll be sent, then? Giving your agreement to the adoption?'

'If it means so much to you.' He got up to pour himself another whisky. 'By the way, as matter of interest, what was the family crisis that stopped you joining me in Italy?'

I paused. 'My son's dog was run over,' I told him.

He turned to look at me in amazement then he threw back his head and roared with laughter. 'Honestly, Elaine, you're *priceless*. Talk about a grand passion! I don't know whether to be insulted or flattered. *Turned down for a flattened pooch!*'

I looked at him, sitting there convulsed with laughter, the whisky slopping from his glass onto the sofa and suddenly I felt nothing more than pity for him. I remembered something he'd told me: *I don't do happy endings.* There would be no happy ending for him either. A shelf full of books wouldn't bring him much comfort when he was old and alone. I thought of the story outline I'd seen on his desk and was tempted to let him know I'd seen it, then I checked myself. He'd agreed to what I asked. There was nothing else I needed or wanted from him – *nothing*. Anything there had been between us in the past was well and truly dead.

I caught the train by the skin of my teeth. As I walked along the carriage, looking for a seat I spotted Amanda, a spare seat beside her. Before I could slip past she looked up and saw me.

'*Elaine*! Come and sit down. You look tired. Had a good day?'

Her words were very slightly slurred and I guessed that Haydn had dined her well and wined her even better. I sat down gratefully in the empty seat beside her.

'Yes, thank you.'

'You don't seem to have done much shopping,' she observed, looking round for non-existent bags.

'No, there wasn't really time.'

'You know, you're always in such a rush,' she said. 'You've been looking really strained and tired lately. You could do with a break.'

I shrugged, surprised at her perception. Amanda always seemed too preoccupied with her own needs to notice anyone else's.

She grasped my arm. 'Go on then – *ask* me. Aren't you dying to know?'

Suddenly I remembered her reason for coming up to London. 'Oh – the audition! How did it go?'

'*I got the part!*' she announced – so loudly that other passengers turned to look at her.

'Really? Congratulations!' I thought of having the house to ourselves once again – of being without her shrill voice and the constant barrage of demands and my heart lifted so much that I felt almost fond of her. I squeezed her arm. 'That's great news, Amanda, and what about Haydn, did you have fun catching up with him?'

She pulled a face, suddenly sober. 'Oh, *him*! I've never seen anyone age so badly,' she said, patting her hair. 'The trouble is he thinks he's still twenty-five. I'll have my work cut out keeping *him* in line, I can tell you!'

Sixteen

When Amanda and I turned into the drive at Beaumont House Ian was just seeing his last pupil out. Amanda buttonholed him at once, eager to regale him with the details of her prospective triumphant comeback. By the time she let him go I'd made some sandwiches and had the kettle on. I looked round as Ian came through the door.

'Hi. Where's Jamie?'

'Your dad has taken him to a cricket match,' he said. 'They've taken Toffee with them.'

'Tea and a sandwich? I asked.

He nodded. 'Please. That was Margaret Harris, my most challenging pupil. I need sustenance after an hour with her.' He glanced at me as I spread the cloth on the table. 'You came home then.'

I looked at him. 'Of course I came home.'

He raised an eyebrow. 'And…?'

'Chris has promised to sign the adoption agreement.'

'And that's all? He doesn't want to meet Jamie – have regular access?'

'No.'

'And he's not going to turn up on the doorstep making demands?'

I shook my head. 'He's not interested. As long as nothing gets into the newspapers that's all he cares about.'

'Huh, charming! And this is the man you almost left me for.'

I sat down opposite him. 'Ian, there was never any question of me leaving you.'

'So you say.'

'I mean it, I promise you. The only explanation I can offer for

216

seeing Chris again is that I never quite drew a line under our relationship when we split up.'

'And you wanted to turn back the clock?'

'No. I think I'd built a rosy picture of what we once had. Now I remember it for what it was, a romantic, girlish dream that ended in probably the worst time of my life. Although I didn't see it at the time I know now that Chris was always self-centred. Success hasn't improved him.' I looked up at him. 'The only question now is, do you still want to go ahead with the adoption?'

'Want to go ahead?' His eyes met mine. 'What do you think? You know what Jamie means to me.'

'Yes, I do. But unfortunately Jamie and I come as a package and if you feel that I've let you down too badly to be forgiven—' He held up his hand to stop me.

'Stop right there. I don't want to go into that.'

'But I think we have to, Ian. I don't want to be *tolerated* just because you love Jamie. I don't want to be the price you pay for something you've set your heart on.'

'That's a brutal way of putting it.'

'But nevertheless that's how it is. I know I've behaved badly. I know I don't deserve your love and trust. I'm just being realistic.'

He was shaking his head. 'I can't talk about this any more tonight, Elaine. Forget the tea. I think I'll have an early night.'

As he made to get up I put out a hand to stop him. 'Ian, please, we can't keep avoiding the subject. Is it possible to mend the damage I've done? I need to know. Can things ever be the same as before?'

He ran his fingers through his hair. 'I don't know, Elaine,' he said. 'I honestly don't know.'

'I'd never spoil things between you and Jamie. You know that, don't you? If the worst happened I'd still want you and he to see as much of each other as possible.'

'I can't discuss it now.' He flung out of the room but not before I'd seen the tears glistening in his eyes; not before I'd seen the deep hurt etched on his face. My heart ached. Just how much damage had I caused? Would he ever find it in his heart to forgive me? How could I have been such a fool?

My appetite gone I stood up and began to take the cloth off the table. Suddenly my eyes alighted on Cecily Harding's watercolour painting of St Ives harbour on the wall opposite and I remembered the peace and beauty of the place. I thought of Amanda's words. *You've been looking strained and tired. You need a break.* Maybe if I put some distance between Ian and myself we'd both have time and space to think things through rationally. Maybe going back to Cornwall would make things fall into place for me. It would do Jamie good too, after all the hard work he had put in at school and with his music. There was still time before he and Ian were due to leave for the Cardiff Summer School. I could rent a cottage in St Ives for a week – we could even take Toffee.

After yet another night in the spare room Ian came down to breakfast looking red-eyed and exhausted. I seized the moment while it was just the two of us to bring up the subject of Cornwall.

'I've been thinking. We could both do with some time apart, Ian.'

He replaced his coffee cup on its saucer and pushed it away. 'Is this your way of saying that you're leaving?'

'*No!* Just that we could do with a break – all of us. Before you and Jamie go to Cardiff suppose I rent a cottage and take Jamie and Toffee, just for a few days?' I leant towards him. 'I'm talking about a holiday, Ian; some time for you and me – specially *you* to take stock; think things through. It's impossible with us all on top of one another.'

He relaxed visibly. 'I daresay Jamie would appreciate it.'

'The thing is would *you* appreciate it?' I said. 'Do you think it would help us come to a decision – about the future?'

'Maybe.'

'Then shall I make arrangements?'

'If you like. All right then.'

'I'll ask Jamie first, of course. I don't want to force him away from his beloved music.'

But Jamie was delighted by the idea. I pointed to the picture on the kitchen wall. 'You see that place? I went there once. I used to know the lady who painted that picture. Would you like to go and see it for real? It's quite a long way but it's worth the drive. What do you think?'

He nodded eagerly. 'Wow! Yes please, Mum. I could go out in one of those fishing boats.'

I laughed. 'Well, I don't know about that. I'd quite like to bring you home in one piece.'

And so it was agreed. First I talked to Mary but she brushed my concerns about letting her down aside with a wave of her hand.

'Just you get your marriage sorted out,' she said. 'For once I agree with Amanda that you need a break. You and Ian both look strained. Maybe a few days apart are just what you need. And don't worry about *Mary-Mary*. Janet and I can manage perfectly well without you. Don't imagine for one minute that you're indispensable, my girl,' she added with a twinkle in her eye. 'Just get your life sorted out.'

I rang Mrs Saunders and left a message on her phone to tell her that Chris had agreed to the adoption and giving her his London address. Then I rang the tourist agency, holding my breath that there would be something available for me to rent at such short notice. To my relief they had a cottage free the following week, not far from the harbour.

The following Saturday Jamie and I set out complete with Toffee in his basket on the back seat. It was surprising how quickly he'd become used to having one leg in plaster. I'd consulted the vet and as Toffee had had his stitches out now he was allowed to be a bit more active.

We made the drive in good time and arrived in St Ives just as the sun was setting. Jamie got out of the car outside the cottage and stared at the harbour, its waters painted golden by the setting sun.

'Wow, Mum. It's nothing like Greencliffe, is it?'

I laughed as I heaved our cases out of the boot. 'Not a bit. Come on, are you going to help me with these cases instead of goggling at the scenery?'

Later, he stared out of the window at the boats, bobbing on the incoming tide. 'I wish Ian could have come too,' he said wistfully. He turned to me. 'You and he are okay, aren't you?'

I looked up in surprise. I'd thought we'd kept our differences to ourselves but it seemed Jamie had picked up on the atmosphere between us. 'Of course we are,' I told him cheerfully. 'We're fine.'

'I've made up my mind,' he said. 'When we go home I'm going to start calling Ian Dad. Do you think he'll like that?'

I swallowed hard at the lump in my throat. 'Very much,' I said. 'I think he'll like that a lot.'

Jamie adored St Ives. He swam in the chilly Cornish sea and scoured the beach at low tide for shells and semi-precious stones.

Most of his 'finds' were just plain pebbles but he was delighted with his collection. We walked and explored coves in the daytime and went down to the harbour in the evening to buy freshly caught fish for our tea. One of the fishermen took a shine to Jamie and after a lot of broad hints he offered to take him out in his boat. Seeing my doubtful expression he held up a small life jacket.

'No need to worry, missus,' he said. 'My grandson's about this young'un's age and I always make him wear this when he comes out with me. This young feller-me-lad'll come to no harm, I promise you.' He laughed, his brown, weather-beaten face creasing. 'You can even bring your little hound if you like,' he said, ruffling Jamie's hair. 'He's not going far with that pot on his leg I'll be bound.'

They went the following day and I watched as the little boat sailed out after lunch on the high tide, Jamie sitting in the stern with Toffee firmly tethered by his lead at his side. I'd decided to spend the afternoon going into the town to look at the shops but instead I found my feet leading me up the narrow, steeply stepped alleyways to where I remembered Cecily's cottage stood high above the harbour. Nothing had changed. Rambling roses still spilled over the stone walls and the scent of lavender filled the soft summer air.

Suddenly there it was at the top of the steps; Cecily's cottage, drowsing in the afternoon sunshine. The scent from the honeysuckle that climbed over the front porch was so evocative that it made my senses reel. Someone else lived there now, of course. There were different curtains at the windows and the tubs outside the front door were filled with golden marigolds instead of petunias. I sat down on the top step and looked at the view – the very view that Cecily had painted in the picture she'd given me.

'I'm so sorry, Cecily,' I whispered. 'Sorry I couldn't have kept Chris on the straight and narrow as you wanted me to. Sorry he didn't turn out to be the man you wanted him to be. I think you'd have liked your great grandson though. I know he'd have liked you.' I swallowed the lump in my throat at the thought of all she'd given up for her beloved Chris and his future. I remembered her words: *It was too late to paint the roses and the sea and all the other beautiful things….* But she did have a little time to paint, I told myself; at least she had a tiny slice of what should have been her life. And she loved Chris very much so I was sure that she'd considered her sacrifice worthwhile.

I stood up and brushed the dust from my jeans. 'God bless you, Cecily,' I whispered. 'Maybe Jamie will repay what you gave up one day. I wish you could have known him.'

I descended the alleyway and returned to the harbour. I treated myself to a cream tea at one of the cafes and sat at a table outside, shading my eyes to scan the horizon, slightly anxious for the return of the fishing boat. Half an hour went by and the sun began to go down then suddenly there it was, scudding through the water, its outboard motor chugging and Jamie waving to me from the stern. I stood up and walked down to meet them.

The fisherman beached the boat and jumped over the side in his big fisherman's boots, lifting Jamie out as though he was a mere feather and setting him down on the hard dry sand. He untied Toffee's lead and lifted him out next and the little dog ran madly around the beach, happy to be free again.

'Mum! We caught ever so many fishes!' Jamie told me excitedly. 'And Mr Tregorran says I can take some home for our tea.'

I laughed. 'Has he been good?' I asked.

The fisherman grinned. 'Good as gold, missus. A born little fisherman you got there and no mistake.' Reaching into the boat he pulled out a creel of mackerel and handed it to me. I shook my head.

'Oh no, you're too generous.'

'Bless you no!' he said. 'Young'un here helped land 'em himself. He's worked for 'em.' He winked at me. 'They'll be the best fish he's ever tasted, you see if they ain't.'

We said goodbye to Mr Tregorran and began to make our way back to the cottage, Jamie proudly carrying his 'catch'. A winding flight of steps led up to the lane where the cottage was and I bent to pick up Toffee. Ahead of me I heard Jamie's excited cry as he rounded the bend.

'Mum, *Mum*! Look who's here!' Dropping his fish he leapt up the last two steps and straight into the arms of the man waiting outside the cottage door. 'It's great here, Dad, but even better now that you're here. I wish you could have come with us.'

Ian looked at me over Jamie's head and the expression in his eyes made my heart miss a beat. I put Toffee down and the little dog ran to Ian too, his tail wagging furiously. I bent to pick up the creel of mackerel.

'Jamie, take your fish through to the kitchen and give Toffee a drink of water,' I said. 'He must be parched.' Reluctantly Jamie took the fish and called to Toffee who followed him into the cottage. I looked at Ian.

'Hello.'

'Hi. Jamie looks happy. It seems your idea was a roaring success.'

'He's had the time of his life. He's been out in a fishing boat this afternoon – hence the fish. Apparently he—'

'*Elaine*....' He took two steps towards me and grasped my shoulders. 'I couldn't stay away any longer. I've missed you so much.'

'Missed me – or Jamie?'

'Both of you, of course. As you said, you come as a package and thank God for that. I can't imagine life without the two of you. I can't function properly without you and Jamie. If there was ever any doubt this week has proved it.'

I looked up into his eyes. 'So, does that mean...?'

'It means that I love you and nothing is going to change that. I never stopped. I was just terrified that you'd stopped loving me.'

'I'm so sorry I hurt you,' I whispered. 'More sorry than I could ever say. And – what happened had nothing to do with not loving you – not for a second.' I slipped my arms around his neck and kissed him. 'Thank you for coming, Ian,' I whispered. 'And for forgiving me.'

He placed a finger against my lips. 'Let's not talk about forgiving.'

'You've made the day perfect. I promise I'll do my best to make it up to you.'

He looked at me. 'Am I mistaken or did I hear Jamie call me Dad?'

I smiled. 'He did, and he's already told me that you're the only dad he's ever wanted.'

Jamie appeared in the doorway, glaring at us indignantly. 'Are you two coming in or what?' he demanded. 'I'm hungry and there's fish to cook.'

Laughing, Ian put an arm round my waist. 'All right, we're coming.'

As we all sat at supper Jamie looked anxiously at Ian. 'It's great that you're here, but we don't have to go home tomorrow, do we? We're supposed to be staying till Saturday.'

Ian looked at me. 'Well, I daresay I could stay on for another couple of days.'

'Wow, wicked!' Jamie grinned. 'There's so much I want to show you, the beach and the harbour and the fishing boats. Did you know that there are real jewels on the beach? I've got some. They only need polishing. I'll show them to you after tea, Dad – it's okay to call you Dad now, isn't it?

Ian laughed. 'You bet it is!'

'There is just one small snag,' I said, glancing at him.

'What's that?'

'There are only two bedrooms here in the cottage. No spare room.'

Under the table Ian's hand reached for mine and his eyes danced as they looked into mine. 'Is that so? Oh dear. Well, I suppose we'll just have to manage, won't we?'